TORMENT

WORKS BY JEREMY ROBINSON

The Didymus Contingency

Raising The Past

Beneath

Antarktos Rising

Kronos

Pulse

Instinct

Threshold

Callsign: King

Callsign: Queen

Callsign: Rook

Callsign: King 2 – Underworld

Callsign: Bishop

Callsign: Knight

Callsign: Deep Blue

Callsign: King 3 – Blackout

Torment

The Sentinel

The Last Hunter – Descent

The Last Hunter – Pursuit

The Last Hunter – Ascent

The Last Hunter – Lament

The Last Hunter – Onslaught

The Last Hunter – Collected Edition

Insomnia

SecondWorld

Project Nemesis

Ragnarok

Island 731

The Raven

Nazi Hunter: Atlantis

Prime

Omega

Project Maigo

Refuge

Guardian

Xom-B

Savage

Flood Rising

Project 731

Cannibal

Endgame

MirrorWorld

Hunger

Herculean

Project Hyperion

Patriot

Apocalypse Machine

Empire

Feast

Unity

Project Legion

The Distance

The Last Valkyrie

Centurion

Infinite

Helios

Viking Tomorrow

Forbidden Island

The Divide

The Others

Space Force

Alter

Flux

Tether

Tribe

NPC

Exo-Hunter

Infinite²

The Dark

Mind Bullet

The Order

TORMENT

JEREMY ROBINSON

BREAKNECK MEDIA

For those brave enough to answer the question...

INTRODUCTION

I wrote and published *Torment* several years ago. It was my first true horror novel and was so...different from what I normally wrote at the time, that I decided to release it under the pen name 'Jeremy Bishop.' The novel sold great but was also surprisingly controversial. While most people loved the story, and the horrors within, a subset of people were enraged by it—and not just because of the content, but because it resonated with them so profoundly that they responded to their fear with anger. This generated some of the most epic one-star reviews I've ever received.

Flash forward to the present. I no longer shy away from controversial topics, and my amazing and wise readers understand that novels with religious context aren't designed to convert anyone. Since *Torment*'s release, my novels have grown stranger, darker, funnier, and more...twisted. So, it's time to welcome *Torment* home and publish the novel again under the Robinson name—in e-book, audiobook narrated by the inconceivable R.C. Bray, and published for the first time in hardcover.

The story itself is exactly the same as before. If you're purchasing again, expect the same experience, but with a brand spanking new cover. If this is your first-time reading *Torment*...buckle up and prepare for re-entry. Things are about to get nuts. In either case, if you enjoy...or are enraged ...by *Torment*, please consider posting reviews at Amazon, Audible, and Goodreads. Every single one helps spread the word.

If you want to connect with me, and an awesome group of fellow fans, considering joining The Tribe at facebook.com/groups/JR.Tribe. We have a good time, keep everyone updated on what's brewing in Hollywood, and give away prizes every dang week. Hope to see you there, and thank you, *thank you* for reading!

—Jeremy Robinson

"It is easy to go down into Hell; night and day, the gates of dark Death stand wide; but to climb back again, to retrace one's steps to the upper air—there's the rub, the task."

—Virgil, Aeneid

TERRA

1

Siberia

Ice cold air seeped through the slate gray stones of the cell wall, infusing the darkness with a biting chill. But it wasn't the frostbite taking root in Matt Brenton's toes that held his attention. Nor the frost coated layer of bile clinging to his ten day old beard. He'd grown accustomed to the company of pain and filth. With each rise and set of the sun—seen only as a reflection of light through the cell door—Brenton's mind slipped further from reality and into a kind of hellish dream world. Pain numbed his mind. Time escaped him. But his captors had taken notice and were making an effort to regain his full attention.

Brenton stared at the hand on the table. Skinny, frail and bloody, it didn't look like his, but the pain pulsing up his arm and radiating through his body confirmed it with each whack of the blade. Brenton twitched as the dull fishing knife neared the third finger of his left hand. He wasn't sure if the rusty odor filling his nostrils came from the blade or his blood, but it centered him enough to speak.

"Wait," he said, his voice like a pitiful stranger's. "Please, don't."

The masked face of his torturer, a man without name who reeked of garlic...or body odor, lowered into view. "Tell me what I want to know," said the voice with no accent. "No further harm will come to you. Just confirm for me what I already know to be truth and you will be set free."

The knife rested on the skin of his ring finger, just above the spot where a wedding ring would soon rest. His mind, desperate for distraction, flashed back to his proposal and found perspective instead.

It was raining. Not hard. But enough to make the oceanside view gray from top to bottom. Decidedly un-romantic. But this was the spot. They had spent several long summer nights at this spot, watching heat lightning and talking about space travel, alternate dimensions and other geeky topics that interested him. He knew Mia was humoring him most of the time. But she listened.

When he dropped to one knee, she listened harder than ever.

He heard no cheer. No hoopla. Just a whispered, yes, and a tight embrace—the kind that says, I will love you until death do us part.

Happily Ever After.

Not quite.

A year had passed since the proposal, eight months more since he'd been deployed, delaying the wedding. At least ten days since he swerved off the road under a barrage of gunfire and a near death run-in with an IED in northern Afghanistan. The assailants took him from the ruined convoy and killed his team. Wounded and blindfolded, he spent the next few days delirious, hungry and in motion. Always in motion. As the air grew colder he realized they were heading north. By the time they reached their destination, his wounds had just begun to mend, but his heart had broken. He knew he'd never see home or Mia again.

The pressure of the blade on his finger ripped him back to the present. He looked into the eyes of his captor, then back to the finger. If there was any chance, any chance at all he could see Mia again, he had to take it. Pain pinched his finger as the blade began to slice. "Okay! All right! I'll say whatever you want me to."

The blade came away.

Brenton looked at his hand. Two fingers lay separated, but the ring finger wriggled at his command—still attached, though bleeding. "What do you want to know?"

"Only for you to confirm our intelligence."

Brenton nodded. "Anything."

His captor walked behind him. A click echoed through the cold air. "What is your name and rank?"

"Staff Sergeant Matthew Brenton, U.S. Marine Corps."

"Please confirm the following." Brenton heard the unmistakable tone that added, "or I'll take the finger." Confirm anything the man says.

"You intended to cross the Afghani border on a mission to infiltrate Russia?"

"I did."

"You are a sniper, yes?"

Brenton squinted. This couldn't be happening. "Yes."

"One of your country's best?"

"Yes."

"Elite?"

"Yes."

"Is it true that your government—the United States government—sent you here, to Moscow, with orders to assassinate President Misha Alexandrov?"

Brenton's eyes widened with a shock near that of losing a finger. "What?"

"Answer the question!" The voice of his captor was closer to a growl and the sound of metal on stone revealed he had picked up the knife again.

"Yes! Yes, it's true."

"What...is true?"

Brenton's head sagged.

He was committing treason on a gross scale, not only admitting to something awful, but an outright act of war. "My orders...were to assassinate President Misha Alexandrov."

His captor walked in front of him again. He held the knife in one hand and a mini-tape recorder in the other. He clicked the stop button on the recorder. "Thank you."

"Please don't kill me," Brenton said, followed by a guttural sob.

The masked man surged forward with the knife, swiping it down, tearing through sinews. Brenton screamed. "Don't kill me! God, please, don't kill me!"

He sobbed and shook as the man stepped back. Brenton's vision narrowed as he stared at the stone floor. The knife fell at his feet.

"I am a man of my word," said his captor, allowing his Russian accent to tinge his voice for the first time. "You are free to go."

Brenton saw the booted feet of the man pivot and walk from the cell, leaving the door open behind him. Brenton sobbed. Spit from his mouth rolled onto his beard and froze to the thickly crusted surface. He fell from the chair to his knees, looking at his freed hands, numb and in-complete—but free. Sobs turned to laughs as Brenton picked up the knife and his detached fingers. If he packed them in ice, maybe they could be reattached?

Loud chopping rotor blades shook the cell, building in pitch as they sliced through the arctic air. Brenton stumbled out of the cell, through a short hallway and into the brightness of a clear day, the sun striking a gleaming white, foot thick, layer of snow. A black helicopter lifted up and peeled away from a cleared helipad. As it flew away, the helo dove down and disappeared below a precipice.

Brenton rubbed his eyes, trying desperately to focus them in the harsh light and absolute cold that crystallized the moisture around his eyes. Then he saw it...the edge of the precipice upon which his cell—a stone shanty attached to a small log cabin—stood. There were no trees. No rocks. No life. Brenton spun around, scanning his surroundings. He saw the same thing in every direction. He'd been marooned on the top of some stone spire in the middle of nowhere.

He clenched his fists and felt a wash of pain from the bloody stumps where his two fingers used to be. He looked at the hand, at the empty ring finger, and refused to give up. He ran for the edge, pushing his bare feet through the snow, one pain-filled step at a time. Reaching the pre-cipice, Brenton fell to his knees and clenched his hands in the snow. The cliff descended at least one hundred feet and ended with a line of boul-ders and jagged edges. He won his freedom from the cell, but he was more of a prisoner than ever.

He would die here.

Alone.

Brenton screamed at the sky, his voice raw and wet. He screamed and screamed, pouring out his anguish to the world. When only his distant echo responded, Brenton held his head in his hands and wept quietly for several minutes, then found his voice. "Christ." The word, meant as a curse, opened his eyes. He hadn't thought about God since childhood. But now, with nothing left but pain and despair, who else was there to listen to him?

"Are you there?"

Brenton looked at the sky. Soft cumulus clouds drifted over the barren plains, their shadows casting a deep purple shade on the flawless sheet of snow. Holding his breath, he listened for a reply. Surely, if there were a God, he would reply now.

God didn't speak.

The only sound came from the gentle touchdown of snowflakes landing on the ground—like quiet flicks of static. In that quiet, Brenton found some kind of peace, perhaps supernatural, perhaps a primal connection with nature. His logic said that a man facing death had no choice but to make peace with his past, accept it for what it was, but he couldn't help wondering if he felt something more.

He turned his eyes up again. "If you're really there, God, Allah, whoever you are, I don't want to freeze to death! I don't want to starve!"

His voice echoed again, bouncing off the distant cliffs and returning faded and distorted. "Please! Get me down from—"

A pop and shift of snow beneath his knees drew his attention down. Before he could realize what the line slicing across the snow beneath him represented, it slipped away and fell, taking his body with it. As he descended through the frigid air, Brenton didn't scream, he simply mouthed a final request, "Let me see her again."

Then his body struck the rocks below. Bones shattered. Brain matter splashed and froze. Guts slid free and melted into the snow. His end had been tortured and horrific, but in death, he had been spared from the horrors yet to come.

2

New Hampshire

Mia Durante descended the stairs two at a time.

"Coming!" She paused at the bottom, in the foyer, where a pile of winter clothes blocked the door. She glanced out the side window as she moved the clothes. Her younger sister and niece waited at the front door, rubbing their arms against the winter chill.

"You can let yourself in," she said as she looked at her reflection in the hallway mirror. All signs of her crying had faded. As much as she needed to talk to someone about what happened the previous day, her sister and niece weren't the right people. She wasn't sure who the right people would be anymore. Matt was her confidante, but now, after what she'd done...

"Um, no, we can't." Her sister's voice contained part annoyance, part sarcasm.

"Why not?" Mia said, as she reached for the knob and found it immovable. She quickly unlocked the doorknob and then the deadbolt. She swung the door open with a grin. "Sorry."

Like rabbits fleeing a forest fire, Margo and Liz dashed into the house, hopping and chattering. "When are going to make me a key?" Margo said. "Better yet, when are you going to sell this shithole and buy a real house?"

She and Matt had bought the fixer-upper, a farmhouse built in 1841, against the recommendation of their real estate agent. It was supposed to have been a bonding experience—the two of them solidifying the foundation, cleaning out the rot and evicting the rodent tenants as a symbol of their growing bond. The house would grow with them, every year the three becoming stronger. At first she laughed off the concept as romantic rubbish, but after realizing Matt's sincere desire to see it through, she signed up for what was sure to be an adventure. Of course, the plan met an impasse when Matt shipped out, and even though he was due back in two months, she'd probably ruined any chance of having a life in this house.

Ignoring her sister and pushing away her concerns, Mia knelt down next to Liz, a seven-year-old with tangled blond hair, and helped her out of her jacket. "Your mother has a horrible mouth."

Liz nodded with a grin. "Grammy says she used to put soap in her mouth."

"She did," Mia said, "but not enough to get it clean." She stood and handed the winter coat to Margo. "Where is the matriarch anyway?"

"Not coming," Margo said, "On a date, if you can believe it."

"Wow," Mia said. Her mother hadn't been on a date in the ten years since their father died. It was a big step...one that her mother had apparently not wanted her to know about.

"I know, right? At least one of us might be sleeping with a man tonight."

Mia stood still for a moment, then tried to conceal her frown by turning away. But Margo saw her.

"Shit, I'm sorry."

Mia waved it off as she walked toward the kitchen and fought against the shaking in her hands. If she let her emotional wall crack she'd confess everything, and Matt needed to hear it first. "Just stop cursing in front of your daughter."

She entered the kitchen, feeling the hardwood floor flex beneath her with each step. The tin ceiling, wood stove, and brick mantle gave the room a warm, country feel, but the drafty windows meant maintaining a large supply of dry wood at all times. The six foot stack in the mud room was just a small part of several cords she had cut herself before winter set in. With Matt deployed, her father dead and Margo's ex-boyfriend an ex-boyfriend, she had no one to help her with the physical work around the house. And Margo, with her perfect nails, certainly wasn't up to the task. After spending the morning hacking and stacking wood, she felt ready for the Durante girls' weekly pizza party.

"Pizza is on the island," she said, leaning into the fridge for a beer. She took two and handed one to Margo, who already had her hand out. She placed her bottle on the counter next to the pizza box, which she opened with gusto. "Voila! Extra cheese with olives, peppers and ham."

"That's gonna taste like shit," Liz said.

Mia couldn't help but laugh and Margo spit out her first swig of beer. "You see?" Mia said, motioning to Liz, who was laughing now too.

The phone rang.

"Clean that up," she said to Margo, and headed for the phone. She pointed at Liz with a grin. "And you!"

Liz laughed. "Open mouth, insert soap," she said, placing her hand inside her mouth.

Mia was laughing when she answered the phone. When the man on the other end spoke, she stopped.

There was no controlling her shaking hands now. She nearly dropped the phone. Margo stopped cleaning. Liz stopped smiling. "Auntie Mia?"

The phone conversation ended with Mia silently placing the phone down and stepping back. A mix of emotions—despair, anger, and guilt—consumed her.

"Who was it?" Margo asked, then got very serious. "It wasn't?"

Mia was already nodding.

"Is he?"

Mia shook her head, no. "Missing in action," she whispered. "For ten days."

Before Margo's comforting hand could reach her, Mia ran for the sink, clutched the sides and vomited until there was nothing left in her stomach. Missing in action left some room for hope, but MIA in Afghanistan could easily end with a videotaped beheading.

"What's wrong, mom?" Liz asked her mother. "Is Uncle Matt not coming home?"

"He's coming home," Margo said, trying to sound confident.

"When?"

"I don't—"

The phone rang again.

Margo sprang for the phone and answered it before Mia could re-move herself from the sink. "Hello... Oh my God. Okay, I will." As though moving through sludge, she placed the phone on the receiver and turn-ed to Mia, who was still bent over the sink.

"Who was it?" she asked.

"Mom."

Mia looked confused. "She knows?"

Margo nodded slowly. "It's on the news."

After quickly rinsing out her mouth, Mia made for the living room. Margo caught her by the arm. "Mia, wait."

They stared into each other's eyes for a moment as Margo attempted to find a gentle way to break the news. She couldn't let her sister learn the truth from a newscaster. "Mia..."

"Just spit it out!" Mia shouted.

"They're saying Matt's a traitor. An assassin. They—"

Mia had heard enough. She ignored the rest of her sister's words and pounded for the TV. She turned it on, changed the channel to a news network and was greeted by a service photo of her fiancé. She staggered back and fell into one of the old La-Z-Boy chairs she and Matt had picked up at a yard sale. Her hand went to her mouth as she heard the words, "...accused by Russia of being an assassin—an elite sniper—sent to kill President Misha Alexandrov."

It wasn't possible. Matt drove trucks. In and out of the military, it's what he loved to do. He drove them for work. He drove them for fun. He drove them for his country. But the Russian military accused him of be-ing an elite sniper?

The words, "act of war" filtered from the newscaster and cut through her chaotic thoughts. I'll never see him again, she thought.

"My orders were to assassinate President Misha Alexandrov." Matt's voice hit her like a wrecking ball. She pitched forward and let out a moan. They were playing a recording. His confession.

"You are a sniper, yes?" an interrogator asked.

"Yes."

"One of your country's best?"

"Yes."

"Elite?"

"Yes."

The ridiculousness of the statements made her laugh with rage, but her mind swirled with doubts. Is Matt a sniper? Could he have hidden something like this from me? Why the hell is this happening? As the questions built and the news replayed the audio recording again and again, she listened to his voice, hearing the fear tinged with desperation, and she wept. She cried for him, knowing what it would take for him to betray his country like that. Hell, she thought, he endured hell, and broke.

Who wouldn't?

And I was here.

Safe.

Feeling sorry for myself.

Feeling alone.

And justified for fucking his best friend.

He'll never know, she thought, and for a brief moment she felt a new emotion.

Relief.

It sent her running back to the sink where she dry-heaved some more of her soul.

3

New Hampshire

"Shit!" she yelled, and pushed the button to hang up the portable phone. Mia missed the days of slamming down a corded phone and hearing the clang of the bell inside. It was much more satisfying. The best you could do with a cordless was throw it across the room, but then you'd be out thirty bucks. And she had more calls to make.

Two weeks had passed since she and everyone else in the world learned about Matt. She felt sure he was dead, and spent the first week at her sister's house, mourning his loss and her betrayal. There was no funeral, however, because there was no body and officially, no one knew Matt's fate. Maybe never would.

Her anguish became anger. Anger became a thirst for justice. Then for answers.

Was Matt really an assassin?

Who was responsible for his death, or capture?

What was being done about it?

Her guilt became a perpetual motivation. She needed to tell him the truth. She needed him to forgive her. To love her, despite her failings. She had no idea if such a possibility existed, but she couldn't live with herself if she didn't get the chance.

She pursued the cause as a reporter. Because she and Matt had yet to marry, her relationship with him was easy to hide. His name was on the mortgage and utilities. They had separate checking accounts. So no one questioned why a small town crime reporter was asking about the biggest story of the year.

Then again, everyone was asking the same questions.

The problem was, no one was talking. Not the president. Not a single senator or congressman. No one. Aside from denying all accusations, the United States government had gone silent on the issue. Business as usual.

Hear no evil.

See no evil.

Speak no evil.

But Mia didn't buy it.

A plane crash yesterday had distracted the media. They could only stay focused on a story so long with no official sound bites. They'd played and replayed the audio of Matt's confession so many times most of the country could probably recite it. The standard group of ex-military, ex-political and ex-presidential candidates had ranted and debated until their voices grew raw.

But the media's distraction didn't keep the government from stone-walling her. The reporter angle wasn't working.

She looked down at the phone. She'd made nearly one hundred phone calls in the past few days. Most had been answered by full voice mailboxes. The few human beings she spoke to had simply said, "No comment," and hung up.

"No luck?" asked Chris Kuzneski, a photographer at the paper and one of the few co-workers she considered a friend. He knew the score and didn't believe Matt was an assassin.

"No one's talking," she said, leaning back in her office chair. Her desk was clutter free, in part because she was a neat freak, but also because no one used paper anymore. Everything she needed, from phone books, to press releases, to word processing could be found on her slender MacBook.

"Have you played the fiancé card?"

She nodded. "Seems I'm not the first person to try. No one's buying it."

"Damn. Have you said please?" Kuzneski flashed a smile, but the look in his eyes posed a question. Is it okay to joke with you?

She smiled, happy for the distraction. "I've said a lot of things."

He chuckled. "I bet."

"Shut-up, Kuzneski. What kind of name is that, anyway? Kuzneski. Sounds like Was Pesky."

"Hey, don't take your frustration out on me," he said, raising his hands in mock defense and stepping back. Not watching his step, he tripped over a trash barrel, toppled into an office chair with a too loose back and tipped ass-over-tea-kettle onto the linoleum floor.

Mia burst out laughing, and everyone in the office turned in her direction.

When Kuzneski hopped back up, they seemed to understand what had happened and went back to work.

"Thanks for helping me up," he said, straightening his shirt.

"What are friends for?"

"Honestly?" Kuzneski said. "Friends need to be honest with each other."

The uncommonly serious tone of his voice held her attention.

"You look like shit. Go home. Get some rest."

She looked unsure. Giving up wasn't in her blood.

But before she could respond, he held his watch out in front of her face. "Besides..."

At first she had no idea what he was trying to tell her. She read the time on his watch. 4:10PM. Normal work hours were until 5PM, but she often stayed late and—

"Shit!" Mia closed her MacBook and shoved it into her briefcase.

"Ten minutes late," Kuzneski said. "Some aunt you are."

"Bite me, Peski," she said as she rushed for the door.

His singsong voice chased her down the stairwell. "You're welcome."

It turned out Kuzneski was being a good friend. He'd set his watch twenty minutes fast so she would arrive at Liz's school on time.

"Hi Auntie!" Liz said as she swung open the door, hopped into the back seat and buckled herself in. Liz's hair bounced as she bobbed her head back and forth for a moment before meeting Mia's eyes in the rearview mirror. She smiled, barely containing her energy.

Mia turned around in her seat. "What's got into you?"

"Nothing," Liz said, but the way she bit her tongue after speaking said otherwise.

Some of the weight that had settled on Mia over the past few weeks lifted as she watched Liz squirm in her seat, doing her best to contain some kind of surprise. While Liz wasn't her own, she was as close as Mia would ever get. She and Matt had talked kids on several occasions. Apprehensive at first, he came around after she began describing what their kids might be like and who they could become. But it wasn't to be. Even if Matt were still around, doctors had long ago pronounced her infertile.

"C'mon Lizard, spill the beans."

Liz giggled and shook her head, but after just a few moments of an old-school stare down, she cracked. She dug into her backpack and pulled out a business size envelope. A nice one, with a shiny blue return address she couldn't make out.

"Did the president tell you where Uncle Matt is?" Liz asked, her grin widening.

Mia's stomach dropped. The question caught her off guard. "Why? No..."

"Did you talk to him on the phone?"

"No, Liz." Mia's frustration was growing despite Liz's continued excitement. "It's not that simple. You can't just talk to —." Her memory kicked in. It couldn't be...

Liz let out a giggle. "I can."

With that, Liz handed the envelope over. Mia glanced at the return address and nearly dropped the envelope. It read:

The White House
Washington, D.C. 20500
202-456-1414

"I won," Liz said. "I won a contest."

Mia didn't bother asking which contest. She knew exactly what this letter regarded. She opened the envelope and read the one-page letter inside.

Dear Elizabeth,

Thank you for your inspiring essay on "What it means to receive the Medal of Honor." Out of nearly two hundred thousand entries from around the country, we have chosen yours as the best, for your honesty, above average writing skill, and evident research. I would like you and one family member to attend a private Medal of Honor ceremony next week, where I will be giving the award to Major Paul Byers. It would mean a lot to all of us if you would attend. A duplicate letter has been sent to your mother at home. Please call to confirm. Thank you very much for entering the contest and I look forward to meeting you for breakfast next week.

Sincerely,

President Robert Collins

A hand-written note read, "Hope you like Eggs Benedict!" and was followed by the president's signature.

Mia stared at the letter, rereading it. She felt sure Margo would let her go with Liz. She doubted being confronted by the fiancé of a man Russia accused of being an assassin would be well received by the president, especially over Eggs Benedict, but she'd get no better chance to find out the truth.

Liz unbuckled and leaned over the front seat. "Did I do good?"

Mia kissed her hard on the cheek. "You did amazing."

"There's just one problem," Liz said, her smile turning quizzical. "I didn't write anything for this contest. I like writing. And I'm smart, thank you very much. But they sent a copy of my essay along with that letter and I definitely didn't write it. It was too..."

"Insightful?"

"Exactly." Liz leaned over the front seat and turned her head toward Mia, her eyes wide with mock suspicion. "So, Auntie Mia, who writes for the newspaper, who do you think wrote it? Hmm?"

Mia smiled wide. She had indeed written the short essay, doing her best to keep the language as simple, and believable, as possible while making a statement that would be profound for a seven-year-old. The odds of it working were slim. Thousands of kids had entered. But like Liz knew, only one of them was actually a reporter, and a damn good writer. She took Liz's hand, locking their pinkies. "Can we keep this a secret?"

"Can I have a hundred dollars?"

"How about a Friendly's sundae on Saturday?"

Liz raised a thoughtful eyebrow and then said, "I'll take a Friendly's sundae right now."

"Done," Mia said, squeezing Liz's pinkie. She showed all smiles on the outside—Liz would keep her secret—but her insides felt like she'd just sucked down a pint of spoiled milk. The odds of her confronting the president about Matt in person defied logic and felt supernatural, like fate, or God. Too bad she didn't believe in either.

4

Washington D.C.

Robert Collins walked through the lobby of the White House West Wing and entered the main hallway. Though his freshly pressed suit itched his skin, he made no move to scratch. He believed the president should be prim and proper at all times. In private, he'd scratch his ass raw, but even a single pair of eyes was enough to make him straighten up, speak deeply and ignore any personal irritations. His hair, graying on the sides, but still black on top, matched his black and white suit, chosen specifically for this morning's medal ceremony and brunch. The press hadn't been invited, but a staff photographer would document the moment and send the pictures out with a press release. If the press came, they'd only ask questions about the Russian debacle. It wouldn't be long before some other kind of controversy or tragedy overshadowed the hullabaloo started by the Russians. The airplane crash helped, but with every crash around the world being front page news since 9-11, it wouldn't hold interest for long. "Let it blow over," he'd told his staff, "then welcome the vultures back."

Four Secret Service officers, three men and one woman, followed close behind Collins. They had been handpicked to watch his back and if need be, take a bullet for him. Tom Austin, the senior agent of the four, was an outstanding agent with a squeaky clean appearance and a record as polished as his now bald head. Collins had heard that the man had some strange hobbies outside of the job—surreal art and painting—but that didn't matter to Collins. Tom was the best Secret Service agent on the job.

Collins strode past the vice president's office, glancing in. The office, as expected, was empty. A hunting trip called the VP north to Maine. He'd

missed out on the Russian fiasco, but called in to brag about the black
bear he'd taken. "Maybe a brown bear is next in our sights, eh?" he'd
joked. Russia hadn't been a bear since the collapse of the Soviet Union.
Mother Russia was hardly more than a cub now.

Passing the chief-of-staff's office, Collins saw the man hard at work.
He gave a quick wave and rounded the corner. Next came rows of small-
ler offices on either side of the hallway, leading toward the Oval Office.
He avoided the glances of the men and women working in those offices.
He knew what they were thinking, and their probing eyes would only
spoil what was sure to be a pleasant morning and a delicious brunch.
The White House cook staff made amazing hollandaise sauce. He kept
his eyes trained straight ahead. Any acknowledgement of the staffers in
the offices to either side might bring on a barrage of questions about
Russia he didn't feel like answering, to them, or the press.

The truth of the matter was that Collins did not take the Russian
claims or threat seriously. Not in the least bit. Russians perfected the art
of geopolitical grandstanding long ago. Several other concerns held
higher spots on his priority list. Bills to be vetoed. Lobbyists to treat to
dinner. Medals to award. Hell, his golf swing had him more concerned.
He didn't need to get into a public, celebrity style, name calling squabble
with a has-been superpower. They could shout until they were red in
the face, nothing more. It was a waste of time. Their own silence proved
that. If they had any real case at all, they'd still be holding press conferences, or harassing the U.N.

Collins smiled as he passed between the dining room adjacent to
the Oval Office and the Roosevelt Room. Someone in the Russian military
was no doubt being deported to Siberia for such a tactical blunder. What
their angle was, he had no idea, but it turned out to be a major league
screw up. Thank God I've got smarter people than that on my payroll,
Collins thought, as he opened the door to the Oval Office and stepped
inside. He left the four Secret Service officers in the hall where they
would take up their normal positions.

He closed the door behind him and smiled. A woman sitting in his
executive chair had her long legs up on his desk. Her skirt rode up to her
thigh and carried his eyes over the rest of her body, up to her blue eyes

and smiling face. She held up a cigar. "Found an old stash of cigars deep in the desk. Think Clinton wants them back or should we have some fun?"

Collins laughed. "Not very First Lady-like of you, dear."

Penny Collins laughed and stood behind the desk. "You know how un-First Lady-like I can be." She put the cigar in the center desk drawer, straightened her dress and met him in the middle of the room. She kissed him lightly on the lips, then straightened his jacket. Because of Collins's large nose, thin lips and short stature, he'd been dubbed the luckiest president to sit in the Oval Office. Kennedy had nothing on him. Penny put Jackie-O and Marylyn to shame. Speculation about how such an average looking man landed such a catch ranged from extortion to true love, but the truth was somewhere in between. He loved sex, and she loved money and power. They provided for each other. His looks were not an issue and hers were perfect.

"You're off to the shops again, today?" he asked.

"Well, you won't find me slurping eggs Benedict with a couple of old guys and some kid." She headed for the door. "I'll be back for our critical meeting after lunch."

Collins smiled. Today is going to be a good day, he thought. "Love you, babe," he said as she left the office.

"Right back at you, Mr. President," she replied in her best, breathy Monroe impression. She straightened suddenly and smiled. "Hello, Tom."

Austin nodded to Penny as he held the door and let her pass. He entered the office as she left and closed the door behind him.

"You're a lucky man, Mr. President," Austin said.

"Tell that to my bank account," Collins said as he sat behind the desk. He opened the desk drawer, took out the cigar Penny had been holding and smelled it. "Damn perfume." He tossed the cigar into the small trash bin next to the desk. "What's up?"

As Austin approached the desk, Collins noticed the manila folder in his hand.

"I went over the guest list for this afternoon," Austin said.

"And?"

"And this." Austin opened the manila folder and pulled out a black and white photo of a thirty-something, dark eyed woman with straight black hair and a pleasant smile. "This is the family member accompanying the girl who won the essay contest."

"What's her name? The girl's? Leslie or something?"

"Elizabeth."

"Right. Elizabeth." Collins wrote the name down on a piece of paper and slipped it into his pocket. "Go on."

"The woman is Elizabeth's aunt, Mia Durante."

Austin paused.

"Doesn't ring a bell," Collins said. "Should it?"

"Not at all. But if she'd been married to her fiancé, her last name would have been Brenton."

Collins sat up straight. "His fiancé?"

Austin shifted his weight.

"What is it?" Collins asked. "Don't tell me there's more."

"She's a reporter. Small town, but still, a reporter."

"Son-of-a-bitch," Collins whispered. "I'll have to cancel."

"They're already here. Stephanie is giving them a private tour along with the medal recipient and his brother."

Collins pursed his lips. "Just keep her away from me. Don't tackle her or anything. Just make sure she doesn't raise her voice or make a scene. If she starts asking questions, conjure up some emergency to get me out of there."

"An emergency?"

"You'll think of something," Collins said with a smile. His day had gone to crap in a matter of minutes, but it could still be salvaged. Austin was on the job. He'd take care of Durante if she became a problem.

5

Washington D.C.

Major Paul Byers followed the group closely, taking in faces, voices and mannerisms. It had become a habit during his time in the U.S. Marine Corps. He'd spent all of 1971 and part of '73 in the jungles of Vietnam. He became adept at learning who he could and couldn't trust with his life by watching them, scrutinizing every move, twitch and grunt. As a result, he'd survived the war with only a few physical scars to show for it. He'd even managed to pull a few of his friends out of harm's way. Now, thirty-seven years late, his actions during a botched raid on a Viet-Cong camp had earned him a trip to the White House. He didn't feel he deserved a medal, let alone the Medal of Honor, but he knew that made him even more deserving in the eyes of those bestowing it. Still, it was nice to be recognized for what he gave to his country...if only they would give out a few hundred thousand more. In his mind, every man and woman involved in that mess deserved a medal.

"Welcome to the East Room," said an enthusiastic young Asian woman after snapping closed the cell phone that had held her attention for the past minute. She'd introduced herself when the limo dropped them off at the White House main entrance—Stephanie Chang, the president's personal aide. Seemed nice enough. Cute too. "This is the largest room in the White House. It's used for press conferences, dinners, ceremonies. Things like that."

The long room featured a large oriental rug with vibrant reds and blues—very royal—which were cut into sections by long streams of light shining through eleven tall windows. Two extravagant crystal chandeliers hung from the ceiling and a lone grand piano occupied the far corner.

"Will Mr. Byers get his medal here?" the little girl asked.

Paul smiled. Elizabeth Durante. She had short-cut blond hair and a smile that melted his heart. Innocence personified, yet incredibly aware and social. They met in the limo and hit it off right away, swapping first grade horror stories, his involving long walks through the snow, hers involving iPods and cell phones. She knew more about the medal that would soon be hung around his neck than he did. Smart kid.

"Oh, no," Chang said as she moved to the center of the room. "Because the press was not invited, this will be a private and casual affair. We'll be doing the medal ceremony in the Oval Office just after brunch."

Elizabeth's eyes grew wide as she whispered, "Wow." The woman holding her hand, Mia Durante, her aunt, frowned. Paul had yet to figure her out. There was something about her. She looked intelligent and nice enough, but her eyes revealed something brewing just below the surface ...concealed, but barely contained.

"After brunch?" Mia asked. "I thought the ceremony was before brunch."

"Change of plans, I'm afraid. That was the president's chief of security who called a minute ago."

"Do you know why?" Mia asked.

Chang shrugged. "Beats me. But what Tom says, goes. Oh, Tom Austin is chief of security. Secret Service. Harmless, really. Unless you mess with the President, of course. From what I've heard, he can be a pit bull when he needs to be."

As Chang led them to a painting and began explaining its detailed past, Paul watched Mia. She bit her lower lip, rubbed her hands on her pants and tapped her foot ever so slightly. She either felt incredibly nervous about being at the White House and meeting the president or something was up. Never one to beat around the bush, he stepped toward her, intent on discovering the truth.

Before he got to her a hand clapped his shoulder. "What'd I miss?"

Paul turned and faced his brother, Mark, whose eyes darted around the room like a mischievous child in a room full of fireworks. The white ring around his collar, signifying his place in the priesthood, seemed to be the only thing holding him back. Then it failed to do even that. Mark made a beeline for the piano while Chang continued her dissertation about the painting, having never seen Mark return from the bathroom or witnessing his sprint to the piano. Paul stood his ground, not wanting to appear as a co-conspirator during the debacle that was sure to ensue...

Now.

The piano roared to life as Mark's fingers flew over the keys, pounding out the notes of Amazing Grace. Paul shook his head with a smile. It sounded great, first because Mark was an accomplished pianist, and second because Mark had refrained from singing. But the reaction from Chang was instant horror.

"Mr. Byers!" she shouted, walking to the piano as fast as she could. "Mr. Byers, please!" The rest of her exhortations became drowned by the echo of notes flowing through the large East Room.

Mark mouthed, "What?" He had no intention of stopping to listen. And Elizabeth's dancing at the center of the room only encouraged him to play with more passion. Mia, however, remained unfazed by the music, Chang's urgent pleas, and her niece dancing like a wounded flamingo at the center of the largest room in the White House.

Paul tapped Mia's shoulder, causing her to flinch. "Didn't mean to startle you."

She shook her head. "Don't worry about it."

"You feeling okay?"

"Yeah, sure. Of course..." She looked him in the eyes. "Why?"

Paul smiled his best grandfatherly smile. He wanted to put her at ease. "You seem a little nervous is all."

Mia looked at the floor and traced the Oriental rug's pattern with the toe of her high heel. "Just ants in my pants."

"About meeting the president?"

"You could say that."

"What else could I say?"

"This an interrogation?"

"Hey, I didn't vote for the guy," Paul said, then pretended to zip his lips. "My lips are sealed."

Mia continued staring at the floor, clearly uncomfortable. Paul decided not to press the woman. He watched Elizabeth dance around the room, kicking legs wildly and swaying arms to Mark's piano playing. "She's something else. Your niece."

Mia smiled and nodded.

"You have any kids?" Paul asked. He caught his breath when Mia froze. That touched a nerve.

Mia turned to him, her eyes already wet and ready to spill over and her bottom lip displaying the slightest of quivers.

Paul's heart went out to the woman. He knew suffering when he saw it. He patted her back and said, "Hey now, it'll be okay. You don't need to talk to me."

To his surprise she leaned on his shoulder. Then she sniffed, wiped her eyes and stood up straight. "I need to talk to someone or I'll burst."

Paul nodded and waited.

"I was supposed to get married later this year." Paul listened though he had no idea where her story would go. Mia took a deep breath and finished, "My fiancé's name was Matthew Brenton."

"Brenton..." Paul blinked. "Matthew Brenton? The sniper?"

"He's not a sniper," Mia whispered. "He's a truck driver."

Paul had no reason not to believe her, and the statements made by the U.S. government supported her claim. "Hey, you didn't write Elizabeth's essay now, did you? That'd be a pretty sneaky way to get an audience," he said with a smile.

Mia chuckled, then took a deep breath, letting her body relax. She crossed her arms over her blue blouse, and said, "I just want to find out what happened to Matt."

"They're not telling you anything?"

Mia shook her head. "Not a peep."

"Have you contacted the media?"

"I'm a reporter."

"Oh." Paul shook his head. He loved his country. Would have died for his country. But things like this—railroading a soldier's family—soon to be or not—for no good reason other to maintain appearances, really got under his skin. When he got back from Vietnam and some of his friends were still fighting, he'd listen to the stories of their frustrated wives, just wanting to know that their husbands were still alive. But they didn't have to listen to their husbands' tortured voices betraying their country in an audio recording. "Was that really him? The recording?"

Mia nodded.

Paul shook his head. "So you're here to ask about your fiancé?"

"Not that it will do any good," Mia said. "I doubt he'll listen to me. Probably have me escorted away is more likely."

"If he doesn't listen to you, maybe he'll listen to a Medal of Honor recipient?"

Mia smiled. "Thanks...and if he doesn't?"

"Well then," Paul said with a smile, "Miss Reporter, we'll have quite the story to tell."

Mark's booming rendition of Amazing Grace ended with a resounding cheer from Elizabeth and a sigh of relief from Chang, who looked at her watch and announced, "They'll be waiting for us in the dining room now. Please, follow me." She waited for Mark to stand and then hurried for the door.

Paul extended his elbow to Mia. "Been a long time since I had a pretty girl to escort to dinner...or brunch."

Mia smiled and linked her arm in his. He grinned and said, "Let's give 'em hell."

6

Mia followed the group, keeping an eye on Elizabeth as she talked up a storm, asking Mark how he learned to play the piano. Paul followed close behind them. With his hands clasped behind his back, straight posture and immaculate military uniform, the man shouted, "war hero." Perhaps with him on her side she really would find out something about Matt?

Chang stopped in front of a pair of cherry red doors. "This is the Family Dining Room where we'll be having brunch. It's used primarily for smaller functions like today. The State Dining Room is where larger functions are held." Her cell phone blurted the Star Trek theme song. Stifling a look of embarrassment, she flipped it open, pressed it to her ear and listened. "Okay," she said, then snapped the phone shut. "Sorry, I'm a bit of a Trekkie."

Mark held his hand up separating his index and middle fingers from his ring and pinkie fingers. "Live long and prosper."

Chang smiled. "Just for that I'll forget the piano incident."

Mark smiled.

"Just don't do it again, okay?"

Mark brought his fingers together. "Scout's honor."

Paul nudged him. "They teach hand signs at the archdiocese now?"

"I can do gang signs, too."

Mia's nervousness grew with each second they stood in front of the dining room doors. She'd only known about the possibility of meeting the president for a short time, not even a full week, but the intensity of worry and anxiety over the impending encounter consumed all her thoughts.

Mark twisted his fingers into a W. "West Coast!"

Mia cleared her throat. "Can we..." She motioned to the door, afraid her quivering voice might reveal her tension.

A quick jerk of the door handle was Chang's reply, as her smile disappeared. "Of course." She entered the room and stood next to a long oval table that reflected the sunlight streaming in through two large windows surrounded by golden drapes. Likewise, the walls of the room shone bright yellow. The whole scene gave the impression of being inside an egg yolk, which was strangely fitting given the steaming plates of eggs Benedict being set on the table by a hurried wait staff.

Mia entered the room last and saw the president standing at the other side of the table. His wide eyes and wider smile seemed genuine, but the president was known for being a charmer.

Chang introduced them one by one to Collins. Mark shook his hand and said, "It's an honor, Mr. President."

Paul saluted and the president followed suit. The president shook his hand with both hands, two peas in a pod.

"Great to finally meet you, Paul," Collins said. "I'm really looking forward to today."

Paul nodded. "Likewise, sir."

Mia's stomach twisted. Would Paul really back her up in the face of his Commander-in-Chief? Or would he be a good soldier and keep his mouth shut, obey orders and all that?

Collins knelt down in front of Elizabeth. "And you must be our essayist?"

"I can probably write better than you," Elizabeth said with her eyebrows and chin raised high. Then she smiled. "But I really want to be an astronaut."

Collins laughed. "Well, if you apply yourself and study hard, I'm sure you'll be whatever you want to be."

"Can I go to the moon?"

"By the time you're ready, we'll be going to Mars."

Elizabeth's eyes opened like blooming flowers. Collins smiled and stood, moving to Mia.

He held out his hand.

Mia took it and shook. "Mr. President."

Mia nearly threw up on the man. She felt positive she couldn't eat anything, let alone make it through brunch without passing out from anxiety, so she decided to get things over with fast. He wouldn't be rude to someone he'd just met, would he? She put on her reporter face and opened her mouth.

"Later," Collins said.

Mia blinked. "What?"

"We'll talk later," he said in a whisper. "No need to talk about...your issues...in front of all these people. We'll talk later, in private. I promise."

Mia couldn't believe it. She just stood there shaking his hand. He'd cleared the air, just like that, diffusing her tension like an emotional bomb squad. He knew who she was and seemed unfazed by it. Could it really be that easy? She glanced at Paul. He raised his eyebrows and gave a slight shrug as though to say, "why not?"

"Okay," she said.

Collins headed back to the head of the table and motioned everyone to sit down. During the next hour of small talk, eggs, bacon, home fries and gobs of hollandaise sauce, Mia felt herself relaxing. She couldn't think of a reason the president should react badly to her presence. She just wanted to know where her fiancé was and what they were doing to get him back. The only possible conflict might come if they were, in fact, doing nothing. But if that proved true, Collins would realize it and wouldn't want to talk to her at all.

Unless that's why he asked for a private meeting? So no one would hear her shouting. Or maybe he'd suddenly be whisked away, avoiding any sort of meeting at all? Mia's nervousness began to claw its way back to the surface. Then Paul came to her rescue, playing devil's advocate.

"Sir, I've been meaning to ask you about the man accused of being an assassin..."

Mia could only guess that Paul had avoided using Matt's name for Elizabeth's sake. The man had tact to spare.

Collins glanced at Mia, then back to Paul, clearly trying to find a connection between the two. "Yes?"

"It's obviously not true, and I understand the need for a media blackout. There's no need to indulge a Russian ruse, but I can't help wondering about the soldier. Is anything being done to bring him home? I'm sure his family must be worried sick."

Collins put down his fork and wiped his mouth with a napkin. During those few seconds, the room fell silent. All eyes turned to Collins.

"I'm sure you understand," Collins said, "that this is a delicate matter." Paul nodded. "Absolutely."

"We can't simply send in a rescue team, breaching their borders, after they've already accused us of committing an act of war." Collins looked at Mia. "At this time, there isn't much we can do."

Mia was about to speak, but Paul slightly lifted his fingers off the table, motioning her to stay calm.

"Sir," Paul said, his voice still calm and utterly respectful, "Do you think something can be done when all this blows over?"

Collins sighed. Mia thought for a moment he would lose his composure, but after twitching his lips one way and then the other, he said, "From what I understand, Mr. Brenton was a fine soldier. He served his country well. But in the end, he—"

A tall, balding man that screamed, "Secret Service" entered the room quickly, followed by a jittery, shaggy haired man that Mia didn't recognize. The man bent down, whispered into the president's ear and then left in a hurry.

Collins looked startled, but then looked back to the Secret Service man and smiled. "That's taking it a little far, don't you think, Tom?"

Mia placed the name. This was the pit bull, Tom Austin. But what were they talking about?

Austin shook his head. "Not me, sir. It's real."

The president just stared straight ahead, like he'd been lobotomized by the man's words. It felt like watching a flashback of George W. sitting in front of the classroom of kids after being told about the attack on the World Trade Center. He just sat...staring...

"Sir," Paul said. "What's happened?"

Collins craned his head slowly toward Paul. "I'm afraid we're going to have to cancel the ceremony today. Russia just declared war."

7

Earth Orbit

Several times each year, a group of satellites launched into space by the Russian satellite communications company, MTI, cross over the airspace of the United States and Europe at the exact same time. The complex dance began in the late nineties, when the first of the now fifty-seven satellites was placed in earth orbit. The last of the bunch joined the group in early 2007. Four times since June 2007, they have formed a perfectly dispersed web of satellites over the western world, just for a few minutes each time.

A few minutes was all they needed.

All fifty seven satellites activated simultaneously. Hatch doors opened noiselessly in space, their payloads exposed to the endless vacuum. This moment represented fifteen years of planning, painstaking calculations, absolute secrecy and a hidden budget that drained resources from the struggling Russian economy. But the long-term plan would return the mother country to superpower status, wipe out all opposition and leave them to reign in a new world order.

The gambit was dangerous, no doubt, but living in the shadow of an overpowering enemy is not a life worth living. The potential benefits outweighed the risks, which had been minimized through detailed planning and now, perfect execution.

The satellites began their countdown when the Russian president publicly declared war. The announcement was designed to confuse the enemy. The Americans would respond with incredulous accusations about the assassination attempt and the unlikely odds that Russia could ever win a war. But the other reason for the announcement was to get the Americans' eyes turned toward Russia. Why shoot the enemy in the back when you can get them to turn around and see it coming. Let them realize they've been throwing a party in front of a lion's den. Then destroy them.

    3...

    2...

    1...

Fifty-seven fifteen-megaton nuclear warheads detonated as one. Their bright plumes of light, seen from the ground, brought gasps of awe, comments of beauty and then—absolute fear.

No traces of radiation reached the earth. Not a degree of heat. Not a wave of pressure.

What struck was invisible and totally undetectable, until the electromagnetic pulse reached out and disabled every electronic device in the western world.

8

Washington D.C.

A panel in the dining room wall slid up to reveal a flat-screen television. Austin turned it on and stood back as the screen lit up, revealing the stern eyes and grim face of the Russian president. The news ticker at the bottom of the screen read, "Russia declares war on the United States." For a moment Mia felt strange and out of place to be receiving the grave news not only at the same time as the president of the United States, but in his presence. She expected him to jump up at any moment and run to some war room or something. But he stayed rooted in his seat at the head of the table, hovering over his scraps of bacon and eggs. She realized then that this was going down in real time. Even moving to another room would mean catching up on what was being broadcast.

"Turn it up," Collins said.

Austin pushed the volume button on the TV several times, then stood back as Misha Alexandrov's voice filled the room. His voice boomed loud and angry, speaking in heavily accented English. "Today the Americans and their allies will learn what it means to mock the great Russia. We will no longer tolerate the insults, economic posturing or flagrant spread of their Christian religion in our great Soviet state! Today, we return to the communism that made this country great! Today, we return to the pinnacle of the world's attention. Today, our enemies will taste defeat."

Alexandrov turned toward the camera, peering into the eyes of billions of transfixed viewers and said. "Today."

Realization slammed into Mia's mind. "Oh God. He wouldn't." She turned to the president. "He wouldn't, right?"

The president looked at Chang, who'd been whispering on the phone. "The VP?"

"En route to a secure location," Chang said, nearly in tears.

Collins nodded, then stood. He looked at the group. "I'm sure this is all posturing...but... Stephanie, make arrangements for them to be taken out of the city."

Chang nodded.

The president headed for the door with Austin in tow. He turned back to the group as he opened the door. "Don't worry, I'm sure everything will—"

The TV blinked out. The lights died. The sounds of the city, which had been penetrating the White House walls as a distant yet constant hum, went silent.

Austin clasped the president's arm, fearing danger. Two more Secret Service men and one woman burst into the room, eyes sharp and wary. As the group stood in silence, waiting for some sign of life to return, Chang gasped. She held up her cell phone. The screen was black.

"Electromagnetic pulse," Mia whispered. She'd seen the supposed effects of an electromagnetic pulse in enough movies to recognize what had happened. With every electronic device rendered useless, no other explanation made sense.

Then the silence broke again. Horns blared in the distance. Grinding metal shook the air. Cars were stalling. Some were crashing. Engines stopped. Power steering failed. Mia's eyes widened as she realized the same effect would be taking place in the skies. With five thousand planes in the sky at any given time in the United States, a lot of people were about to die.

Then a new sound intruded—shouting voices and heavy feet. A flurry of men burst into the room all shouting at once. Collins held up his hands and they fell silent. "How long before we're back up?" he asked no one in particular.

A young man with large ears stepped forward. "The generators are being refitted with shielded parts. White House power should be restored within the minute. Same with our military bases, silos and radar systems. We should assume our satellites are being destroyed as we speak. They'll want us blind."

A man pushed through the group with an old rotary phone. He lay on the floor and slid under a china cabinet.

Mia's mind spun as the new events unfolded around her, building like a hurricane and dispersing all her worries and thoughts about Matt like dust in a storm. She wanted to say something, to contribute somehow, but all she could do was watch and marvel at Collins's calm in the face of war.

"When the lines are up, I want all forces put on red alert. I want planes in the sky and our—"

The old metal bell on the phone cut painfully through the air. The man on the floor slid out from beneath the pantry where he'd plugged it into the wall and answered. "White House."

Mia couldn't understand the man on the other end, but she could hear his shouting voice. She knew the news was bad when the man on the floor opened his eyes wide.

"What about the missile defen—"

Then she heard the tinny voice on the other end shout, "It's all gone! Get out! Get out now!" The line went dead. The man on the floor hung up the phone and looked at Collins. His face paled as he swallowed. "ICBMs in the air, sir. The missile defense networks in Europe and Alaska have already been hit."

"How many?" Collins asked, his voice quiet and deep.

"Everything they've got. They've targeted Europe and our allies around the world as well. Several European allies have already been hit."

"How long?"

The man sniffed. "Five minutes."

Collins took a long deep breath while Mia tried hard not to vomit. The United States was about to be nuked into oblivion. With Washington D.C. no doubt first on the hit list, they had slightly less than five minutes to live.

She reached out and took Elizabeth's hand.

She looked at Mark.

His eyes were closed, his lips moving fast. Praying. Paul sat rigid next to him. He looked ready to snap into action like a true war hero, but what could he do against a nuclear assault?

Collins waved the man with the phone over. He took the phone, placed it down and dialed a five digit number. "General Long, this is President Collins. Are you aware of our current situation? Good. What's the status of our nuclear arsenal?" Collins listened and nodded. "Good, good. Listen...launch everything. Predefined targets in scenario Omega. Yes. Yes. Right now. Get them off the ground and out of our subs before a single U.S. city is struck. I want them wiped off the damn planet. There is no way I'm going to let those sons-a-bitches rewrite history!" Collins slammed down the phone causing everyone in the room to jump. Not because of the loud clang of the phone's bell, a sound Mia no longer missed, but because he'd just ordered the outright extinction of the human race.

Austin caught her eye as he moved forward and whispered into Collins's ear. Collins nodded. "Do it."

Austin looked up at the group of men. "Listen up. Initiate the Orion Protocol. Get everyone you can, but do not wait. The train leaves in sixty seconds. We launch in two. Go!"

The group of men exited the room like a torrent of water, flowing into the hallways. Three of the remaining Secret Service agents rushed out with Collins and Chang. Austin began to follow then stopped at the door. He looked back at the stunned group still sitting at the table. "You can sit there and die or you can come with me, but keep up, because I'm not going to wait."

Mia was the first on her feet, scooping up Elizabeth and chasing after Austin, who was already out the door. Paul and Mark followed close behind as Austin led them down a staircase to the first floor, across the center hall and into a library lined with books. Mia paused for a moment, surprised to see one of the bookshelves hanging open like something out of Indiana Jones. Austin appeared in the doorway from below. "Hurry it up!" he shouted. "We're leaving in thirty seconds!"

Mia and the others rushed through the doorway and down fifty cement stairs. At the bottom they entered a large cavity that housed what looked like several small subway cars, but they were unlike any subway cars she'd ever seen. They sat high on a single track that ran under the center of the car. Austin waved them on as he held the door open. "Move it!"

Mia ran through the doors and put Elizabeth down. The inside of the car looked like an actual subway, with seats on the sides and poles in the middle. As Paul and Mark entered, Austin let the doors close and stepped inside. Mia could see other groups of White House staff flowing through several doors throughout the chamber, all scrambling into the other cars.

Austin picked Elizabeth up and held her tight to his chest as he sat down.

"Hey," Mia protested, but the look in Austin's eyes told her to shut up.

"Hold on," he said so seriously that she instantly complied, grabbing on to one of the poles.

The car lifted slightly and then took off like a rocket. Paul, caught off guard, fell to the floor and slid to the back of the car where he crashed into the wall. But no one could help him. As the car climbed rapidly to its top speed of two hundred miles per hour, the G-forces held everyone in place. But then, as quickly as it started, the car came to a steady stop. Mia looked out the window and gasped. Had they just covered the distance between Washington D.C. and Area 51?

Paul stood up with a groan and followed Mia's eyes. "Now what the hell is that?"

9

Mia stumbled from the railcar, pulling Elizabeth by the hand. They had entered a massive chamber, lit by rows of halogen lights that wrapped around the tall cylindrical space. The chamber stood perhaps three hundred feet tall and twice as wide, but the four objects contained within commanded all her attention.

"Auntie Mia," Elizabeth said, "you're hurting my hand."

Elizabeth's pained and nervous voice yanked Mia away from the view. She looked back at her niece and saw her large, bright blue eyes brimming with tears. Realizing in that moment that Elizabeth would soon be the only family she had left—Matt, Margo and Mom would soon be reduced to ashes—she picked the girl up in her arms and held her tight to her chest. She chased after Austin, who was halfway to one of the strange looking...things.

"You want me to carry her?" Paul asked, as he took her arm, half walking, half running next to her.

"I got her, thanks." Mia said.

"You know what these things are?" Paul asked.

Mia looked at the four bell shaped objects. Each craft stood seventy-five feet tall and had a sixty foot diameter at the bottom. The underside had a curved surface coated by millions of smooth, black panels. The black skin looked familiar to Mia, but in her panic she failed to place the image. The stark white surface of the object Austin led them toward gleamed bright in the halogen light, obscuring most of the external features except a large American flag and rows of small portal windows.

"Salvation, I hope."

"The Lord is my light and my salvation—whom shall I fear?" Mark said as he joined their mad rush to the strange structure. "The Lord is the stronghold of my life—of whom shall I be afraid?" He looked at Mia. "One of the Psalms. Can't remember which one under the current circumstances."

Mia quickened her pace as they neared a ramp that led up to a large open, steel doorway. Austin stood by the hatch, but no longer waved for them to hurry. He looked past them, his eyes pinched with sadness. She turned to Mark as she stepped up on to the ramp. "You're not afraid?"

Mark climbed onto the ramp, followed by Paul. "Actually, I'm scared shitless, but you were asking for salvation. I just want to not be nuked."

Mia couldn't help but smile as they rushed up the ramp and past Austin. Mark somehow gave her hope that everything might be okay. Perhaps this was all a cosmic misunderstanding? Maybe the missiles could be called back? Her smile disappeared after she passed through a long hallway and entered a large room.

Fifty chairs, laid back like recliners, filled the room. Attached to each chair was a restraint system, like you'd see on a roller coaster, but much more rigid. Collins, the three Secret Service agents and Chang were in the process of pulling the bars up over their chests. Once in place, the black padding around the bodies, heads and chest expanded, locked them in tight.

A loud clang sounded from the hallway behind them. Tom had closed the door. Mark ran to one of the small portals. He turned back as Tom entered the room, "We have room for at least forty more people!"

"No time!" Tom said as he jumped into one of the chairs and pulled the bar up over his chest. As the padding inflated he said, "I suggest you strap yourself in. We launch in thirty seconds."

Mia's eyes widened as the word "launch" took root in her mind. "Oh, God." She flung Elizabeth into the nearest chair and yanked the bar up over her small chest. It seemed loose on her small body. "Will this work for a child?" Mia shouted as her hands began to tremble.

"No...time..." Tom said, barely able to breathe, let alone speak in the tight grasp of the chair.

Mia leaned down and kissed Elizabeth. "I love you."

As the pads on Elizabeth's chair began to expand, Mia jumped into the next chair. Paul and Mark were both strapped in already, pads constricting their bodies. She slid into position, sat up and grabbed the safety bar. As she pulled the bar up and over her body, a loud mechanical voice filled the one-fifth occupied room, "Ten, nine, eight, seven..."

Mia grunted as she pulled down on the arm and locked it into place. The pads began to fill with air, but were still a few inches from her body. She turned her head slightly and looked to the side. She could see through one of the portals. People poured from the small train cars still, all running toward the crafts. Soft thuds drifted from the hallway. People outside were banging on the hatch. Had anyone else made it? Would they reach the other...

"Three...two..."

Orion.

In that final second, Mia's subconscious finished putting together the pieces of what was about to happen. Collins called this project Orion. Tom said they would be launched. Matt's third passion after trucks and the military was space. He read everything he could about it, absorbing every bit of it as though he'd get to visit the moon someday. And she'd suffered through more than a few documentaries. One such documentary discussed possible methods for propelling spacecrafts through space at enormous speeds. Solar sails, ion propulsion, laser sails and all sorts of other fancy theories. But one struck her as being absolutely outlandish. Orion.

In short, small nuclear explosives would be dropped out of the spacecraft's rear and detonated two hundred feet back. Massive shock absorbers in the back of the craft would take the impact, and the craft would be shot forward. Repeat this in rapid succession and you've got the making of an amazingly fast ship...or in this case, escape pod. But the project was supposed to have been scrapped. Concerns over fallout stopped the project short. But here, in Washington D.C, thousands upon thousands of people would be exposed to the full blast, radiation and fallout from the Orion engine. To save themselves, they were about to kill thousands of people...a few minutes before the Russians.

"One."

The ship shook violently.

Screams from outside filtered through the steel walls and rumbling engines. Then with a violent kick, the voices fell silent. The people and trains outside the portal disappeared in the billowing smoke.

A tremendous pressure clasped her body tight. Mia looked down and realized the restraints had compressed around her body. She couldn't move.

Then the ship lifted off, sucking what little air remained in her compressed lungs, denying her the opportunity to vent her fear, anger and vast terror with a scream.

Sam Black climbed out of his car. He'd managed to turn the wheel just as his car lost power. He had avoided hitting the car in front of him, but careened over the curb and up onto the sidewalk of Pennsylvania Avenue. He'd expected Secret Service men to swarm the scene, followed quickly by police and firemen. But no one showed. Looking out the windshield, he could see why. By the lack of sound, he judged that every car within earshot had died. "What the..."

Sam caught sight of the front tire that had struck the curb first. "Aww, hell." The tire was flat and the rim bent. "Dammit."

Recently divorced, working as a line cook and paying alimony, a new tire, let alone a front axle was far above his budget. A shrill scream took his attention away from the latest miserable chapter of his life. A woman across the street, standing with the White House as a backdrop, pointed toward the horizon. "They're going to crash!"

Sam followed her pointed finger and saw the faint image of a 747 falling nose down, far in the distance.

A heavily mustached man stepped up on the curb next to him. "Think it's the terrorists? First the power and now this."

Sam turned to the man, "The power?"

"Power's out everywhere...in everything."

Sam turned back to the plane in time to see it disappear behind the city's buildings. A woman across the street screamed. She'd seen it, too. A distant boom pealed through the air like thunder and smoke rose to the sky. Then the ground began to shake. "What the hell? No way could we feel that plane hit."

The mustached man nodded. "Must have been ten miles away."

A line of people filled the sidewalk in either direction, moving forward slowly, pointing and talking. Sam lowered his eyes from the smoke-filled horizon to the green grass of Lafayette Park's famous Ellipse.

"Ho-lee shit," the mustached man said. "What's going on?"

Four massive holes opened up at the middle of the Ellipse. Large disks of grass had sunk down and were now sliding beneath the park. Already, the four openings looked like half-moons.

"What the..." Sam stepped forward, intent on getting a good look. This would be a good story to tell his kid. Might give him some leverage over the ex. Dad witnessed history being made, kid, be proud.

Seconds after the spaces opened fully, a massive rumble shook the ground and smoke blasted from three of the four holes. A moment later, smoke burst from the fourth hole.

The sidewalk full of onlookers began stepping back. Sam stayed still, rooted by curiosity. Three white domes emerged from three of the holes, huge gleaming bodies rising from the ground. Plumes of smoke billowed out around them.

Sam stepped back as he realized that whatever these things were, they had rockets attached to them and he had no idea how far the heat would reach. He saw people getting back into their cars. He did the same and then realized his electric powered windows were down. He jumped out and headed for the next car on the road, never taking his eyes off the rising behemoths. When the fourth object began to rise he knocked on the window of the mustached man's car. The door flung open, "Get in man, get in!"

Sam climbed in and slammed the door as a wall of steam and smoke overtook the street full of dead cars, then rolled over the White House itself. The smoke settled and cleared as the four craft rose up into the sky, one lagging behind the others by several hundred feet.

"Ma-aan," the mustached man said, "What the fu—" The man caught his breath as three small objects fell from the undersides of the higher three crafts, which were now a thousand feet off the ground and rising.

"What are those?" Sam asked.

An instant later, Sam's eyes registered a bright white flash, a pain like someone striking his full body with a massive fist, and a twist in his gut. He vomited as his bowels loosened and he felt blood seeping from his nose, eyes, ears and mouth. On top of all that, he was blind and deaf.

Sam never saw the three higher crafts launch skyward at amazing speeds, riding shockwave after shockwave of small nuclear explosions. He had no idea the fourth one had been knocked off course by the explosions from the first three. And when the fourth ship launched its small nuclear device horizontally rather than vertically, Sam had no way to know it had landed just outside the mustached man's car.

Then they both ceased to exist.

10

Over Washington D.C.

Points of light danced in Mia's vision as she fought against the restraint system and crushing G-forces, struggling to catch a breath. The restraints were designed to keep the force of lift-off from tearing apart a human body, but did nothing to prevent the sudden increase in pressure, which significantly lowered blood pressure and the flow of oxygen to the brain. As the rapidly accelerating escape pod approached 8 G's, known as the maximum G-force, unconsciousness loomed for Mia. Realizing this, she struggled to look out the portal. She felt sure it would be the last time she saw Earth's blue sky.

But the view from the portal was solid white. Mia thought her failing mind was playing tricks, but color variations kept her focused. Then the white disappeared, replaced by a vibrant blue. She could see the tops of clouds in the distance. They'd passed through the clouds and were rising quickly. The scene looked beautiful and serene, and for a moment, allowed Mia a reprieve from the horrible pressure and shaking. As the clouds faded from view, the blue hue became deep, like the depths of the ocean.

The colorful dots that filled her vision turned white and stationary. As she winked in and out of consciousness, she realized the stationary points of lights were stars. Then something else, something she wished was an illusion, passed by in the distance. A long, black-tipped cylinder rocketed past in the opposite direction. Then she saw more—missiles descending from space to Earth. Her consciousness faded, and with the last of her lucidity she took one last peek through the portal. This time she saw new missiles, more than she imagined possible, rising up from the same country that would, within seconds, no longer exist.

Then the oxygen-sucking maximum G-force robbed her of conscious-ness.

Tom Austin woke as the forces pushing against his body disappeared. He lifted his hands to his head and rubbed his eyes. He didn't remember passing out, but knew he had. Having no memory of the restraint system releasing him was proof of that. He sat, pushing with his hands and shot out of the chair. He spun toward the ceiling and collided with it.

Zero gravity.

From maximum G to zero G, Austin thought. That's just great.

He shoved off the ceiling and took hold of his chair. He knew there was no up or down anymore, but the designers of the Earth Escape Pod obviously hadn't taken that into account. His eyes still perceived an up and down, but his body had no clue, and he felt the confusion in his stomach. Fighting the urge to puke, Austin focused on the few men and women in the room who were now under his direct care as the ranking Secret Service agent on board. President Collins's chest rose and fell—unconscious, but alive. Around the president lay the three members of his Secret Service team: Daniel White, the skinny, blond-haired, emerald-eyed electronics wiz, Joseph Garbarino, the burly Italian Stallion, and Erin Vanderwarf, one of the few female field agents in the service, whose full pouty lips and long lashes made her one of the prettiest, too, despite a rugged build. All seemed fine.

Austin turned his attention to their guests. He flung himself from chair to chair, covering the empty spaces between him and Paul Byers, the war hero. Byers looked dead, but a quick check of his pulse revealed otherwise. Paul's brother, the priest, was already beginning to stir. Before his eyes got to the next passenger, her name echoed through the room.

"Elizabeth!" Mia shouted as she flung herself from the chair and catapulted through the air, up and above her young niece. Tom pushed off Paul's chair and intercepted Mia as she approached the ceiling. Gripping a handhold, he snagged Mia's wrist with his free hand. The force of Mia's movement pushed them both flat against the ceiling. He looked at her as confusion flooded her eyes.

"We're in space," he said. "No gravity."

She looked at him, eyes wide and nodded frantically. She understood, but the information clearly unnerved her. Tears filled her eyes. "My sister. My mother."

Mia hadn't asked a question, but Austin heard one. He closed his eyes and gave a gentle nod. "Everyone is gone."

When she began to cry, he didn't know how to respond. He barely knew this woman. His instincts leaned toward survival, not mourning. But he wasn't without sympathy. He gave a tug on her hand and she floated into his embrace. He held her, floating in zero gravity for nearly a minute while she cried into his shoulder. Then she pushed away slowly, wiping away her tears. "Thanks."

He offered a thin smile. The woman was resilient, he gave her that much. She didn't break down or cry out. She mourned briefly, and now, like him, was setting her mind on their current predicament. "Push off the ceiling, gently. You won't slow down until you hit something."

She nodded quickly again and looked down at the floor, ten feet below. "An object in motion..."

Austin smiled and finished, "Tends to stay in motion. Yes."

Austin let go of her arm and she pushed off the ceiling gently, but not quite evenly. She spun on her way to the floor, bounced off one of the laid-back chairs and caught herself on the floor. She righted herself. Without a comment or look back at Austin, she pulled herself to Elizabeth's side. He watched as she checked the girl's pulse.

"She okay?" he asked.

Mia nodded. "Should I wake her up?"

"Best if they wake on their own. Let the mind recuperate first."

Mia turned her gaze from Elizabeth to the portal. "Have you looked?"

"What?"

"At Earth," Mia said. "Have you looked?"

Austin felt a wave of anxiety wash through him. He'd been so focused on his duties that he'd forgotten all about the dangers they'd just escaped. The dangers that more than six billion other people had no way of avoiding. He doubted the few people who made it to the underground facilities could survive. In an all-out, no-holds-barred nuclear war, even a mountain could be flattened by repeated strikes.

As Mia made her way across the long room, guiding herself along rows of chairs, Austin pulled himself along a row of handholds built into the ceiling. At least the designers had gotten that right. They reached the slightly curved far wall at the same time and met at the dinner-plate sized portal, side by side, legs floating out behind them. It reminded Austin of looking through the underwater portal of his childhood home's pool, but the aqua tinged view of his brother on the other side wasn't there. Instead, he witnessed the most vile sight he had ever seen in his life. A swirl of black filled earth's atmosphere and absorbed the light cast by the sun. Pulses of orange marked the detonation of still descending nuclear devices, further reducing the world to ash. Stabs of blue revealed the ocean below, but the vivid colored planet that only a few minutes ago stood out as a pearl in the universe had been reduced to a black and gray swirled marble.

As the planet spun beneath them, Austin began to wonder how what he saw was possible. The entire planet had vanished beneath a roiling thick cloud of smoke and fallout. The fiery flares continued, but he no longer saw pulses of light, more like bolts of orange lightning, slipping through the sooty atmosphere.

"Is this real?" Mia asked.

"It's real," he whispered, then cleared his throat. "I'm not sure how it's possible. I suppose no one really knew what unleashing that amount of destructive energy would do."

Austin returned to the view of Earth, watching the flashes of orange cut through the black atmosphere. "Looks like some kind of chain reaction was triggered. Maybe volcanoes...or some kind of lightning. I don't know."

Mark, the priest, silently floated toward them. They moved aside as he arrived and looked out the portal. He stared in silence for a moment. He asked no questions. Made no comment. After a minute, his lips turned down.

"Better make your peace," he said and then pushed away from the wall. He floated across the room like an apparition, looking both of them in the eyes before spinning away.

ORBIT

11

Earth Orbit

Vanderwarf, the lone female Secret Service officer stood far to the side of White, one of her three male counterparts, with her arms outstretched toward his face. She held a plastic bag open with tightly clamped fingertips and a turned away face. She'd wedged her feet beneath two handholds so that she could stand on the ceiling, while White held on with both feet and hands so that his violent vomiting wouldn't simultaneously launch him across the room and send an arc of bile into the zero-G environment.

Cleaning liquids in zero-G was a challenge.

Cleaning puke was hell.

To his credit, White didn't seem embarrassed by being the only one to react badly to the lack of gravity. He just latched on and puked when he needed to and acted like his cool, collected, quiet self when he could hold his stomach down.

Mia had watched the action from the corner of the room where she'd been holding Elizabeth since the girl woke up a half hour ago. The fourth Secret Service man, Garbarino, sat brooding, dismantling and reassembling his sidearm, allowing the parts to float in front of him. When he needed a part, he'd just pluck it from the air. Paul and Mark stood by a portal on the far side of the room that looked out at the amazing view of the stars. They'd been talking seriously the whole time, but didn't seem to be arguing. Collins stood by a portal on the near side, hands against the steel walls, peering down at the swirling black world below that looked more like an alien planet than the world they'd called home only forty-five minutes ago. He had yet to say a word.

Five minutes after checking everyone for injuries, Austin left the room and sealed them in. He wanted to make sure the rest of the pod was intact before letting them settle in.

Settle in? Mia thought, like we'll ever "settle in" anywhere again. This capsule is our tomb.

She squeezed Elizabeth and kissed her head. She couldn't bear the thought of watching Elizabeth die or vice-versa, of having Elizabeth watch her die. But what was the point of living now anyway? Survival instinct? They could do nothing meaningful with their lives now. The human race had been reduced from more than six billion to ten. Maybe they would be better off just ending it all, like some Stephen King novel, everyone can just shoot each other in the head. The Secret Service team packed enough hardware to get the job done.

A form rose up from the floor, lacking any kind of grace, and hit the ceiling. Chang. She'd been crying quietly since waking. The dynamic duo of Paul and Mark had tried to console her, but to no avail. They gave up and took up the position by the portal. Chang pushed gently off the ceiling and floated toward Mia. Her eyes were swollen and red, but the tears had stopped, or perhaps she'd just run out.

Swinging her arms like a kid on a balance beam, Chang tried to slow her approach, but only managed to flip herself over. "Whoa!"

Elizabeth ducked as Chang's rear end struck Mia's face. The impact felt more embarrassing than painful. Not wanting Chang to bounce off like a pinball and spin around the room, Mia took hold of her legs and held her tight. Both looked toward the other's face.

"Sorry," Chang said. Then she squinted awkwardly. "You know you're standing on the ceiling?"

Mia looked at Chang's face, askew with confusion, upside down...yet right side up, and snorted.

And for some reason, Lionel Richie's Dancing On The Ceiling popped into her head and she sang, "Oh what a feeling, when we're dancing on the ceiling."

Then she laughed, slowly at first as she attempted to conceal her smile behind Chang's upturned leg, but then breaking out into an uncontrollable laugh. Chang joined in, then Elizabeth, and the three unloaded a world's worth of anxiety by finding humor in their current, ridiculous situation. Across the room, White vomited loudly and they laughed even more. "Thanks," White said after finishing. Vanderwarf just smiled at them. Everyone else seemed too preoccupied with their own thoughts to notice the laughing women.

Mia righted herself and Elizabeth so that their feet were once again facing the floor. The move sent a wave of nausea through her body, but it passed quickly. She came face to face with Chang as they both reached out for something to stop their movement. "You okay?" Mia asked once her movement had stopped.

Chang nodded. "It's just a hard concept to get used to—the end of the world, living in space, never finishing the final season DVD of Battlestar."

Mia smiled. She hadn't liked Chang much when they first met. The woman had seemed uptight. But Mia could now see that had been her "at work" personality. This was the real Chang. A little goofy. Very clumsy. A Battlestar Galactica nerd. And they shared a sense of humor, even if it was inappropriate.

"How about you?" Chang asked.

How could she answer that question? Americans had a slew of stand-by answers to the question: Okay. Not bad. Same old, same old. They were reserved for small talk with strangers or reuniting with friends, but almost never were questions meant to garner anything other than one of the standard answers. Anything more became annoying. But now, America and its societal norms no longer existed. Besides, it seemed like Chang actually wanted to know. "My fiancé was Matthew Brenton."

A pang of guilt struck when she said the word fiancé. If life on Earth hadn't come to an abrupt end and Matt had returned from the war, and learned the truth...? But the world had ended. Clean slate, right?

Chang's smile disappeared. "Oh."

"Yup."

"So..." Chang said. "Your fiancé is the scapegoat...for all of this." Chang motioned toward a nearby portal with a view of the Earth.

"I came to ask the president if he knew where Matt was being held or if he was even still alive. I know the answer to the second question now." Mia noticed Elizabeth floating around their legs and smiled. "I've still got my Liz, though."

Elizabeth smiled and floated to one of the chairs. Chang lowered her voice. "Does she understand what's happened? That her mother is..."

Mia was impressed that Chang remembered Margo had been a single mom. But she probably had to remember little details like that all the time. "I'm going to avoid the subject for as long as possible. Children are supposed to be more adaptable...or flexible, or something, than adults, but she's dealing with enough already, and she's not talking much. I'll wait for her to bring it up, if she decides to. Did you lose...have a lot of family?"

"Actually, no. No husband. No kids. Only child. Mom died three years ago. Dad was an asshole." Chang smiled. "The people in this room are the ones I saw most of the time for the past few years. The rest are probably floating in one of the other pods."

"Other pods made it?" Mia asked.

"At least two of them," Chang said. "That's what the Byers brothers have been looking at."

"Then there are other survivors?"

"Probably not many, but some, yeah."

Mia started moving toward the nearest far side portal to get a look for herself, when the steel door next to her clunked loudly as it unlocked and swung open. She bounced out of the way as Austin floated into the room. "Sorry," he said. "The door didn't hit you, did it?"

Mia shook her head, no.

"Good," Austin said. "I need you for a minute."

"Me?" Mia asked. "Not one of them?" Mia motioned to the rest of the room.

Austin looked around the rest of the room and frowned slightly. "Just you." He looked at Chang. "Can you watch Liz?"

Mia realized Tom was making an effort to be extra friendly, even using Elizabeth's nickname, but she still felt uncomfortable that he wanted her, exclusively, to join him. "Why me?"

Tom fixed his eyes on hers.

"Now."

He slipped back through the door without another word. She looked back at Chang, whose face had lost some of its regained composure
and asked, "Keep an eye on her?"

Chang nodded. "No problem."

"You listen to Ms. Chang, Liz," Mia said to Elizabeth. "I'll be right back."

Elizabeth saluted in response, then floated over to Chang. "Can we
talk to the president?"

As Chang answered, Mia followed Austin through the door, wondering what he intended to talk about...or do...and in that instant, realized she was trapped in an oversized escape pod with a bunch of total
strangers under extreme circumstances. If one of them went on a
rampage, there would be no place to hide.

As Austin locked the door behind her, she realized that if he intended to take advantage of the situation...of her...no one would come to her
rescue. The loud hiss of the thick door being sealed told her no one
would even hear her scream. As Tom pushed off the door and slid
through the zero gravity tunnel, straight toward her, she prepared for a
fight.

12

Mia braced herself against the tunnel wall as Austin drifted toward her, arms outstretched, hands open, ready to grab. Her thoughts turned toward her karate training. Before becoming a reporter and after a near death car accident in high school sidetracked what was almost a starlet singing career, she found a home in the martial arts. It began as physical therapy after the accident, but soon became a passion. She quickly became a black belt and began teaching adult and children's classes of her own. The problem with karate instruction in rural New Hampshire is that it doesn't pay the bills. She took a job with Foster's Daily Democrat as a reporter, thanks to her night-school degree in English and a friend in circulation. The karate came in handy once, with an unruly interviewee, but she'd been out of practice since. As Austin's thick hands reached out toward her, she wished she'd stuck with it. Not that it would do her much good in zero gravity.

Just as Mia was about to lash out with a kick to his groin, Austin reached past Mia's head, took a handhold and pulled himself further down the tunnel. "This way," he said.

Mia did her best to conceal her sigh of relief and focused on slowing her breathing as she followed after Austin. She couldn't crack up now. She'd survived the worst the world had to offer and for Elizabeth's sake, would do her damnedest to pull them through this and provide her with some semblance of a life.

But what kind of life could she really offer the child? A life worth living? There were no other children. No trees or grass. No pets. She would grow up in a space the size of a large house, with no gravity, no fresh food, nothing that resembled any semblance of a human life on Earth. And all she'd have for company, aside from her aunt, was a small group of adults, at least one of whom was likely to go insane and kill the rest. Astronauts were screened, trained and mentally prepared for living like this, but this group...she doubted any of them, with the possible exception of Austin, had the right stuff.

For a fraction of a moment she wondered if killing Liz and herself was the right thing to do. It would be merciful. But grossly wrong. The notion soured her stomach, helped along by the zero gravity. She felt herself losing control, the sinews that held her emotions in check were stretched tight and breaking one at a time.

Ping.

Ping.

Ping.

Don't lose your fucking mind! she thought at herself. Liz deserves to live and you're going to make damn sure her life is the best it can be, given the circumstances.

She focused on moving instead of the hopelessly horrible life that awaited Liz. The stark white octagonal hallway stretched on for another ten feet before coming to a three way intersection, each direction blocked by a steel hatch. It was wide enough for two people to pass without collision, or float side-by-side. She passed under a recessed light and paused a few feet back from Austin, who opened the hatch leading left.

"In here," he said.

Mia slid into the room behind Austin and found herself in a digital wonderland. The room held two comfortable looking chairs, bolted to the floor, covered in straps. Surrounding the chairs was an array of computer monitors, glowing buttons, gauges and a long window that provided a stunning and horrific view of the molten Earth below. Austin took a seat and motioned her to take the other. She sat down next to him, but floated up a little.

"Use the Velcro straps," Austin said. "They'll hold you down."

Mia took a pair of straps and pulled them tight over her thighs. She did the same around her waist. Strapped down and comfortable, Mia looked over at Austin. He sat silently, rubbing his forehead with his fingers. After nearly a minute, the silence and view of Earth began to drive her mad. "What is this place?"

"Command center," Austin said. He'd apparently been waiting for her to speak. "All the systems on board are controlled from here. Every room can be monitored, every hatch sealed, every light turned off and on. We can also see the status of Earth. We'll know when it's safe to return."

"Return?" Mia asked. "How will we ever return?"

"The computer monitors Earth's survivability, testing for radiation, breathable atmosphere, yadda, yadda, yadda. When it determines that it's safe to return, it sounds a warning and ten minutes later we descend back to the surface in a free fall followed by parachutes. It'll even put us back on U.S. soil."

Mia's eyebrows rose. "Thanks for the detailed description, but that's not what I meant."

Austin looked at her. "What did you mean?"

"I mean, look at it," Mia said, her voice raising an octave. She thrust an open palm toward the view of Earth below, still churning with destructive swirling clouds and stabs of luminous orange. "We destroyed the planet. There's no going back."

Austin looked at the view and nodded. "Yeah...it looks like we're screwed." He looked at her and smiled. "But don't tell anyone else that."

Mia shook her head and smirked. She couldn't believe humor still existed, but as her smile grew, so did Austin's. He flipped his hand like he was opening a notebook and began writing in it with an imaginary pen. "Note to self. Mia Durante. Finds global annihilation humorous. Subject requires further observation."

Austin closed the imaginary notepad and looked back at her like he'd done and said nothing. In that moment she learned two things: 1. Austin was okay. 2. He had a weird sense of humor.

"So," she said. "Why am I here and not one of your Secret Service guys? Or the president for that matter?"

Austin leaned back in his chair and tapped out a steady beat with his fingers on the armrests as he thought. He looked at her and noticed her eyes on his fingers. "I play the drums." He turned his head toward the button covered ceiling. "Pretty soon everyone on board is going to realize that the United States no longer exists. I'm pretty sure this has already dawned on Collins. He can't be the president of something that is not there. My team will realize this as well and figure out they no longer need to protect the man. Their motivation has been removed."

Mia nodded. She hadn't thought this far ahead yet, but it all made sense. The destruction of the United States made them all equals. The president, the priest, the war hero, the Secret Service, the reporter, the aide and the little girl—all on even ground. She frowned. Julia Child couldn't come up with a better recipe for chaos. "So, let me ask again. Why am I here?"

"Other than a pretty face to distract me from the view?"

Mia raised a no-nonsense eyebrow, which made him smile.

"I've been watching the group." Austin flipped a series of switches.

A line of screens arranged beneath the long window.

Several views of the large, lounge chair-filled room appeared. Each screen focused on an individual or pair. "You want the quick and honest answer?"

Mia nodded, looking at each screen.

"You're the only one not cracking up." Austin pointed at the shot of Collins, still staring out the portal. "He hasn't moved, not even a twitch of the finger. He'll probably come back to us, but for now he's in LaLa Land and like I said, he's lost whatever sway he had over people now that his position no longer exists."

He pointed to the next screen showing the still sick Secret Service man and the woman tending to him. "White is obviously physically ill, but I'm hoping he'll come around. Vanderwarf seems okay, but was going to be transferred next week because she's got a thing for Danny-boy there. She's going to be preoccupied with him until he's not launching puke and then she'll have to deal with the loss of her parents, five brothers, two sisters, her son and...her husband. White has resisted her advances, but she's a looker and an affair was bound to happen. Of course, that's not an issue now, is it?"

The next screen showed Garbarino, still reassembling his handgun. "Garbarino has me worried. He's the quiet type. Never says much. But he's got a temper. Removing your sidearm, let alone disassembling it and reassembling it in view of the public is a huge breach of protocol. He's no longer thinking about right and wrong. I guarantee you he's already figured out that the president and me are no longer his bosses. And he's distracting himself from dealing with what happened. Not a good thing."

He moved on to the next screen showing Chang talking with Elizabeth. "Frankly, Chang has surprised me. She cried for a long time, which is perfectly rational, then pulled herself together. She'll be helpful, but she's young and emotional. Elizabeth..." He looked at Mia. "I don't need to explain her. Cute kid, though."

Mia smiled.

"And that brings us to the brothers grim. And I mean grim as in depressing, not the fairy tales, though the line these two are spinning is just as morbid as the original stories." Austin flicked another button, activating a directional microphone attached to the hidden camera. Paul's and Mark's whispered voices filled the room.

"I don't know," said Paul.

"I'm telling you... Did you see the clouds down there?" Mark's hushed words were hard to make out. The next two sentences were a mix of slurred syllables.

"Then how come we're still here?" Paul asked, a little anger in his voice.

Mark shrugged and spoke, but his words were once again unintelligible. What they could see was the Bible in the priest's hand. He smacked it against his brother's chest every once in a while for emphasis.

Paul rubbed the back of his neck. "Maybe."

Austin turned the sound off.

"I see what you mean," Mia said.

"I've only caught bits and pieces of the load the priest is selling, but it's no good. We need to keep paranoid religious talk to a minimum. Nothing freaks people out faster." Austin turned back to the view of Paul and Mark and snorted. Mark was turning through the pages of the small Bible. "Wouldn't you know it? The only print book in the world to survive just had to be the Bible."

Mia frowned hard.

"What?" Austin asked.

"That's just sad, I guess. All the books on Earth are gone."

"That's sadder than all the people on Earth being gone?"

"No, just different. Books represent hundreds, sometimes thousands of years of accumulated history. Everything mankind has ever discovered or created was recorded in a book. Now it's all dust."

"Not quite," Austin said. "A digital copy of nearly every book ever printed is stored on board, along with data and information that's never seen print. What do you read?"

"Run for your life action stuff."

"Ugh, no thanks. I've had enough of the real thing."

"To each his own," she said. "So...is there a point to all this? You told me why they're not here, but not why I am here. Why are you showing me this? Telling me about the others? Why are you telling me about this...ship, or escape pod—"

"Earth Escape Pod."

"Whatever. What's the point?"

"Someone needs to be in charge."

Mia's forehead scrunched tight. What the hell? "We have a president."

"Who's no longer a president of anything."

"We have you."

"People tend not to trust gun-toting ex-Secret Service men." Austin opened his coat, revealing his sidearm. "It implies they don't have a choice."

"Then lose the gun," Mia said.

"Not a chance."

"Why?"

"Because there are three other people on board with guns, and I don't know if they're trustworthy yet. Like I said, Garbarino has me worried."

Mia could see his line of thinking. She wasn't cracking up. Yet. She didn't carry a gun. She was pretty, strong and had no previous affiliation with any of them except— "Elizabeth."

Austin nodded. "She makes you a mother figure. Mother figures are trustworthy. She also gives you the most motivation to come out of this in one piece. The rest of us are just fighting for our lives. You're fighting for two."

Mia sank into her chair. He was right. But she still wasn't convinced he wouldn't do a better job. He was dealing with the annihilation of the human race better than all of them. "What about you? Why aren't you cracking up?"

Austin leaned his balding head back into the chair and closed his eyes. "When I was eight, my father and I were driving cross country. We'd just entered Arizona when this wall of sand came from the south and swept toward the north. To us, seeing it from a distance, it looked beautiful. My father wisely stopped on the side of the road while we watched the sandstorm pass. When we started back on the road again, we found a small town a few miles ahead. It'd been directly in the path of the storm. The first person we saw was an eight year old boy. He was missing an arm. His mother lay in the sand with a shingle buried in her forehead. We counted twelve dead that day. People missing limbs, heads, or otherwise impaled by debris. Cars were overturned. Windows broken. Shards of metal, glass and wood everywhere. The sand was soaked with blood. It's amazing anyone survived. That was my first experience with death. I've been to thirty-four funerals since, seven in 10th grade alone. There wasn't much left of my family when..." Austin motioned to the view of Earth. "...this happened. Death just seems to follow me around and I've been ready for it for a long time. It's why I can take a job where getting shot for someone else is part of the deal. It's also why I'm the wrong person to take the lead right now. I'm good at dealing with death and with preventing death, but I'm not so good at what needs to happen next."

Mia met Austin's eyes. "And what's that?"

Austin forced a smile as he turned the security monitors off. "Life."

13

Paul Byers spun through the air, enjoying the lightness zero gravity provided his aging body. He'd been limber and fit once, with an athletic build and square jaw, but time and post-traumatic stress syndrome had taken their toll. His body was still in fairly good shape for a man in his late fifties, but the heroics of his stint in Vietnam would never be repeated. His slower body was still capable of enduring some physical strain, but his mind had never been the same. It had taken him years to overcome the fear, anxiety and insomnia caused by surviving the war and saving his friends. He often envied the unconscious men he pulled from the jungle. They couldn't remember what happened that day. Occasionally, he envied the few that didn't make it.

Counseling had overcome his thoughts of suicide, but he never felt far from the brink. And now...now the feelings were bubbling to the surface once again. The stress of escaping the planet, surviving the destruction of civilization and his brother's endless harping taxed his mental capacity to process, compartmentalize and block his emotions. Everyone called him a hero, but he was really just a tired old man who once again began to envy the dead. Their lives ended in a wink. His would drag on for who knew how long.

If not for the blessed lack of gravity distracting him from the full burden of his emotions, he'd already have cracked.

Paul drifted over the rows of chairs, pushing himself smoothly through the air. He'd told Mark that he needed time to think things through, but he really just didn't want to hear any more preaching. He loved Mark. They were closer now than they ever had been. Disagreements over the war in Vietnam had caused a divide between the two long ago, but time and Mark's joining the priesthood and learning the fine art of forgiveness had healed the wounds. Mark occasionally insisted they "talk God" and Paul usually didn't mind. He knew his brother's desire to "save" him was genuine and an honest expression of love, so he put up with it and sometimes even found it interesting. But now, in light of all that had happened, it drained what little psychological reserves Paul still clung to.

He watched the other survivors. The Secret Service man who'd been puking had finally run out of juice. The woman was now stroking his head. Odd couple, Paul thought.

The creepy Secret Service man still played with his gun. Paul didn't like the looks of him. If Paul was headed toward the edge, that guy had dropped over the side when they reached orbit.

Pushing himself away from the Secret Service people, Paul watched Collins, apparently lost in thought. He moved toward Collins, hoping to probe him for information about the craft that had whisked them away from harm—and into space. But when he reached the wall and caught a profile of Collins's face, he stopped. Collins looked further gone than the rest.

A whimper turned Paul around. In the corner of the room he saw Chang and Elizabeth. Where was Mia? He hadn't seen her leave. Elizabeth was crying lightly as Chang did her best to distract her with an impromptu, low gravity game of patty-cake.

"C'mon Liz. Hit my hands," Chang said. "Do you know how to play patty-cake?"

Elizabeth shook her head, no.

Chang rolled her eyes and stood up, but her movement launched her off the floor. She hit her head on the ceiling and stayed there, floating above Elizabeth as Paul approached. "What seven year old girl doesn't know how to play patty-cake?" Chang said to Paul.

"Apparently this one," Paul said. He flashed a smile to Elizabeth and nearly felt his heart break as she smiled back and reached out to him. He took her hand and lifted her up. She floated to him and he wrapped his thick arms around her small body. Her blonde hair floated freely around her head, tickling his nose, making him smile.

"Will Auntie Mia be back soon?" she asked.

"I'm sure she will, honey," Paul said. "I can stay with you until she gets back. Would that be good?"

Elizabeth nodded and held on tighter. In that moment Paul's concerns and fears melted away, replaced by a sense of responsibility and purpose. He saw his own frailty as selfish indulgence and stuffed it away. This innocent child would need his strength. He might not be a hero any more, but he was a prime candidate for being a surrogate grandfather.

Elizabeth leaned back and looked into Paul's eyes. The dark blue of her eyes pierced him as much as her question. "Are we going to die, Mr. Byers?"

Paul glanced out a nearby portal and saw the burning remnants of Earth. He looked away quickly and returned his gaze to her eyes. "Not a chance," he said.

"How do you know?"

"He doesn't," Chang said from above. "He's just trying to make us feel better."

Paul looked up as Chang moved toward the wall and pulled herself down to the floor. "First, I'm not trying to make you feel better. Second, you're not helping. So shut it or go hang out with the glee squad over there." Paul motioned toward Garbarino, who looked up and shot a sarcastic smile at him.

Guess I said that too loud, Paul thought.

Chang became upright on the floor again and pursed her lips. She sighed and looked down. "Sorry. Just having a hard time."

"Which is perfectly normal," Paul said. "Just keep it to yourself for now, okay?"

"Okay."

"Do you want Mr. Byers to hold you, too?" Elizabeth asked, which got a chuckle from Chang. But the smile disappeared at the sound of a gun being cocked.

Paul turned around as Garbarino slid down from the chair he'd been sitting on and stood at the center of the room. "All right, listen up, people. You've done enough crying, puking and palling around. It's time to get some shit squared away."

Garbarino seemed oblivious to the fact that he was waving his weapon around in his hand as he spoke. Or maybe it was his silent way of saying, "Don't even bother arguing." Either way, it made Paul nervous.

He looked toward the four hatches that entered the room. All were firm-ly closed. Where were Mia and Austin?

"So gather round," Garbarino said, "and I'll fill you in on how things are going to work around here."

"S'cuse me, son, but I think I'm still in charge," Collins said as he turned away from the window.

"Really?" Garbarino asked. "Because it looks to me that all you're good for right now is feeling sorry for yourself."

"I am the President of the United States of—"

"Nothing!" Garbarino shouted.

"Joseph, don't," Vanderwarf said.

"What's the problem, Erin?" Garbarino said. "You know it's true. I doubt even half of us in here even voted for him, anyway. It's a whole new ball game folks, and if you don't fall in line, you're off the team. Un-derstand?"

Garbarino met Paul's eyes and locked on to him. Perhaps seeing him as competition for alpha male—leader of the pack. Paul had seen similar behavior during the war—men forming pacts with each other, re-arranging the chain of command when their lives were at risk. Paul also knew not to argue with the man. Not now. Not until someone took that gun away.

"Understand?" Garbarino said, casually bringing the gun around toward Paul...and Elizabeth.

Paul put Elizabeth down and raised his open palms to shoulder height. "I understand perfectly," he said. "You're the boss."

14

Mia watched as Austin showed her the basic controls for the escape pod. Luckily, the designers had thought to include a touch-screen, user friendly interface. Their forethought made operating the very complex systems easy enough for anyone accustomed to using an ATM. Diagnostics, flight control, temperature—everything could be controlled from this single room. Austin had a working knowledge of how the system was supposed to work, though he'd only trained on it once. But he worked through the tiered options like an old pro, learning as he went and trying to give Mia the impression he knew the system inside and out. She saw through his charade, but decided not to say anything. Paying attention seemed the better option.

"So," Austin said, "Here is the food and water supply indicator. Plug in the number of people on board and it calculates how long the supplies will last. How many do we have on board?"

Mia counted on her fingers. "Ten. I think."

Austin typed in ten and hit enter. The screen displayed three different answers based on different ration options. Five years, seven years and ten years.

"Ten years..." Mia said. She couldn't imagine spending ten years living in orbit. Not to mention that ten years in zero gravity would leave them too weak to live on Earth again. Their legs would break beneath them as their bones thinned and muscles faded to nothing; zero-gravity living provided very little in the way of a workout. "How long will that—" Mia motioned to the view of Earth, "—last?"

Austin shook his head. "The only way to learn the effect of worldwide fallout is to have a worldwide nuclear war, so we'll be the first to know. Typical fallout settles on the ground within about two weeks. But this...this is something different. I think we somehow changed the fundamental makeup of the planet. I'm not sure the planet can recover from this."

"So we'll die up here?" Mia asked, keeping her eyes on the roiling Earth atmosphere. "In ten years?"

Austin shook his head. "Air won't last more than six, and that's assuming the scrubbers never fail."

They stared in silence at the view. Mia knew that in the weeks to come they would all become accustomed to the sight of their dead planet. In years its role in the sky would become as mundane as the moon's. A dead world they could never again visit.

"What happens..." Mia started, "if you reduce the crew number to one?"

Tom closed his eyes and sighed, then plugged the number change in to the computer. He sat back as the results displayed on the screen. "Seventy years."

"What about two people?"

Austin typed the new number. "Thirty-five. What are you thinking?"

"There are no stasis chambers or any sci-fi stuff like that on board, right? We can't just sleep through this?"

Austin shook his head, no.

"Then we need to decide, everyone lives for six more years..." Mia looked at the floor dreading the cold, Spock-like suggestion. But it made sense. "Or seven of us die now and maybe the two survivors live long enough to return to the surface and repopulate the planet."

"Adam and Eve?"

Mia nodded. "Something like that."

"So who's the lucky man?" The edge in Austin's voice revealed his dislike for the idea.

"I didn't say I would be the woman," Mia said.

"Your math did. You said seven would have to die now. That leaves three. Elizabeth. You and...?"

Mia's shoulders sank as she sighed. "It was just an idea."

One that would once again put her in the arms of another man. Guilt twisted her insides. No matter how long she lived, or if they ever returned to Earth, she would have to carry the guilt of what she had done until she died.

Austin nodded slowly. "Unfortunately, if things don't change down there in the next few weeks...it's probably a good idea."

Mia turned to him and looked in his eyes. He was serious. The idea, at first logical and clean, became messy with thoughts of how the others might be convinced of its validity...or even if they would have to be convinced. Could she murder the others to save the human race? Could she live with that for the rest of her life, too? Her thoughts turned to the lessons taught to her in Sunday school during the few years her parents had gone to church. God had supposedly destroyed the world once, leaving only a few survivors. "Noah," she said.

"What?"

"Nothing."

"You said, 'Noah.' I might be agnostic, but I know the story. You think God is cleansing the Earth of man's wickedness?"

Mia smiled. The idea felt ridiculous. "Please don't lump me in with Mark. Besides, if that was the plan, God screwed up this time. I don't see any animals on board."

Mia's smile faded as she saw Austin's brow furrow. "What?"

"The genetic material for a massive amount of life on Earth is stored on board. Seeds for plants, eggs and sperm of animals and the equipment to artificially bring them all back."

As the blood drained from Mia's head she became light-headed. The similarities to the Ark story were hard to shake. Mia's intellect swiftly ruled out the possibility. "Noah was saved because he was a good man. Holy or whatever. That certainly doesn't describe me and I doubt it describes anyone else on board."

"What about the priest?"

"When you find a holy priest, I'll become a believer." Mia said with a smirk.

"Elizabeth," Austin said.

Mia frowned. "Yeah..."

"And the priest did save the Bible," Austin said. "He might have us all converted by the time we—"

"Earth Escape Pod Alpha, Earth Escape Pod Alpha, come in." The male voice broke through the conversation and repeated like a scratched CD. "This is Earth Escape Pod Beta. We have you in sight. Do you read? Earth Escape Pod Alpha..."

Tom flipped on the clearly labeled microphone and spoke. "Earth Escape Pod Alpha, we read you loud and clear."

"Austin, is that you? It's Reggie."

Austin smiled. "Reggie you son-of-a-bitch. You made it."

"Barely, but we're alive."

Austin covered the microphone with his hand and turned to Mia. "Reggie is...was the head of the president's nighttime guard. He's a good guy." He uncovered the microphone and asked, "How many made it on your end?"

"Thirty-one. Most of them are pretty wigged out. Secretaries and general staffers mostly. So I took charge. How about you? How many on board?"

Austin let out a slow breath before speaking. "Ten. Including the president, Garbarino, White, Vanderwarf and Chang."

"The gang's all there, huh? What about the civies you were babysitting?"

"They're all here," Austin said.

"Hello," Mia said.

"Who's that?"

"Mia Durante, one of the civies," Mia said. "And the one in charge, so you can talk to me now." She smiled at Austin as he made a face that showed he was impressed by her forward approach. He began flicking on the security monitors.

After a moment of silence, Reggie spoke again. "Austin?"

"You heard her, Reg," Austin said, looking away from the monitors. "She's the bo—shit."

Mia turned to the security screen that held Austin's attention.

She could see Garbarino aiming his gun at Paul, who had his arms raised.

Elizabeth stood between the two men.

"Looks like you were right," Austin said. "We're far from holy."

Mia unstrapped from the chair and pushed off toward the exit, moving for the hatch. Austin followed close on her heels.

As they exited the control room and entered the long tubular hallway, Reggie's voice faded behind them. "Austin? Durante? Hey, hello? What the hell is happening over there?"

15

Austin had no idea what to expect as he pulled himself through the hallway. Having not witnessed the event that caused Garbarino to draw his weapon, he wanted to believe that Paul might be just as much at fault as Garbarino, but at his core he knew the truth—Garbarino had crossed the line. Whatever Paul had done to aggravate him, however grievous, he should not be pointing his weapon toward Elizabeth. Even more disconcerting was that in the snippet of video he got a peek at, neither White or Vanderwarf did anything to stop Garbarino. They fell in line without a second thought.

Mia reached the white octagonal hatch and took hold of the large metal handle.

"Hold on," Austin said.

Mia glared back at him, arguing with those deep brown eyes. He reached her side and said, "You need to stay calm. No shouting. No quick movements."

Mia looked down at his hands. "Where's your gun?"

Austin opened his jacket revealing his 9mm holstered under his left arm.

"You don't want to..."

"If someone comes unhinged, the last thing you want to do is upset them. A gun tends to do that," Austin said.

Mia pursed her lips nervously. Austin took her hand. "Just stay cool. Take charge. I'll back you up."

"And if he loses control?"

"I'm a quick draw."

Mia nodded, pulled the handle and yanked open the door. As they floated into the room side by side, Garbarino glanced in their direction, but never took the gun off Paul. "Hey Tom," Garbarino said. "Nice of you to finally join us. You been screwing your new girlfriend?"

"I'm not his girlfriend," Mia said. "And he'd be smiling if I screwed him."

Garbarino glanced at Austin, saw his frown and smirked.

Atta girl, Austin thought, disarm him with humor. He drifted toward Elizabeth and Paul with two intentions: taking a bullet if need be—a concept he'd grown accustomed to—and reaching a good position to return fire. Though his job no longer required him to protect anyone, his instincts still commanded him to do so.

Since his childhood experience in the desert, surrounded by death, he'd had an overwhelming desire to protect people. Some law enforcement types enjoyed solving cases, catching criminals or pouring over evidence. Austin just wanted to save people, directly, at the source. He'd stand in front of the next sandstorm if it meant saving a life. That was his purpose in life. He always wondered when the reaper would come to make the final trade. He'd kept his distance thus far, but maybe this would be it? As Austin reached Elizabeth and stood in front of her, he hoped not. It would be an awful thing for her to see—a man shot in zero gravity. And Mia—he looked forward to getting to know her better.

"I'm not going to shoot the girl," Garbarino said as he watched Austin stand between them.

"You're not going to shoot anyone," Mia replied, getting his full attention again. Three of the reclining chairs stood between them. A mere fifteen feet. She moved around the closest. Ten feet away.

"That's close enough, lady," Garbarino said.

"Okay," Mia said. She held on to the chair in front of her and pushed herself down into a standing position. "Here's what's going to happen..."

Garbarino cocked an eyebrow and snickered.

"You're going to put the gun away."

"You think you're taking my gun?"

"I said put it away. You can keep it." Mia gripped the chair, expelling her nervousness and fear into the cushion. "Then we're going to find the crew quarters, clean up, have something to eat and get coordinated. We have a lot to do."

Garbarino laughed loudly and let his aim lower some. He turned his full attention to Mia. "And who the hell put you in charge?"

"I did," Austin said, hoping Garbarino wouldn't react negatively to his voice and the authority it carried. Garbarino had been under his command for only six months and they'd had two arguments in that time. Neither required writing a report, but Austin always knew Garbarino held some resentment toward him.

"Oh really," Garbarino said. "How noble of you." He turned back to Mia, this time moving the gun toward her. "Well I've got news for you. I'm in charge, now. What I say goes."

"You think because you have a gun, that makes you the best leader?" Mia asked, slowly moving toward Garbarino.

Austin knew she was pushing Garbarino on purpose, trusting that he really wouldn't shoot her without good reason. But she couldn't have picked a more dangerous game. The man wasn't in his right mind. With Garbarino's attention diverted, Austin decided to take action. He slowly ducked behind the nearest chair. Using them for cover, he drew his gun and glided over the floor, moving effortlessly and silently toward Garbarino.

"That and the fact that the rest of these fruit loops are out of their gourds," Garbarino said.

"They're not the ones waving a gun around in a space station. What happens if you blow out one of the windows?" Mia let it sink in for a moment. "You'd kill us all. Just put the gun away and we can all figure things out together."

"We can still have a democracy," Collins said from the opposite side of the room where he had moved when the confrontation first began.

"Shut up," Garbarino said. "No one cares what you think now."

Austin paused between chairs. He caught Mia's eye and showed her his weapon.

"Garbarino," Mia said loudly, keeping his attention on her, "Just put the gun down and we can work this out. Please."

He turned and faced her. "You think because you went to some fancy college that you can tell me what to do? You think you're smarter than me?"

"I went to community college," Mia said. "I'm a journalist for a small-town paper. That's all."

Garbarino slid over the chair between them and got in her face. "Then what the hell makes you think you'd be a better leader than me?"

C'mon, Mia, Austin thought as he slid into position behind Garbarino. The others, who had all seen him by now hadn't raised the alarm, which was good. It meant that White and Vanderwarf were neutral at the least, on his side at best. But that might also mean they were too shook up to be useful. Just keep his attention for a few more seconds, he willed her.

"I'm motivated," Mia said. "I want my niece to live. I'm fighting for more than myself."

"Gonna have to do better than that," Garbarino replied.

"I made contact with another EEP," Mia said. Garbarino's face softened. He thought they were it. The only ones. "I spoke to your friend, Reggie. He's alive too. He has thirty-one people on board. We would have searched for the other two EEPs if you hadn't pulled us away."

Garbarino leaned away from Mia, his muscles relaxing.

"We're still here," Mia said. "The human race still exists. But we can't keep killing each other. Maybe it will be a month. Maybe a year. I have no idea. But we'll get back to the surface. We'll start again. You know we can."

"Not too bad," Garbarino said as he began to holster his weapon. "You might have a future in politics."

Austin rose up behind Garbarino, stopped himself silently by grabbing the chair and reached around Garbarino's waist, grabbing the gun. He simultaneously placed his gun against the side of the man's head. "Sorry, buddy. I'm still going to need the gun."

Garbarino sneered and tightened his grip on the weapon. Austin knew this was a major risk, but the man could not keep the gun. How could they trust he wouldn't snap again? Next time he might kill someone. Better he die now than to let him kill an innocent.

"You blew it, Garbarino," Austin said. "You can have it back when I trust you again."

Garbarino let go of the gun and Austin took it.

"You did the right thing," Austin said.

Garbarino glared at him. "Go fu—"

"Something's happening!" Collins shouted from the far end where he stood peering through a portal at the view of earth. "Oh, God, something's happening! The clouds. They're fading. I can see the ocean!"

Everyone forgot the confrontation and moved toward the windows. They looked out in groups of three, peering through the windows. Collins was right. The dark swirling clouds faded. The stabs of orange light disappeared. Gaps in the cover slowly appeared revealing splotches of blue, brown and green. Their world still existed below the clouds.

Over the next half hour, the group watched in silence as the clouds continued to fade as though some magic force had called them back from whence they came. Austin could think of no rational explanation for it. How could that much ash and fallout simply be sucked down from the atmosphere? He couldn't explain it, but he could embrace it. He smiled wide, meeting Mia's eyes. She returned the smile. Then he felt a hand on his shoulder.

Garbarino.

"Sorry, boss." Garbarino said. "I lost it."

"Understandable," Austin replied, then smiled. "I'm still keeping the gun."

Garbarino nodded. "Fair enough... You think we'll go back soon? You think anyone survived down there?"

"The computer determines when it's safe to return, you know that." Austin didn't want to answer the second question, not truthfully anyway. He knew Garbarino had lost a wife and son. Their loss was probably what tipped him over the edge earlier. He needed hope. "Look at it," he said, turning to the view of the cloudless Earth, glowing brightly, free of darkness. "Someone must still be alive down there."

Austin felt guilty for not pointing out the pock marks that revealed the locations of thousands of nuclear explosions. From this distance they looked like dirty specks on a lens, but to be visible from space, they had to be huge. And there were so many...he doubted anyone could have survived the initial attacks, let alone that swirling storm of fallout that consumed the entire globe afterward.

"Attention, crew," boomed a female voice over the intercom, "Attention crew. Optimal conditions have been reached. Please takes your seats and prepare for descent in ten minutes."

The group stood back from the windows as a collective. "That can't be right," Austin said.

"Computer failure?" Paul asked.

Mark shook his head, no. "Hand of God. That's what."

"Not now, Mark," Mia said more harshly than she meant to. "Everyone strap in and get ready to go. Chang, take care of Liz."

Austin looked over the rest of the group as they began sitting on the chairs they'd climbed out of only two hours ago. They listened to her. She'd taken charge. Though it seemed all for nothing now. Returning to the surface within two hours would be a death sentence. They'd all die from radiation poisoning. No matter how clear the atmosphere became, the surface of the planet would still be coated by a layer of radioactive dust.

Chang took Elizabeth's hand and pulled her toward the nearest chair. Elizabeth reached back for Mia, "Auntie!"

"You'll be okay, Lizzy."

Austin could see it broke Mia's heart to leave Elizabeth again, but if they managed to survive, this would probably be the first of many tough calls she'd have to make in the coming years.

"Tom, come with me." Mia pushed off the wall and headed for the exit.

"What's the plan?" Austin asked as he drifted up next to her.

"Find out if the computer is right."

"If it's not?"

"We try to stop it."

"If we can't?"

"Then it's been nice knowing you."

Mia reached the hatch, yanked it open and looked back at Austin. "But if it's right. Well then, we're going home." She pulled herself through the hatch and was followed by Austin...and Garbarino.

16

Floating to the command center, Mia looked back over her shoulder and said, "If the system is wrong—" She saw Garbarino right behind Austin. She didn't know his intentions, but he was unarmed. "If the surface is still radioactive and there's no air to breathe, will the EEP protect us once we're on the ground?"

"Should," Austin said.

"If it's not damaged," Garbarino added. He sounded much more put together. "They're designed to block out the radiation in space. They should be okay against fallout, too."

Entering the command center, Mia and Austin took the seats and strapped themselves down. Garbarino stood behind them. A digital display counting down read 6:45

6:44

6:43

"You double check the readings," Mia said. "See if the system really is detecting optimal conditions or if it's just the landing system on the fritz. I'll try to get in touch with the—"

"Earth Escape Pod Alpha, are you there?" Reggie's voice was insistent. He must have been trying to reach them for some time.

"Is that Reggie?" Garbarino asked.

"I'm here. We're here," Mia said.

"Bout damn time, Durante. Our system seems to be having a glitch. Wants to send us back down to Earth. Tom, if you're there, any idea on how to stop this thing?"

"Working on it now, Reg," Tom said.

There was a pause.

"You just started working on it, or already were?"

"Already was," Garbarino said. "We're having the same problem."

"Shit," Reggie said. "Have you heard from Delta? We haven't been able to reach them."

"We had..." Mia glanced at Garbarino. "...a distraction. Just got back to the command center now."

Reggie's sigh came over the speakers loud and clear.

"The systems check out," Austin said. "Unless the software is totally compromised, it's really detecting a habitable atmosphere."

Garbarino let out a victory hoot.

Austin turned back to him. "Make sure the others are all strapped in. Gently. And get yourself ready. We can ride out the descent in here."

Garbarino gave a nod.

"And make sure buckles stay on until we're on the ground. Could be a rough landing."

"You got it," Garbarino said as he pushed for the door.

"This looks like the real deal, Reg. Better get your people strapped down."

"Got them strapped in tight as soon as the alarm sounded. What's your countdown at?"

Austin looked at the readout. "Four minutes fifty seconds. You?"

"Looks like we got a head start. Two forty."

"You remember the protocols?" Austin asked.

"Guinea pig goes out first. Then everyone else. If we're out of visual range, GPS trackers should lead us to each other, assuming the satellites are still functioning."

"We have guinea pigs on board?" Mia asked, confused.

"As senior security officer on the EEP first to the ground," Reggie said, "I'm the guinea pig. I'll be outside and breathing Earth air before you're on the ground." His hopeful words sounded forced, but at least there was a fraction of hope now.

"Whoa!" Reggie's voice was so loud the speakers crackled.

"What is it, Reggie?" Austin asked.

"Earth Escape Pod Delta. She just passed by. Nearly hit us."

Austin and Mia leaned against their straps and looked out the long window. The white hull of EEP Delta came into view. The bell shaped ship was indeed descending, and would at any moment drop into Earth's atmosphere.

"We have to assume it's either a ghost ship or everyone on board died for some reason," Reggie said. "So I'll still be the first man on the ground, agreed?"

"Agreed," Austin said.

"I'm strapping in now. Won't be able to talk until I'm on the ground."

"Copy that, Reg, take care of yourself."

"Good luck," Mia said.

Reg laughed. "We're either the luckiest or unluckiest people in the history of mankind. Guess we'll find out when we get down there. See you then."

With that, Reggie went silent.

They watched as EEP Delta succumbed to Earth's gravity and became a white spec over the North American continent. Just as the Delta ship disappeared from view, Beta passed by and began its drop.

"Better activate the chairs," Austin said.

Mia wasn't looking forward to the crushing pressure of the restraint system again, but she also didn't want to become a smear on the ceiling.

"Handle over there reclines the chair. Once you're back you'll see the restraining bar. Pull it over your chest to activate the pressurized cushion system."

"Pressurized cushion system?"

"I couldn't remember the actual name. Just made it up."

"Reassuring," Mia said, then reclined her chair and pulled the bar up over her head.

As the padding filled with air around her, he added, "Prepare for the wildest ride of your life."

"Wilder than the takeoff?"

"About the same, but the view will be better."

Mia remembered looking out the portal as the EEP blasted its way into space. "You saw the missiles, too?"

"Worst thing I've ever seen in my life."

"And this will be better because?"

"The world as we know it is already gone. Everyone is dead."

Their eyes met. He smiled. "Even if we explode on reentry, or die of radiation poisoning, or have to live in the EEP for six years, things couldn't possibly get any worse."

17

The physical toll of reentry seemed paltry compared to the pulsing acceleration of liftoff. Mia's stomach lurched when gravity took hold, but other than that, she remained fully conscious and aware. The view out the window shifted from dark space, to deep purple and then to clear blue sky. Not a cloud in sight. The view through the command center window was much more expansive than the small portal had been, but she still could not see the ground.

And that's what she really wanted to see.

She expected the world to be scorched and decimated. Ruins of the human civilization. Over time, what was left would be reduced to dust, and future generations, born from the children of the few survivors, would build a new world. Villages at first. Then small cities. Migrations would come next. Trade routes. Countries. Wars. Human civilization would be remade and probably, someday in the future, undone again.

She wondered for a moment if this could have happened before. Maybe the flood was some kind of man-made cataclysm? she thought. Six thousand years in the future, our descendants might debate the mythology surrounding the time when God burned the Earth, sparing those who fled into space, in EEPs that contained all the knowledge and life of the previous earth. The knowledge, all digital, wouldn't survive long. Batteries would die and the technology to recreate them wouldn't exist for a long time to come. But in the years to come, using the technology on the EEPs, they would recreate Earth's animal life.

She knew it was all ludicrous, but that didn't keep her from hoping.

What else is there to hope for? she wondered.

The parachutes deployed and jolted the EEP hard, slowing the descent to a swaying flutter.

She unlocked the bar restraint and pushed it back over her head.

"What are you doing?" Austin asked.

"I want to see." The cushioning system disengaged with the removal of the bar and she could move again. She undid the Velcro snaps and pushed out of her chair. But she didn't make it far. While gravity was now tugging her toward the Earth's core, her brain had yet to readjust. Some part of her mind expected to float free of the chair, but she merely bounced in the seat.

Austin chuckled. "Heavier than you remember?"

"Hey," she said, before standing and leaning toward the window.

"When we touch down, you'll want to be back in the chair and strapped in," he said, undoing his own restraints. "It could be rough."

The EEP had swayed back so she could see only sky. "Won't the shock absorbers take most of it?"

"Unless we land on a ledge and flip over."

She looked back at him. "That could happen?"

"If it's a short fall we could end up upside down or on our side. If it's a long fall, the EEP would right itself—it's bottom heavy—but the parachutes might not slow us down again."

Mia frowned, but felt the EEP sway in the other direction. She leaned over the command console and looked out the window. As the world below came into view, Austin joined her.

"Oh my God," she whispered.

"Well, that's not what I expected."

A residential neighborhood, seemingly untouched by the war, stood one thousand feet below. Things looked different in the distance—darker—but this small part of the world looked livable.

"Do you think there are survivors?"

"I don't see how it's possible. Then again, I don't see how this is possible either. I was expecting ruins everywhere." As the EEP spun around, Austin saw a gleaming white circle below them. "There's EEP Beta."

Mia strained to see. The massive spacecraft had come to rest atop of a house, now flattened beneath it.

"EEP Alpha, do you read?"

Austin toggled the com system.

"We hear you Reggie. What's the score?"

"The system was right. I'm on the ground. The air is breathable. The Geiger counter is pinging at normal levels. No fallout anywhere. It's like the missiles never dropped."

"Have you seen any survivors?"

"Not a one." Reggie was quiet for a moment. "No animals either. No birds. No bugs. Somehow this neighborhood survived."

A stiff breeze caught EEP Alpha and began pulling them away from EEP Beta. "Looks like we're going to touch down a few blocks away," Austin said. "Stay where you are. We'll come to you."

"Copy that, Austin."

Austin motioned to the chairs and sat down. "Better strap in, we'll be on the ground in thirty seconds."

Mia nodded, took her seat and began to lift the bar restraint over her body. But before she did, Reggie's voice came over the speakers again. "Oh my God, I see survivors!"

Mia and Austin launched from their chairs and looked out the window. EEP Beta was further away, but still visible. They could see Reggie in front, waving his arms, and his group of survivors exiting the EEP behind him. Further down the street, a crowd of people approached.

"Looks like the whole neighborhood," Reggie said. "Sounds like they're shouting something."

"What are they saying?" Austin asked, while keeping one eye on their distance from the ground. Maybe fifteen seconds left.

"Can't tell. They're all shouting. Making it hard to hear." Reggie's voice grew louder as he spoke to the people, who were now just a few feet away. "One at a time! I can't hear you!"

A new voice, feminine, came over Reggie's mic. "Please run! I don't want to hurt—"

"Reggie..." Austin said. Something about the woman's voice bothered him. But he didn't get any further.

"What?" Reggie said, "I don't—" The scream that followed was horrible, like something from a B-movie actress, but worse because it came from the voice of a man.

"Fuck," Austin said.

They were far from the action now, but the jerky violent movements of the mob as they descended on the survivors, coupled with Reggie's scream told him everything he needed to know. They were being slaughtered. The last thing he saw was a group of the mob peel off and head in their direction. Then a tall power line passed by the window.

He shoved Mia into her seat and dove into his. "Hold on!"

The impact came a moment later. The EEP shook and screeched as they plowed through a house, scraped across the open street and slammed into a second home. The EEP tipped for a moment as the full parachutes tugged, but the heavy base settled to the ground with a thud.

They were still for only a moment when Austin leapt from his seat and yanked her up. There was no time to ask about injuries. No time to ponder what had happened. They needed to move.

"There an armory on board?" she asked.

Austin nodded. They were on the same page.

Though the neighborhood looked as American as they come, he didn't know where they had landed. What he did know was that the locals were hostile and would reach them inside five minutes.

They had to run.

They had to fight.

The war, it seemed, wasn't over.

TORMENT

18

America

"Everyone up!" Mia shouted as she rejoined the others. She felt happy to see Garbarino and Paul Byers jump up at the ready.

When Austin added, "Move! We have hostiles incoming!" Vanderwarf and White stood. Austin pointed to them, "You two, weapons cache. I want a firearm in the hands of everyone over seven years old in under a minute." He turned to Garbarino and Byers. "Joe, break out the survival packs. One for everyone."

Garbarino waved for Paul to follow him, then looked back. "What about the kid? She won't be able to carry it."

"I'll double up," Austin said.

"So will you," Mia said to Garbarino as she pulled Liz free of her restraints and picked her up. "I'm carrying Liz."

He frowned for a moment, but then nodded. It made sense.

"Explain the situation to them while I check things out." Austin said as he moved around Mia and headed for the exterior hatch.

Mia watched him unlock the hatch and step outside, no pause or consideration given to the survivability of the atmosphere. When she turned back, Mark, Collins and Chang were staring at her wide-eyed.

"What's happening?" Collins asked. "Is it the Russians? Did they survive somehow?"

"We're in a residential neighborhood," Mia said, and then thought about her next words. She didn't want to scare Liz further. She could feel the little girl's limbs shaking as she silently held on tight. "EEP Beta landed a few blocks over. They...encountered a large hostile group."

Chang sucked in a breath. "They're dead?"

Mia shot her a look as Liz tightened her grip.

Chang looked at the floor. "Sorry."

Mia tried to think of a way to say things without Liz understanding. She decided on military speak, which she knew thanks to Matt. "They're KIA," Mia said. "Yes. Some of the group is coming this way."

"Hence the backpacks and weapons," Mark said. "We're on the run."

Vanderwarf and White reentered the room, each carrying a small arsenal—several handguns, spare clips, two shotguns and three MP5 submachine guns. They laid them out on a reclining chair. Mia had spent a lot of time at the shooting range with various men in her former life and was a pretty good shot. She felt thankful for that as she took a Sig Sauer handgun and four spare clips, and shoved them all into a pocket with one hand while holding Liz with the other.

Collins took a handgun as well.

He didn't look comfortable holding it.

"You've shot before?" Paul asked him.

"I've only fired a gun a few times. My father took me hunting. Never liked it." He moved the weapon up and down, feeling its weight in his hand. "Not sure I could shoot someone."

Mia let out scoffing laugh. "Says the man who pushed the button."

Collins stiffened. "Hey—"

"No time for talking, you two," White said. "Focus on surviving or you're likely not to." He held a handgun out to Mark. "Not going to be a stereotype, are you?"

"Hardly," Mark said, taking an MP5 and a Sig Sauer.

Vanderwarf squinted at him, motioning to the MP5. "You know how to use that?"

"The handgun, yes." He held up the MP5. "This thing, no—"

Garbarino and Paul returned, a slew of backpacks on their backs and in their arms.

Mark pointed to Paul, "—but he does." After taking two spare clips for the MP5, Mark handed the weapon to his brother, who had just deposited the bags at their feet.

Paul inspected the MP5, checked the clip and chambered the first round. "Thanks."

"Don't mention it," Mark said as he slipped on his backpack.

The exterior hatch swung open. Austin entered and found several weapons aimed in his direction. He paused for a moment, realizing he'd almost been shot, then stepped in and claimed a second handgun for himself. "Those who have never fired a weapon, please don't aim or fire at something until those of us with experience say so. The switch on the left side is the safety. Switch it to the off position—" He demonstrated this for them. "—point it at your target and pull the trigger."

"Right," Chang said. She placed her handgun in her backpack and slung it over her shoulder. She still wore her work clothes. She wasn't wearing high heels, but her shoes weren't exactly made for running. "How far do we have to go?"

While most of the people looked at her the way they might a mental patient, Austin said what they were all thinking. "As far as we have to, now—"

A distant scream cut through the air.

"What's that?" Chang asked.

Austin moved to the hatch, leading with his gun. "They're coming." He turned back to the group. "Get those packs on and grab as many weapons as you can carry."

Garbarino picked up two handguns, one of them being the weapon taken from him previously, and a shotgun. Vanderwarf and White had the MP5s and one handgun each. Collins took the second shotgun.

A gunshot echoed loudly inside the EEP sending hands to ears.

"Fuck!" Garbarino shouted.

"They're here!" Austin squeezed off two rounds. "Garbarino, take them south. I'll slow them down!"

Mia followed Garbarino out of the EEP and on to the street of the McMansion lined neighborhood. The blacktop street smelled of new pavement and was bisected by two bright yellow lines, perhaps days old. The maple trees lining the street were bare, and the grass brown, but being the middle of February in what looked like the American Northeast to her, that was expected. What wasn't expected was the temperature, which Mia pegged around eighty degrees. Other than that aberration, the neighborhood looked like so many others hastily built over the previous ten years. There was no rushing mob, but she did see two bodies lying face down one hundred feet away. As the others exited and followed Garbarino around the backside of the EEP, Mia stopped by Austin. "You shouldn't stay by yourself."

"I'll be fine."

"You could die."

"I know I'm not paid to do this anymore, but it's still my job." Austin motioned toward Liz. "And it's not like you can help."

"What about Garbarino? Why did you put him in charge?"

"He'll toe the line as long as he feels respected," Austin said. "If I don't make it back, he's in charge in a fight, you're in charge of everything else. He'll go for that."

"If he doesn't?"

Austin looked over her shoulder. "Then you'll have help."

Paul had waited for her. He stood there, brandishing his submachine gun like a true war hero. And he'd heard everything.

"But that's not going to happen," Austin said. "I just want to give you a head start. I can catch up."

A terrified voice called out from the distance.

"Is that one of ours?" Paul asked.

"Wrong direction," Austin said, taking aim past the two bodies he'd already shot. "Now go!"

Paul took Mia by the arm and led her around the EEP. She was surprised to see Garbarino waiting there for them and wondered if he had heard any of their conversation. But he just waved them on, shouting, "Move your asses!"

Two shots rang out from Austin's position.

Mia saw the rest of their crew jogging down the street, away from the EEP and the oncoming crowd. She looked back the way they'd come. It didn't feel right, leaving Austin. But then Liz leaned back, looked her in the eyes and said, "What the hell are you waiting for, Auntie Mia, move your ass!"

She started forward. Then two more shots set them all to running, like horses out of the gate. They didn't slow until they caught up to Collins, who was already out of breath.

Mia thought about it and realized she'd never seen photos of or heard news about this president going out for jogs. In fact, she seemed to recall he had heart problems. Great.

Two blocks from the EEP, more gunshots rang out. Then a scream. A man's scream.

Then silence. They all stared back at the EEP, waiting for Austin to come running, but he didn't.

After a moment, Mia turned to Garbarino, placed her hand on his arm, and very intentionally said, "Lead the way," all the while feeling like she'd just handed them all over to the devil.

19

Within twenty minutes, Mia, Collins, Chang and the Byers brothers lagged behind their three Secret Service escorts. Mia was in shape, but lacked endurance, especially when carrying a fifty pound seven year old. Liz seemed to sense this and tapped her shoulder. "I can run now," the girl said. "I'm not afraid anymore."

Mia looked the girl in the eyes. "You sure?"

She nodded.

"Stay right next to me."

The nod continued. Mia put her down, then put her hands on her knees while she caught her breath. The brothers and Chang stopped with her, while Collins walked on ahead, his body soaked in sweat.

Garbarino heard the number of moving feet behind him change and turned around. "Hey! Keep moving."

"We need to rest," Mia said.

"Those people might still be chasing us," he said, stomping toward her.

"There hasn't been a sound or a gunshot for a while," she countered.

Garbarino stood above her. "That's probably because Austin is dead and those sons-a-bitches are sneaking up on us. Now..." He took her arm and yanked her up. "Move!"

"Hey!" Liz shouted and went to hit Garbarino, but Mia caught her little fist.

She stood face-to-face with the man, and when she did she realized she stood a good two inches taller. "Right now, if those people charged us, I wouldn't have the energy to run. We've been through a lot and the non-stop adrenaline rush of being launched into space by a series of nuclear blasts, watching the world be destroyed, floating in zero gravity, dropping back down to Earth and then being attacked by crazed survivors, is starting to wear off."

Garbarino's face slowly fell as he listened to her. The words seemed to suck the energy out of him. He looked around the neighborhood. "Houses up there look big. Might be a good place to hole up."

Mia looked up the road and saw several new and very large houses. They were the kind contractors built in a month, the kind she mocked when she drove by, but right now they looked incredibly normal and inviting. She smiled. "Thank you."

"Let's move," Chang said. "Maybe the plumbing still works."

Mark followed after her. "I could go for a shower."

"I'll take a bath," Paul said, loping ahead of the other two, looking ridiculous with his submachine gun.

Mia took Liz's hand and nodded at Garbarino. "You did the right thing."

"Yeah, well, let's hope it doesn't get us killed." He motioned for her to get moving and followed behind her. She looked back and was happy to find him walking backwards, keeping watch behind them.

They reached the line of massive homes five minutes later and selected a three-story giant. The choice had nothing to do with how opulent the house was, with its perfectly shaped, leafless hedges, a waterless fountain and a new BMW in the driveway. The third story fire escape appealed to all of them. If trouble came through the front, back or garage doors, they had an alternate escape route. The third floor would also offer them an excellent view of the neighborhood and anyone that might be looking for them.

While the others let themselves in through the unlocked front door, Mia stopped in front of the house. She pulled her handgun from her pocket and ejected a single round. It landed on the sidewalk. She bent down and positioned the round so that it pointed toward the house.

"What are you doing?" Liz asked.

"Leaving a message."

"For Mr. Austin?"

"Yup. For Mr. Austin."

She stood and scooped up Liz. "Can he be my new daddy? I've never had a daddy."

Mia laughed. "You like him that much?"

She bobbed her head up and down. "And you can be my new mommy."

"Liz..." Mia didn't know what to say. She had avoided the subject for as long as possible, but now it seemed Liz needed to process the loss.

"I know she's dead," the girl said. "Everyone is dead. Except for us." Tears formed in her eyes, causing Mia to tear up as well.

This is a new world, Mia thought. As awful as it felt, if Liz was going to survive, she would have to get tough. They all would. And she swore to herself that this was the last time she would cry. Blurry crying eyes couldn't aim a gun very well. And they didn't evoke confidence in the people she now led.

A knock on the door turned her around. The priest stood there with the shotgun. "Shake a leg, ladies."

Mia wiped her eyes and put Liz down. "I'm your mommy now. I'll keep you safe. I promise."

"And Mr. Austin?"

Mia smiled. "I'll let you ask him."

"You don't want to marry him?"

The smile faded.

"You still love Uncle Matt?" Liz answered the question in her own mind and shook her head. "You're right, I don't think he would like that."

Liz ran to Mark, who was waving her on. She left Mia standing alone on the sidewalk, frozen with guilt. For a moment she wished one of the savage survivors would leap out from behind a tree and tear her to pieces. She deserved nothing less. She had betrayed the man she loved. Over what? A little boredom. Some lonely nights? Her fucking libido?

"Mia!" Mark was whispering now, but more insistent. His voice snapped her from her reverie. She turned toward him and found Liz waving her in, too. If it weren't for Liz she might put the gun in her mouth and escape this horrible world once and for all.

After scanning the area, she entered the house and closed the solid red door behind her.

An open concept interior and a group of relieved faces greeted her.
Mark had just taken a seat behind a baby grand piano.

The three Secret Service agents and Collins were searching through
kitchen cabinets and sharing a box of Funny Bones.

Paul exited a bathroom and announced, "Water's running."

Garbarino entered from the garage. "Power's out, but they have a
generator and a really big propane tank."

Chang sat in a reclining chair, scanning a DVD collection. "They
have Khan!"

Mark poised his hands over the piano keys.

"Everyone shut up!" Mia said in such an angry voice that it came out
as half growl. "Are you all insane?"

When no one answered, she continued.

"There are people outside who want to kill us. With their bare
hands. They already killed at least thirty-one other survivors and maybe
Austin." She looked at the agents and Collins. "You going to offer them
cookies and spoiled milk when they come knocking?" Mark came next.
"Are you going to provide the soundtrack while they tear us apart?" She
turned to Chang. "You may never see Star Trek again." Paul. "You may
never take a hot shower." Garbarino. "And if you plan on keeping us alive
by ringing the fucking dinner bell, then go right ahead and start the generator." Did you notice how quiet it is out there? No cars. No electricity.
Not even a fucking cricket! They'd hear the generator for miles away."

Everyone stood in silence, staring at her.

She pointed to the three people in the kitchen. "Blockade the back
door." Garbarino and Paul. "Garage." Mark and Chang. "Front door."

She moved to the stairs, pulling Liz with her. Garbarino stood in
front of her, blocking her way. "And what will you be doing, fearless leader?"

Mia took her handgun out and chambered a round. Garbarino
stepped back and tensed. She saw the gun in his hand slowly rising. "If
you'll get out of my way, I'm going to go make sure there isn't an army of
people upstairs waiting to kill us once we've barricaded ourselves in."

The idea that someone could already be in the house hit Garbarino
hard. He stepped aside and motioned for Paul to follow him.

As Mia stormed up the stairs with Liz in tow, she heard furniture moving behind her. She stopped at the second floor and looked down at Liz. The girl wore a large smile. "What?"

"You cursed," she said. "A lot."

Mia let out a small laugh. "Yeah, I did."

"Why?"

"I don't know," Mia said. "I was angry."

"Mommy said that swear words aren't really bad. It's society that says they're bad. But they're still just words. And most of the time they make people smile."

Mia laughed again. It sounded like something Margo would say.

"But now," Liz said, "Everyone is dead. So we can decide what's okay to say, right?"

Mia felt wrong smiling, but couldn't help it. "I suppose. But what if the others disagree?"

Liz stood quiet for a moment, pondering the question. Then she shrugged. "Fuck 'em."

Covering her mouth, Mia laughed hard, but stopped just as abruptly. She held the gun up. Liz went silent and fell in behind her. She'd heard it too. Footsteps. Above them.

Someone was home.

20

"Stay here," Mia whispered to Liz. She'd quickly checked the second floor bedrooms and deposited Liz in a closet. The girl shuffled back into the closest, hidden behind a rack of hanging suits that must have come from a Big n' Tall store.

The stairs to the third floor were at the center of the hall and ended at a closed door. A thick, beige carpet covered the steps and concealed her approach. She paused at the top of the stairs, trying to remember how police officers breached a room, but then realized every image she had of the maneuver was from a TV show.

With her left hand on the door knob and the gun in her right, she slowly turned the handle and nudged the door open. Other than the bottom of the door brushing against the carpet, she managed complete silence.

The third floor was one large room. Four skylights above and a large, front looking window filled the room with the tangerine glow of the setting sun. She searched the long room for any sign of the person she'd heard and found nothing. There were two arcade games; the screens blank. A mini-bar filled the back corner accompanied by a card table and dart board on the wall. The front half of the room held two plush couches and a TV screen that looked big enough to service a stadium theater. But the centerpiece of the room was a pool table. Ornately carved from red oak, the table sat at the center of the space. A large stained glass fixture hung above it.

The most interesting thing about the pool table was what lay on the side.

A bullet.

Her bullet.

She walked toward the round, staring at it. "Austin?"

"Didn't want you to shoot me." Austin's voice came from behind her. A small bathroom was hidden behind the stairs. He stepped out, wiping off his face with a hand towel.

She wanted to leap at the man and hug him. Having written him off as dead, she felt glad to see him. She lowered her gun.

He walked to the pool table and picked up the round. "Thanks for the message. I came in through the fire escape after checking out the back-yard."

"How did you get here so fast?" she asked.

He took out a pool ball and rolled it across the table, bouncing it off the cushion. "I wasn't that far behind. Wanted to make sure you weren't being followed."

"You were watching us?"

He nodded. "I was in the woods behind the house."

"Could'a told me."

"Worried?" he asked with a grin.

"Asshole."

Austin laughed and looked beyond her. Liz was standing there. He stopped smiling.

"Don't worry, Mr. Austin. We decided that curse words weren't off-ensive anymore," Liz said as she entered the room and sat on a couch.

"I told you to wait," Mia said, a touch of anger in her voice.

Liz shrugged. "I thought it was safe to come out with them." She thumb-ed over her shoulder as Mark arrived, carrying a novel. Paul and Chang followed him, also carrying novels.

"There a book club I don't know about?" Austin asked.

"Only form of entertainment that's not going to get us killed," Mark said.

"Running for your life isn't entertaining enough?" Mia asked.

"Food's here," Collins announced as he entered carrying two brown bags full of non-perishable food.

White and Vanderwarf followed, hands empty. Garbarino was last. He closed and locked the door at the bottom of the stairs then joined them at the top. He looked honestly pleased to see Austin. "You made it."

Austin stopped the rolling pool ball. "One almost got me. Snuck up behind me while I was distracted."

"Were they armed?" Garbarino asked.

Austin shook his head. "They were...insane. No weapons. Came at me with hands and teeth. Like animals. A few of them weren't any trouble. But if I wasn't armed...or if the rest of them showed up." He shook his head again, this time looking at the floor. "Wouldn't have turned out the same."

After a moment of silence, he moved to the end of the pool table and reached under it. He motioned to Garbarino. "Help me on this end. Vanderwarf. White. Get the other side."

Together, the four of them moved the heavy table in front of the fire escape door on the side of the house. With the downstairs sealed, the second floor door locked and the pool table blocking the only other exit, they were sealed in tight.

As night settled, the group ate boxes of Hostess comfort food, spoke little, and one by one dropped off to sleep. Vanderwarf and White lay down behind the bar. No one could see them, everyone knew the two were dealing with the destruction of the world in their own, primal way.

"Going to have to start repopulating the planet sooner or later," Paul had whispered to Mark, but the priest wasn't laughing. Despite his normally humorous personality, he had fallen more serious as the sun descended and the sunset turned blood red. But if darkness filled his thoughts, he kept it to himself and eventually nodded off. Paul slept on one of the couches, snoring lightly. Chang had found a bean bag chair and fell asleep halfway on, lying on her back with her head cocked back and her mouth wide open. Collins fell asleep as he often did in the Oval Office, head down on the table. He'd started playing solitaire, but wasn't having any luck.

Liz fell asleep on Mia's lap while she sat in a comfortable chair to the side of the front window. Had it not been pitch black outside, it would have offered her a view of half the neighborhood for nearly a mile. Austin sat on a stool across from her, arms folded across his chest keeping watch in the other direction.

"Strange, isn't it?" he said quietly.

"What is?" she replied.

"That sound."

She listened, but could only hear the breathing of several sleeping people and Paul's snoring. "I can't hear anything."

Austin picked up a pillow from the arm of the couch and tossed it at Paul. The man snorted, rolled over and fell quiet. "Outside," Austin said.

She reached forward slowly and opened the small window. She held her breath and listened. At first she heard nothing. But after a few moments she heard...something. High pitched. Reverberating. Very distant. "What is it?" she asked.

"Screaming," he said.

Goose bumps sprung up on her arms. He was right. Once he identified the sound, she could hear it for what it was—screaming, from hundreds, if not thousands of people. "What's going on out there?" she asked.

As though in reply, a light outside clicked on.

Austin sprang up.

Mia gasped.

"Motion sensitive light in the driveway," he said. "Must have a battery backup."

She heard nothing but "motion sensitive."

Someone lurked outside.

She shifted for a view of the driveway and saw a man. He moved quickly, but not in a single direction. Like a squirrel in the road, unsure of which way to run from an approaching car, he leaped one way and then the other. She could hear his panicked breathing, squeaking with fear.

"Should we help him?" she asked.

Austin shook his head, no. Instead, he whispered, "Close your window."

She did so, quickly and quietly, careful not to jostle Liz and wake her up.

"I don't think he could have heard us."

"It's not him I'm worried about." He motioned to the others. "It's them. I don't want them to wake up. I don't want them to see."

"See what?"

"You didn't hear the voices?"

She shook her head, wondering if her hearing sucked or if Austin just had really good ears.

"The people who attacked me. Who attacked Reggie. They all shouted warnings first. Apologies. Like they didn't want to be doing what they were about to do. Like it horrified them. I could hear them coming." He motioned out the window. "And so can he."

The man was still running in circles. Then, through the closed windows, Mia did hear another voice. A woman's. Then a man's. She couldn't make out the words, but she could see them. Running shadows. Three of them.

The panicked man finally saw them coming. Or maybe heard them. And turned to run in the opposite direction. But he was so out of his head with fright that he turned and sprinted into a tree. The three descended on top of him before he could stand. The woman went for his neck with her teeth, cutting off his scream. The two men tore at his stomach. Blood pooled around him as they slaughtered the man.

From beginning to end, the attack lasted only fifteen seconds. The two men and the woman stood above the body, wailing. Crying like children. They disappeared into the night again, leaving the dead man behind, his entrails looping over the driveway, his blood glowing bright red under the halogen glow of the motion sensitive light.

Mia and Austin stared down at the body in silence.

When the light blinked out again, Austin whispered, "We'll go out the back in the morning. Get some sleep."

She thought sleep would be impossible, but she sat back, closed her eyes, and when she opened them again, the view of stars outside had been replaced by blue sky. For a moment, lost in the comfortable place between sleep and reality, she forgot everything that had happened.

That's when Liz started screaming.

21

Mia launched from her chair, wrapped her hand around Liz's open mouth and turned her away from the large window. She thought the girl had seen the mauled body in the driveway. Why didn't we cover the window last night?

As Liz filled her lungs to scream again, Austin knelt in front of her, ready to talk her down from her panic. But he quickly realized what was happening. "She's still asleep."

"Someone shut her up!" Garbarino hissed. He jumped to his feet, holding his weapon. The screaming got his hackles up.

Mia shook her arm. "Elizabeth! Wake up! Liz!"

The girl screamed again.

"They're going to hear her!" Garbarino said.

Mia knew he was right. Her high pitched squeal could probably be heard for blocks, even with the windows shut. And who's to say the killers she and Austin saw the night before weren't waiting outside already?

White and Vanderwarf emerged from behind the bar, weapons at the ready. "What's happening?" Vanderwarf asked.

"Kid's having a nightmare," Collins answered as he stood up and approached Mia. He knelt down in front of Liz, next to Austin and before anyone grasped his intentions, he reached out and slapped the girl across the face.

"Hey!" Austin shouted, shoving his former boss away. Collins fell back, unhurt.

The scream didn't come again. A gentle crying took its place. "My face hurts," Liz said.

Mia glared at Collins for a moment before picking up her niece.

He held his hands up.

"It worked, didn't it? And it sure as hell beats him—" He motioned to Garbarino, "—putting a bullet in her."

Austin saw Garbarino's weapon lower. Had he been bringing it up to fire? There was no way to be sure, so he let it go. He didn't chastise Collins any further, either. The slap wasn't hard enough to break the girl's jaw and she did stop screaming. But was it too late already?

Austin moved to the window and looked out over the neighborhood. The houses, all various shades of beige, glowed yellow in the morning sun. When his gaze turned to the driveway, his heart hammered in his chest.

Mia rubbed Liz's cheek. "You're okay, baby. You're okay."

"I had a bad dream."

"I know."

"You were dead," Liz said before looking at the others. "They were all dead. And I was alone."

"You're not alone," Mia said, wrapping the girl in her arms. A gentle touch on her shoulder took her attention away from Liz. It was Austin. He motioned toward the window with his eyes. There was something outside he wanted her to see. His silence meant he didn't want the others to know.

She looked around the room. With Liz quiet, they all went about their morning rituals. Collins mixed instant coffee into a mug of cold water. Paul was in the bathroom. Mark sat on one of the couches, reading from his small Bible. Vanderwarf, White and Garbarino sat around the card table, opening a fresh box of Hostess cakes. Chang was just waking now. From the tired look in her eyes, she'd slept through the morning theatrics.

Mia stood slowly, holding Liz in her arms, and turned to the window. She kept Liz looking in the opposite direction as she looked, first at the empty neighborhood, and then down to the driveway. She gasped at what she saw.

A dried bloodstain covered a large swath of pavement, but the body, and every scrap of eviscerated organ was missing.

"He's gone... scavengers?" she asked, quietly.

"I don't think so," Austin said. "There'd be something left behind. Bones."

"Maybe they moved it?"

He shook his head. "We haven't seen a living animal or insect since we landed."

"Maybe they came back for him?" Mia asked.

"Came back for who?" It was Chang. She'd snuck up behind them while they looked out the window. She followed their eyes toward the driveway. "Oh my God. Is that blood?"

Mia put Liz down and gave her a little shove toward Mark. "Go talk to Uncle Mark."

Liz obeyed, sitting down next to Mark. He saw what was going on and put his arm around the girl. He opened the Bible and said, "Let me tell you a story."

With Liz preoccupied, Mia turned to Chang. "Stay quiet."

Chang looked back into the room. The others were getting on with their morning, some were even smiling. She nodded. "Whose blood is that?"

"A man was killed there last night," Austin said, his voice devoid of emotion.

"Last night? You saw it?"

Austin looked Chang in the eyes. "Not a word." He waited for her to nod again, then turned to the others. "We're heading out in thirty minutes. Eat, drink, pack what you can carry."

"What's the plan?" White asked.

"We don't even know where we are," Vanderwarf added.

"We're in Rhode Island," Austin said, holding up a map he'd found while searching the end tables on either side of the couch. "We'll head north, through Massachusetts and New Hampshire."

"Won't it be colder up there?" Paul asked as he exited the bathroom.

"It should be colder here," Austin said. "It should be freezing. But it's not. I think it's safe to assume the weather patterns and seasons have changed."

"Then why head north?" Paul asked.

"Fewer targets," Collins said and then turned to Austin. "Northern New England—Vermont, New Hampshire, Maine—don't have a lot in the way of strategic targets. It's mostly trees and very few people. With each nuke costing a good chunk of change to maintain and launch, it's less likely the Russians directly targeted that area of the country."

"You think there might be survivors?" Garbarino asked, sounding hopeful.

"I'm hoping so."

"The kind that doesn't want to kill us?" Chang added as she headed for the bathroom.

"Yeah," Austin said. "That kind."

Mia glanced out the window and saw movement. She held her breath as she leaned over for a better look. She did an admirable job of hiding the quick intake of air, but Austin noticed. He glanced back at her, despite all eyes being on him. Her eyes were wide with urgency. He took a step back and followed her gaze.

He had a harder time hiding his surprise, "Fuck."

But no one seemed to notice, as Chang distracted them by saying, "Dude, haven't you heard, if it's yellow, let it mellow—"

Austin's mind raced. Was he seeing things? He didn't think so. Then how was this possible? The man standing beneath the window, only five feet from the front porch, was the same man they'd seen slaughtered the night before. He was still fidgeting. Still panicking. And the wild-eyed man seemed perfectly healthy despite being nearly naked and covered in caked-on blood.

And if he's here, the killers that tracked him down might not be far behind.

Chang's voice cut through his thoughts. "If it's brown, flush it down."

Austin snapped around, and hissed an angry, "No!"

But his voice was lost among the chuckles of the others.

"Chang!" He said, louder. "Stop!"

She turned to him. "What?" But his warning came too slow. She'd already flushed the toilet. Despite there being no running water, the toilet tank still held enough for one flush. The third floor toilet roared as water shot into the toilet bowl and flowed through the plumbing toward the basement.

Chang understood her mistake as soon as she saw his eyes. She cringed. "Sorry."

"Tom," Mia said, her voice a barely controlled whisper.

He moved back to the window and looked down. The panicked man had stopped in his tracks and was looking up at them. He met Austin's eyes. The man's stare rooted Austin in place and filled him with some kind of primal fear. But the stranger seemed just as afraid.

The fear-filled stare-down was broken when the man whipped his head to the left. He looked up again and mouthed a single word. "Run." Then, he ran.

Tom turned to the others. "Pack up. We're leaving now."

Garbarino stood. "Why? What's—"

The sound of breaking glass silenced him.

"That was downstairs," Paul said.

Austin threw on his backpack and drew his weapon. "They're coming through the windows."

"Fuck," Vanderwarf said. She stood, backpack on and weapon at the ready a moment later. The rest of the group quickly followed.

Garbarino, Austin, Mia and White ran for the pool table blocking the fire exit door. They had it moved out of the way in seconds. Garbarino reached for the deadbolt. Just as he was turning it, Austin's hand slapped over his, stopping him.

"Wait," Austin urged.

Garbarino's eyes were wide. "Fuck that!" He tried turning the lock again, but Austin held it tight.

"Wait," Austin repeated.

Garbarino glared at him for a moment. "For what?"

"If there's more than one, we want to give them all time to get inside, so we can get out. And as soon as we open that door, the ten of us need to run down two flights of stairs. They won't have to go as far. The only chance we have at a head start is if they're—"

The door at the bottom of the third-floor staircase shook as several fists pounded against it. Austin removed his hand from Garbarino's. "Go!"

The locks flew open and Garbarino launched himself out onto the small landing. The morning sun warmed him, and he saw no danger. He took the stairs two at a time, leading the line of survivors down the side of the house. Dead grass crunched beneath his feet when he reached the bottom and knelt in a firing stance. He checked both directions. "All clear," he whispered as the others joined him.

Austin was the last one down. When he reached the bottom, he noticed the banging inside the house had stopped.

The killers were coming.

Austin waved them toward the backyard where a line of trees marked the beginning of a large patch of wilderness. "Into the woods!"

The backyard was a wide open patch of dead grass. Other than a swing set and a candy cane-shaped septic system vent, there was nothing to hide behind. They were totally exposed. But there was no choice. They had to run.

The group moved as one, like flocking birds, crouch-running across the grass. But a child's toy tripped Vanderwarf and sent her to the ground only five feet from the back of the house. White turned around and stopped. He reached down to pick her up. With his head down, he heard the dull thuds of someone running inside the house. Thinking he had at least ten seconds before the person reached the barricaded back door and perhaps another minute after that, he didn't bother raising his weapon.

When the window exploded from the inside out, he was totally unprepared for it. A woman flew through the air, shards of glass covering her face, arms and naked upper torso. White and the woman hit the ground a second later and before anyone, including White, who had the wind knocked out of him, could respond, the woman shouted, "I'm sorry! I don't want to—" She drove her rigid fingers into his throat with unnatural strength. Her fingers disappeared into his neck up to the third knuckle.

White twitched beneath her.

Vanderwarf screamed and kicked away from the woman and her now dead lover.

The woman wailed, as though wounded.

A single gunshot silenced her.

Austin.

The bullet struck the woman's forehead and sent her flailing backwards.

"Vanderwarf!" Austin shouted. "Move!"

Though horrified, Vanderwarf's instincts and training kicked in. She climbed to her feet and ran toward the others. Glass exploded again as a second body emerged from the house. It was a man. Nearly naked. His body charged like a killing machine on speed. But his face was twisted with agony. The expression locked solid as Austin fired a second shot, piercing the man's brain and sending him to the ground.

The silence that followed lasted only a moment.

Voices—a sea of them—rose up in the distance.

"The woods," Austin growled. "Now!"

There was no pause. No looking back.

They ran like prey.

Like the man killed in the driveway the night before.

The same man who followed them now.

Unlike the others, he looked back, eyeing the bodies on the grass—watching their eyes—and then followed the group into the darkness of the dead woods.

22

Three hours and five miles later, the group stopped to rest. The forest seemed endless, stretching on with no sign of life since they'd left the suburban sprawl. Modern man, it seemed, had yet to subdivide or pave this stretch of wilderness. No one complained about it. The dead woods were preferable to any living thing they had come across thus far.

Sitting on their backpacks, the group ate energy bars and drank bottled water. Their survival packs held enough food and water for two days, maybe three if they stretched it. The food taken from the house might keep them going for another day. But food wasn't the issue so much as water.

Without water, they could only last three days.

But they were on foot. And sweating a lot. Austin gave them five days at best, without restocking their supplies. If they were going to make it to the northern woods of New England, they would need a lot more.

They ate in silence, catching their breath. When Chang lay down and closed her eyes, Mia nudged her leg with her foot. "Uh-uh. Your legs will cramp up."

"Already cramped up," Chang said with a huff. But she stood again and stretched instead.

Mia knew that if they rested too long, getting started again would be nearly impossible. Judging by the position of the sun, noon had already come and gone. They needed to find a place to spend the night, not because it would get cold, but because they needed a defensible position to sleep in.

Austin had whispered that suggestion to her as they walked. He still wanted her to be in charge despite him being the best man for the job. If ever people needed to bury their own personal hang-ups, it was now.

But she knew that wouldn't happen. Life and death situation be damned, people would always act like people—selfishly.

Except for me, of course. She nearly laughed at the thought.

In fact, she was being selfish. The more people who survived this mess, the more there would be to protect Liz. To populate a future world where her niece wouldn't be alone.

Is that selfish? She wondered. To want the best for my family?

She looked over at Liz sitting next to Mark who was, at her request, reading to her from the Bible again. Her hands were folded in her lap. Her small body leaned against Mark's arm. Her head tilted toward the small page.

Mark's voice offered soothing words, but she couldn't make them out. She suspected he was reading from the Psalms. She thought those were comforting, but wasn't really sure. Whatever he read, it definitely had a calming effect on Liz.

But Mia wouldn't feel calm until they were all safe. "Two minutes," she announced. "Then we're heading out."

She received a series of grunts in reply. No one was happy about it, but no one argued, either. She looked at Austin and he gave her a subtle nod that said, "You're doing good."

Garbarino stood, repacked his supplies and began stretching. After touching his toes, he began wandering around the group, watching the woods. He stopped behind Mark, and Mia could tell he was eavesdropping. Mia watched his face. Was Garbarino interested in finding God?

When she saw his face twist with disgust, she knew the answer was "no."

Garbarino snatched the book out of Mark's hands.

"Hey!" Mark protested, but Garbarino was already walking away.

A moment later, he read the passage aloud. "'The horses and riders I saw in my vision looked like this: Their breastplates were fiery red, dark blue, and yellow as sulfur.' Garbarino shook his head, but kept reading. "The heads of the horses resembled the heads of lions, and out of their mouths came fire, smoke and sulfur.'" He paused reading again, appeared shaken up for a moment, but then set his jaw and continued reading, this time laying on a thick southern accent. "'A third of mankind was killed by the three plagues of fire, smoke and sulfur that came out of their mouths. The power of the horses was in their mouths and in their tails; for their tails were like snakes, having heads with which they inflict injury.' This is bullshit you know?"

"Just give it back," Mark said, reaching out his hand.

"You were reading that to a kid?" Chang asked.

"I like it," Liz said.

Garbarino started his preacher impersonation again, reading the next verses. "'The rest of mankind that survived these plagues still did not repent of the work of their hands; they did not stop worshiping demons, and idols of gold, silver, bronze, stone and wood—idols that cannot see or hear or walk. Nor did they repent of their murders, their magic arts, their sexual immorality or their thefts." He closed the book and threw it at Mark.

The Bible bounced off the priest's chest and fell to the leaf littered forest floor. Liz knelt down and picked it up, handing it to Mark.

"That what you think happened?" Garbarino asked, and then laughed. "Looks like God got his math wrong. A lot more than one third of the population is dead."

"Joe," Austin said, his voice serious.

"We don't know that," Mark said.

Garbarino scoffed and threw his hands up in the air. "Look around you, man. Everything is dead. Everything!"

"Garbarino..." Austin's voice was nearly a growl.

Chang frowned. "There were people—"

"They're all crazy. Gone cannibal or something!"

The metal chink of a round being loaded caught Garbarino's attention. He turned and found Austin's sidearm aimed at his face. "Shut. The. Fuck. Up," Austin said.

Garbarino stared at him. A mixture of surprise and anger flashed across his face.

Mia's hand came to rest on the weapon, pushing it toward the ground. "I think what Tom is trying to say, Joe, is that your voice is giving away our position and if you're not quiet we may find ourselves overrun by the very cannibals that you so kindly reminded us about."

The tension in Garbarino's face dissolved. He spoke in a whisper, pointing at Mark. "He shouldn't be reading that to her. To anyone."

Mia agreed. If she had known exactly what Mark had been reading she would have kept Liz away from it. She knew some parts of the Bible taught things like love, patience and kindness, but so much of the rest was doom and gloom. And there seemed to be enough of that in the world already. "Please keep that book to yourself," she said to Mark.

He said nothing, but looked sad as he put the Bible in his pocket and packed his bag.

"Pack up," Mia said. "We're leaving."

Collins, who sat twenty feet away from the others stood slowly and slung his backpack over his shoulder with a grunt. When Mia walked past with Liz in tow, he said, "You should have been in politics."

"I've been thinking a career in the Marines might have been better."

"You'd probably be dead if that were the case."

Mia looked at the former president. His statement struck a chord. Matt had been a Marine. "Well, if the Grim Reaper ever retires, I'm sure you could easily fill his shoes."

As soon as the words came out of her mouth, she realized she blamed him, in part, for what had happened. If he'd handled the Russian accusations better, this could have been avoided. If he hadn't returned fire with everything in the United States arsenal there might still be a human race—a place for Liz to grow up.

Collins seethed. "If your fiancé hadn't been caught, none of this would have happened."

Mia turned toward him, determined to not lose her cool like Garbarino. "Caught? He wasn't caught. He was captured. And tortured. And in case you're wondering, I blame that on you as well."

Collins just stared at her, a breath away from blurting out a reply, but years of political coaching taught him to hold his tongue when angry. He'd already said too much. Any more might turn all of them against him, because everything was his fault. Luckily, everyone else who knew the truth was dead. If he could keep his secret, there was nothing to worry about.

But if the truth got out, that Matthew Brenton was indeed an assassin ordered to kill the Russian president, he doubted he'd have long to live.

Mia turned and stormed away, pulling Liz behind her.

Collins watched her go, remembering that she was a reporter. If she thought on it too much, she might realize what his use of the word "caught" implied. And while no newspapers or pundits remained to tell the tale, it wouldn't be hard to inform what was left of human society. If it came to that, he thought, feeling the cold metal of his shotgun, things could get complicated.

23

They came across the cabin before the sun set on their second day back on Earth. The cabin looked quaint, but the bank auction sign on the front door, dated two years previous suggested the interior would be neglected. The white paint covering the outside looked like dry skin, peeling and flaking away. A fridge sat on the now dead, overgrown lawn that encircled the home and reached out to the wall of dead trees surrounding the clearing. The cloudless sky above turned a deep purple as the sun began to descend.

"I've seen this movie," Mark said as the group stood in front of the cabin. "It doesn't end well for the people inside."'

No one argued. The cabin was straight out of a B-grade slasher flick.

"We could follow the driveway," Paul said. The dirt driveway twisted into the woods, disappearing in the distance. "There might be someplace better to hole up."

"No," Austin said. "This is good. Nice and solitary. If someone approaches through the woods, we'll hear them coming." The endless rows of dead trees had carpeted the forest floor in so many dry branches that it was impossible to walk without stepping on them. Anyone approaching the cabin would sound like they had a string of lit firecrackers tied to their feet.

"Unless they come up the driveway," Garbarino said.

"We'll take shifts watching," Austin said with a nod. "Pair up, one agent to one civilian."

"Pair up with one of them?" Garbarino said. He motioned to the others. "No offense, but they're liable to get me killed."

"Would you prefer to have two of them on watch while you slept?"

Garbarino pursed his lip. There was no arguing that.

"What about her?" he asked, pointing to Vanderwarf, who had been quiet all day. She stood at the back of the group, arms crossed head down. "She's useless now."

"Vanderwarf!" Austin snapped.

She went rigid and looked up, eyes wide. "Sir."

"Are you with us?"

"Yes, sir," she said. Her training, which had taken a backseat while she adjusted to the horrors of the new world, was the best in the world. She set her mind to the task at hand, but her lower lip never quite stopped quivering.

Austin turned to Garbarino, "She'll sleep first and take the last shift with Paul. She'll be fine."

"Sorry to point this out," Mark said, "but the ratio of agent to civilian isn't one to one. How will we all go on watch?"

"Not everyone will," Austin said. "Paul is with Vanderwarf, last shift." The pair looked at each other and nodded.

"Mia, you and Garbarino take second shift." Neither looked happy, but they didn't complain.

Austin looked Mark in the eyes. "And you're with me, starting now."

Mark sighed. They had walked all day, covering fifteen miles. They stopped only to eat and use the bathroom, which was whatever dead tree they could hide behind. His legs were sore and his eyes heavy. If he lay down, sleep would come in seconds.

"Don't look so down, Father," Austin said. "God is your strength, remember?"

Mark frowned at the remark. He knew Garbarino was hostile to the idea of God, but had not yet realized Austin was, too. In fact, as he searched the other faces, he saw sympathy in the eyes of only one of them. Liz.

Austin entered the cabin first, weapon at the ready. Garbarino followed. They searched the four-room dwelling as a team, covering each other in case something wild lurked inside. They found a sparsely decorated, hastily abandoned home. The kitchen cabinets and wood stove were both missing, but a stack of old, stained mattresses filled the back bedroom. They saw few personal items, but the front bedroom showed evidence of at least one teenage gathering—empty beer cans and cigarette butts.

As Garbarino began dragging the old mattresses out into the empty rooms, Austin stepped outside. "It ain't pretty, but it's safe and dry."

"Everything is dry," Paul said before entering.

It was true. They hadn't seen a cloud in the sky since returning and even the woods lacked the earthy smell of decaying vegetation.

Austin remained outside with Mark as the rest of the group entered the house and settled in for the night. He sat on the dilapidated front steps and helped himself to half a protein bar and a sip of water. Mark stood by the driveway, turned toward the woods.

They stayed like that for thirty minutes.

As the sky turned dark purple, Austin said, "Thought you were tired."

Mark seemed to not hear him, but then bobbed his head and turned around. He walked right up to Austin and sat down. "Dead tired. I was just giving you time."

Austin looked at him. "Giving me time?" Austin had been giving Mark time. It seemed both of them knew this conversation was going to happen.

"You had to work up the courage," Mark said.

Austin's eyebrows rose high on his forehead.

"Questioning a man's religion isn't an easy thing to do."

Austin smiled. Mark was right about that. It wasn't easy. But it was necessary. "I would appreciate it if you kept that book to yourself. We don't need them to be any more afraid than they already are."

"Actually, I think they could use a lot of what's in the Bible."

Austin let out a gentle laugh.

"If you'd read the whole book, you would know it's a message of hope."

"If delusions give you hope."

Mark just shook his head. "I'll keep it to myself until someone asks. That good enough?"

"Works for me," Austin said.

Mark placed his shotgun across his lap. The hard weapon felt wrong to him, but if wielding it could keep these people alive a little longer, he would use it. "They're going to, you know? Ask."

"What makes you so sure?"

"You haven't really looked around, have you?" Mark said. "Sooner or later, you'll open your eyes. You'll see what I see. Then you'll ask."

The cryptic reply left Austin feeling frustrated. It struck him as the kind of vague, fear-inducing rhetoric that got people to put on white robes and drink poisoned Kool-Aid. "Just keep the Bible-thumping in your head and don't scare the kid."

Mark gave Austin a pat on the shoulder. "In case you haven't noticed, tough guy, she's not scared. Not like the rest of you." He stood and left the porch, taking up his position in the driveway again.

Austin sat in silence, thinking about what Mark said. Other than the nightmare, in which everyone had died, she hadn't panicked. She cringed at the violence, tensed when things got tense, but in general, she seemed peaceful. At peace.

When he couldn't figure out why, Austin pushed the train of thought from his mind and focused on listening instead. Inner peace never saved anyone from a post-apocalyptic nightmare, not in the movies, not in real life.

Two hours later, Mia and Garbarino took watch. Not that you could really call what they were doing watching. The darkness was nearly complete. The moon hid below the horizon. The stars, despite there being more than either had ever seen before, did little to light the deep woods. The only sound each could hear was the breathing of the other.

For the first hour, neither spoke.

At first out of dislike for each other, and then out of fear that they'd be heard. But as the night wore on and their comfort in the dark grew, Mia found herself reviewing the events of the day. And despite Garbarino's theatrics, she appreciated that Garbarino had looked out for Liz's well-being.

"Thanks," she said.

The sudden break in silence made Garbarino jump. "Fuck," he muttered. "Scared the shit out of me."

"Weren't asleep were you?"

"Not a chance. Not out here. What the hell were you thanking me for, anyway?"

"Today, with Liz."

Garbarino knew what she was talking about because the interaction with Mark had been the only noteworthy event of their day. "Sure thing. Think the boss-man had a talk with him."

Mia nodded in the dark. "That's what I was thinking, too."

"Cause otherwise he would have partnered with you." Garbarino followed with a Cary Grant-like impression. "I think he's sweet on you, kid."

Thankful that the darkness hid her flush cheeks, Mia said, "I'm not his type."

"C'mon, don't tell me you haven't thought about repopulating the planet with the man?"

Mia could feel the heat radiating from her face now because she had, in fact, thought that very thing. But not for the reasons Garbarino suggested. Giving Liz a family to grow old with had nothing to do with passion. Besides, it was too soon.

Too soon for what? she asked herself. She hadn't seen Matt in nearly half a year, and now he was— Stop trying to rationalize your betrayal! some part of her screamed.

With Mia silent, Garbarino continued. "At first I knew I was stuck with Chang, which could be okay if she lost a few pounds. But with White out of the picture—"

"That's cold," Mia said.

"That's the world. Of course, maybe Austin is thinking the same thing. You've got something exotic about you, but Vanderwarf, with those Angelina lips. You might end up with me."

Mia couldn't stop herself from laughing. For a moment she wondered if Garbarino might take offense at the blatant insult, but he laughed too.

"Please," she said. "Collins is my runner up."

"Then the old man and the priest, right?"

"Nah, if that doesn't work out, screw repopulating the planet. I'll take Vanderwarf myself. She's way better looking than the rest of you."

Their laughter slowly faded and silence returned.

A few minutes later, Garbarino spoke again.

"You're all right, Durante."

"Thanks Garbarino." Mia rubbed her sore legs. "So, what's your story?"

"What?"

"Why did you join the Secret Service?"

"I suppose you could say I was recruited. Good with a gun. Former Marine. Not afraid of taking a bullet. Never questioned orders. Scored high on the IQ tests."

"Perfect human shield, huh?"

"Something like that."

"And now?"

"Now? You know the score. Every man for himself. There is no greater cause to live for beyond staying alive now. It's different for you. You have the girl. Me? I didn't have many people in my life before. I was dedicated to the good ol' U. S. of A., but that asshole, Collins, had to go and blow up the world. Didn't have to end that way."

"No," Mia said. "It didn't."

"Heard your boyfriend was Matt Brenton. Yeah?"

"Yeah."

"Good Marine? Convoy crew right? Driving trucks?"

"Yes to all three. His convoy was attacked in northern Afghanistan. That's where they took him."

"Huh," Garbarino said.

Mia couldn't see his face, but the sound of Garbarino's voice implied a confused expression. "What?"

"Supplies were airdropped up there. Truck convoys were too dangerous. Hell, they were dangerous in Iraq. They were suicidal in Northern Afghanistan."

It was Mia's turn to be confused. "Huh."

"Looks like you've got a mystery to solve, Scooby Doo."

"Looks like," Mia said, and then fell silent. She spent the next few hours thinking about what Garbarino said. If he was right, it meant that she'd been lied to. By Matt. By Collins. The new information refocused her thoughts on a question that had been nagging her all day: why did Collins say Matt had been caught?

24

After sleeping for nearly seven hours, Paul felt fairly refreshed despite it still being pitch dark when Mia woke him for his shift with Vanderwarf. He wasn't sure what to expect. He hadn't said more than two words to the woman. After what happened to White, he expected she'd been a wreck. He didn't know how close the two had been, but the connection between the two was impossible to miss. To his surprise, when they sat down on the front porch, she seemed ready for anything.

Except silence.

Only ten minutes passed before she said, "We didn't sleep together."

Paul looked over at her. He could see her silhouette against the dark purple, star-filled sky. The sun would be up soon. "I think you have me confused with my brother."

She offered a light laugh. "Just need a friendly ear, not forgiveness."

"A friendly ear, I can do," he said.

"Behind the bar," she said. "He was crying. Didn't want you all to see."

Paul wasn't sure what to say. There was nothing wrong with a good cry, especially given the circumstances, but he, like everyone else, had been so sure the pair had been having sex. The surprise kept him silent, which suited Vanderwarf fine. She wasn't finished.

"I wanted to," she said. "God, I wanted to. He was all I had left in the world, you know? You have your brother. Mia has Liz. I had Dan. But..."

She sniffed back fresh tears.

"He had a wife. Kids. He was going to leave her. Leave them," she said. "And now that they had been taken from him—"

"He felt guilty," Paul said.

"Yeah."

"Makes sense."

"Yeah." She sniffed again. "I spent the night rubbing his back and holding him. Comforting him, you know? I didn't have kids. Can't say I've ever been in love before. But I knew, that night, when he cried for his kids, for his wife, that I loved him for it. He was a good man."

"Sounds like it."

"He didn't deserve what happened to him."

Paul thought on this for a moment. He'd seen plenty of death in his life; men killed more violently than Daniel White's fate. "No one does," Paul said. "Death is the enemy."

"Why did they kill him?" she asked, barely controlling a sob.

Paul put his hand on her back. "The people we saw. Somehow they lived through what we only saw from orbit. Maybe it drove them mad. Changed their minds somehow. Made them killers."

"You heard what she said?"

"Yeah," he said, not wanting to remember the horror in the woman's voice before she jammed her hand into White's throat.

"It was like she didn't want to do it, but couldn't stop herself."

"And if that's true?"

"I can't hate her for it."

"Pity, then?"

"Maybe," Vanderwarf said. "I can't imagine living that way. It'd be—"

Snap.

The pair held their breath for thirty seconds.

"Could it have been a branch falling from one of the trees?" Vanderwarf asked, her voice a whisper.

"Suppose," he replied. He looked up at the sky. The deep purple had lightened further. He could see Vanderwarf next to him. Her cheeks were wet with tears, but her sadness had been replaced by a set jaw and a hawk-like gaze locked on the woods. Her finger was on the trigger of her MP5. Safety off. Ready for business.

Snap.

"Or not," he said.

They stood as a pair, both holding MP5s sporting thirty-round magazines. Both had two spare magazines. Firing eight hundred rounds per minute, the pair could mow down a good sized mob in seconds.

Snap.

But this wasn't a mob. Whoever was approaching the cabin was alone, and from the sound of it, still at least one hundred yards off. They ducked behind a ruined picnic table and focused on the gnarled trees blocking their view of the approaching target.

"Should I wake the others?" Paul asked.

"I'd prefer not to be out here alone but shouting for them will give away our position. If we hear more than the one, we'll wake the others and bug out."

Paul gave a nod. "Good enough."

Crack.

This one was loud.

Close.

A shadow slid between the trees, emerging into the clearing as a silhouette—dark against a darker background.

"It's a man," Paul whispered. The body shape was easy enough to see. But the details were lost. Another few minutes, Paul thought, and there will be enough light to see by.

The man took a step toward them, his movements jerky, uncoordinated.

Paul and Vanderwarf looked at each other.

"You know what he looks like, right?" she whispered.

"Mmm." Paul wasn't willing to give the notion any more thought than that. But he did look like a zombie. The classic brain-loving Romero variety.

Then the man moaned and Paul's heart beat hard.

Vanderwarf's breathing grew heavy.

Then the man spoke. They were too distant to hear the words, but he had clearly said something.

"Zombies don't talk," she whispered.

"Maybe these do?" Paul said and peeked up over the table.

He sat back down quickly.

The man had cut the distance in half. He held his index finger to his lips, signaling for her to be quiet. He pointed to his eyes with two fingers, then toward the man, saying, "Take a look."

Vanderwarf slowly raised her head, but before she cleared the top of the table, the man spoke again. "I'm sorry," he said clearly.

Her eyes went wide and she stood up straight. The man stood with his back to her now, but she recognized his form just as easily as she recognized his voice.

Paul tried pulling her back down, but she yanked away from him. He didn't know why until she spoke.

"Dan?"

Paul stood just as Daniel White turned around. His throat was coated in dry blood, but there was no wound. Had what they all seen been an illusion? Did the woman really punch him in the throat? The blood could have been hers. She had jumped through a window. The strongest evidence was his presence. He was alive.

White looked Vanderwarf in the eyes, his expression flooding with relief. She lowered her weapon and stepped around the picnic table. "Danny, how?"

He wept. "I'm sorry," he said.

"Don't be sorry," she said, reaching out for him.

He reached for her. "Erin. Run away."

Paul felt the words like a battering ram to the head. Run away. But Vanderwarf was too distracted by White's apparent resurrection to really hear what White was saying. He raised his weapon to fire, but the couple reached each other at the same moment, their outstretched arms wrapping in a tight embrace.

"No!" Paul shouted too late.

The front door of the cabin burst open. Austin and Garbarino stormed out, weapons raised, too late to stop what happened next, but in time to witness it.

"Daniel!" Austin shouted.

Daniel's eyes glanced at Austin, full of regret. Then he bit down.

Vanderwarf's scream ripped through the air, a high-pitched wail that woke the others and faded with a liquid gurgle. Blood sprayed in pulsing geysers as Daniel pulled away the meat surrounding her jugular. Her body went loose in his arms. He held her there, weeping as the life left her body.

Screaming erupted from inside the cabin. Chang had looked out the window. Collins's voice came next, unintelligible shouting.

Then a gunshot.

Just one.

Never one to waste ammunition, Austin had aimed carefully and fired once. The shot punched a neat hole in the side of White's head and punched out the other with an explosion of brain matter. In the silence that followed, everyone heard the small chunks of White's brain hit the dead grass and dirt driveway. That detail caused Garbarino to vomit over the side rail of the front porch.

"The fuck," Garbarino said, catching his breath and wiping his mouth. "What the fuck!"

The three armed men surrounded the dead pair.

"What happened?" Austin asked.

"Came out of the woods," Paul replied, pointing to the gnarled trees. "Didn't recognize him until he got close. Tried to stop her."

"You knew?" Austin asked.

"He was apologizing. Looked torn up about what he was about to do."

"Just like the lady who got White yesterday?" Garbarino asked.

"But she didn't get him," Paul said. "Not really. Cause he was alive a minute ago. Knew her name, too."

The front door opened and closed. Mia stood on the porch, her hand to her mouth. "What happened?"

"White came back," Garbarino said. "Got Vanderwarf."

"They're dead?"

Austin answered by pointing to an old blue tarp lying next to the porch and speaking to Paul. "Grab that."

The three men quickly covered the bodies with the tarp. "Pack up our supplies," Austin said to Mia.

"But they're dead."

Before Austin could explain, a distant snap cut through the trees. Then another. And another.

Voices followed—a chorus of them.

"Go!" Austin shouted, training his handgun on the woods.

Mia disappeared inside the cabin and reemerged thirty seconds later carrying four backpacks. Chang followed with Liz. Collins and Mark came next. Mia dispensed backpacks and the four men threw them on.

Austin spun around, trying to determine which direction was north, but before he could give the order to move, something burst from the woods. He turned, took aim and held his fire. He recognized the man.

But Garbarino didn't hesitate. He tracked the man's dash across the grass, held his breath and pulled the—

"Wait!" Austin shouted, pushing Garbarino's hand to the ground.

At the sound of Austin's voice, the running man screamed, holding his hands over his head. In his confusion, the man stumbled and fell. He flailed in the dead grass for a moment before returning to his feet. When he saw them standing there, he turned and ran back the way he'd come, but a breaking branch from the woods turned him around again.

"Friend of yours?" Garbarino asked.

Austin could have recognized his panicky run. He'd seen it twice before. "He's not one of them."

"It's him?" Mia asked, watching the man.

"Him, who?" Collins asked.

"We saw him the first night," Austin said. "They killed him."

"They killed him?" Garbarino said, "But..." He looked at the faded, blue tarp.

One of the two bodies was sitting up beneath the tarp.

Garbarino jumped back, taking aim. "Shit!"

The group turned as one and took a collective step backwards.

"Oh my God," Chang said.

After a moment of shock, Austin turned around, looking for the panicked man. He found him at the end of the driveway. He was out of breath, eyes wide, but no longer running. He met Austin's eyes for just a moment and gave a slight tilt with his head that said, follow me.

"Up the driveway," Austin said. "Follow him."

The man ran from view.

"Go!" Austin shouted and the group listened, chasing after the man.

Austin stayed behind, listening to the woods. The approaching army was still a good distance off, but had somehow tracked them here. They followed White, he thought. He knew we were heading north through the woods.

"I don't want to hurt you," Vanderwarf's voice came from the tarp, hands lifted up and searching for a way out.

The form of White rose up next to her. "I'm sorry."

"So am I," Austin said.

At the sound of his voice, White and Vanderwarf began violently clawing at the tarp. The sounds of anguished weeping followed.

Austin silenced them again with two bullets and then chased after the others. He hoped it would be the last he saw of White or Vanderwarf, but at his core he knew he'd see them again.

25

The driveway wound through the woods for nearly a mile. Its circuitous route slowed their actual progress, but freedom from fallen branches and dead brush allowed them to move much faster, and in near silence. Before long, the snapping branches and chorus of voices behind them faded away.

The man who'd been murdered in the suburban driveway led them to a dirt road lined with tall, dead grass. Austin eyed it, weapon in hand. It would be the perfect place for an ambush.

But none came, and five miles later, when the group had settled into a steady pace, he holstered his weapon and focused on keeping the group together. Chang and Collins often lagged behind, asking for frequent breaks, but their guide never stopped. They all ate and drank on the go. Bathroom breaks were accomplished by two people running ahead, ducking behind a tree, and then rejoining the group as they passed.

After the sixth mile, Chang caught her second wind and walked with Mia, Austin and Liz. She watched the way their panicky guide would run ahead and then stop, looking back over his shoulder to make sure they were still following.

"He's like our own personal Gollum," she said.

"Like in the swamp," Liz added.

"You've seen Lord of the Rings?" Chang asked.

"Seen it?" the girl replied. "My mother read it to me."

"That seems a little...odd," Chang said.

"Why?"

"You're like, what, eight?"

"Seven."

"Exactly."

"So?" Liz said, her voice filled with defiance. "I'm probably smarter than you."

Chang laughed. "You might be right about that."

"Keep it down Frodo and Bilbo," Mia said.

Their guide had stopped up ahead when the brown dirt road turned black.

"The road's paved," Austin said.

"Is that a good thing or a bad thing?" Chang asked.

"No idea," Austin said, "But the plan is to head north. And that's north." He took his handgun out again. "Let's just be ready for anything."

But no one was ready for what they saw upon reaching the blacktop. The pavement began at the crest of a hill that descended into a city surround by miles of suburban sprawl. Thick clouds, alive with heat lightning, hovered over the city, filling the air with a turbulent orange glow. The city itself was in ruins. Most of the buildings lay flattened, all leaning away from a massive impact crater created by a nuclear warhead that detonated a mile outside of town. Some of the buildings on the other side of town looked intact, but most had folded down like card houses.

Their guide shuffled away as they grew near, ever nervous, never trusting. But no one paid him any attention.

"Damn," Garbarino said at the site. "This place got pancaked."

"It's not the last time we'll see this," Austin said. "Try not to let it get to you."

"After the things we've seen already," Paul said, "This is actually easier to swallow."

"Wholesale destruction has nothing on the living dead," Mark added.

"What's wrong with the crater?" Mia asked.

"Other than the fact that the missile that created it killed all the people living in that town?" Garbarino said.

"Look at it," she insisted. While the rest of the bleak landscape appeared a horribly clear image, the crater looked as though it had been created by a pointillist painter. Stranger than that, the whole thing seemed to be—

"Moving," Austin said.

"The whole thing," added Collins. "What the devil? Is the ground melting?"

"Whatever it is," Mia said, "We're steering clear of it."

Austin turned toward their guide, who began heading down the hill. "Where are you taking us?"

The man stopped, looking terrified that he'd been addressed. His whole body shook with each rapid fire breath. "Go," he said. "Go now!" His voice cracked from fright.

"Where?" Austin repeated. He didn't know if he could trust this man anymore than the killer mob. Just because he hadn't tried killing them yet, didn't mean he wouldn't later on, maybe after rejoining others like him.

"Away!"

Austin looked behind them. The dirt road stretched far into the distance, fading into thick forest. "There's no one back there. We lost them."

The man hobbled closer, shaking as he pointed back down the road. "They are coming. They are always coming."

Austin turned to the road again. He saw nothing. Heard nothing. "You can see them?"

With a violent shake of his head, the man said, "I can feel them." He pounded his chest. The impact of his own fist made him flail in anguish. He spun around, as though trying to escape himself, and fell on the ground. As quickly as he fell, the man was back to his bare feet and moving down the hill. "Down is away. Away. Always away!"

This time he didn't look back or wait for them to catch up.

"You're not going to the crater?" Austin shouted after him.

The man shook his head so hard and nearly fell down the hill.

"C'mon," Mia said, and followed after the man.

"What if it's a trap?" Garbarino asked.

"You want to go back?" Mia said.

No one did. They followed the man down the hill. Twenty minutes later, they entered the city. The clouds overhead moved slowly across the sky, pulsing with energy. Beneath them, the temperature felt ten degrees hotter.

Walking through the city streets, Chang began to cry.

Businesses, homes and apartment buildings alike had all fallen toward the east, shoved over by the massive explosion.

"You're crying now?" Garbarino said.

Mia put a hand on his shoulder. "Ease up."

"I'm not ragging on her," he said. "I just don't get it."

Chang sniffed away her tears. "It's just sad, you know? People lived here." She pointed to the sign of a mom and pop bookstore. "Built their dreams here. Raised their children. It wasn't just their lives that were taken, if was life in general. It's all just gone now."

Garbarino stopped in his tracks.

Austin stopped, on edge. "What is it?"

"The bodies," Garbarino said. "Where are all the bodies?"

He motioned to the empty street. "No one was out walking their dog? Or riding their bike?" He approached the wreck of a car in the middle of the street. The vehicle stood empty. "Or driving to work? The bodies are all gone."

Mia searched the city around them. He was right. They hadn't seen a single dead body since stepping off the EEP.

"Where are all the bodies?" he asked again.

A distant roar rolled over them, like a low cord on a cello mixed with a high pitched scratch. The sound had a physical effect on their bodies. Most got goose bumps from head to toe. Liz wet herself. Collins gripped his chest and fell to one knee, breathing in gulps. Chang's crying became a blubbering mess of tears and whimpers.

Up ahead, their guide, who had continued on without them, screamed as though pierced by a sword. He flailed on the ground, wailing and clawing at the pavement. After bloodying himself, his senses returned enough for him to crawl off the street. Once back on his feet he ran toward a convenience store that still stood.

Mia picked up Liz and instinctively chased after the man. Something else was in the city. Something that made her feel a level of dread she didn't know was possible.

The others followed in silence.

"I peed," Liz whispered.

"It's okay, baby," Mia said, holding the girl tight. "It's okay."

Though all the windows were blown out, the metal cage that kept burglars out was down and locked in place. They entered through the broken front door and worked quickly to blockade it with a floor display, an ATM machine and a smoothie maker. After finishing, they retreated to the back of the store and sat, hidden behind an aisle of cereal, potatoes chips and beef jerky.

It wasn't until they were all safely hidden that Austin noticed their guide was tucked in along with them. Like he was one of them.

But he wasn't. The man shook with perpetual fear. His nearly naked body was covered in dry blood and grime. And he stunk like something dead. But he could talk, so Austin asked him the only question on his mind right now. "What's out there?"

A shudder ran through the man's body. "No name...no... A hunter. Delights in pain. Delights in pain."

Delights in pain.

The words triggered a memory in Mia's mind. She looked at the man anew, seeing past the dirt and blood, really seeing his features for the first time. She imagined a pair of round wire-rimmed glasses on his face. "Shit," she whispered.

All eyes turned toward her. When the guide met her eyes, he looked away, cowering. She slowly raised her weapon toward him.

"What are you doing?" Austin asked.

She nodded toward the man. "Delights in pain. Two thousand eight. Boston. Ringing any bells?"

Collins was the first to place it. "Dwight Cortland."

The name caused everyone in the room to shift away from the man. He didn't notice. Just kept biting his nails, which had begun bleeding.

"I covered the story," Mia said. "He killed eighteen women in five states. Said they all asked for it. Said they delighted in the pain."

Dwight gripped his chest, digging into his own flesh. He whipped his head toward the exit, breathing rapidly.

"Gonna make a run for it?" Garbarino asked, taking aim with his weapon.

Dwight shook his head and didn't stop. When he spoke, his voice sounded like it was being filtered through a guitar wah-wah pedal. "No, no, no. They're coming." He stopped suddenly and looked Mia in the eyes. "They're here."

26

A half hour passed in nervous silence, listening for the voices that would herald the arrival of the horde. Dwight the Delight, the serial killer from Boston, reacted first, detecting something the rest of them couldn't. At first, he whimpered quietly with each shift of the breeze through the metal cage walling in the storefront. But his control over his emotions grew more tenuous with each passing moment. He grew agitated, shifting from one foot to the other while squatting behind the aisle. He hummed. He licked his dry lips. They could all see the tension in his body.

As panic claimed whatever self-control the man had left, he seemed about to bolt.

As the first distant call of the horde reached them, he turned toward the blocked exit.

That's when Garbarino pistol whipped him from behind.

No one complained.

Had to be done.

They all knew it.

"Thanks," Mia said.

Garbarino nodded.

"Here they come," Austin whispered. "Stay down. Stay quiet."

The voices grew louder, accompanied by the shuffling of hundreds of feet.

At first, the sound was like a choir of sobbing voices. The infinite sadness of the sound broke Mia's heart. The people outside would kill her. She had no doubt about that. But listening to them; they were pitiful. To be pitied. Horrified. Sad. Tired.

Individual voices emerged from the din as some walked past the small convenience store.

"I can't stop it," a man said to himself. "Why can't I stop it? God..."

Between sobs, a woman spoke. "The blood." Her body shook. "All that blood."

Several more people spoke in other languages, some easily recognizable—French, Japanese, German—but others sounded older, and some Native American, or at least what Mia thought sounded like Native American.

"I'm so sorry," a woman said.

Everyone in the room tensed. The voice belonged to Vanderwarf. She and White had joined the mob. Two more voices, two more mournful killers in the army.

Liz covered her ears, blocking out the voices. Her elbow struck a can of soup on the bottom shelf. It only fell a few inches before striking the linoleum floor, but to the group hiding behind the food aisle, it sounded like a gun shot.

Tension knotted Austin's back as he slowly peeked around the end of the aisle. The orange sky flickered outside the store, darker than before as night fell. But that didn't hold his interest. Standing at the window, fingers interlocked in the metal links of the barrier, was Vanderwarf, her eyes locked on his. Those beautiful eyes. Those full lips. Both expressed immense sadness.

"I'm sorry," she said. Slowly, she began shaking the barrier. "I'm so sorry!" The shaking became violent, attracting attention.

"No!" someone shouted.

"Run away!" said someone else.

"Make it stop!"

The shaking grew louder as more bodies joined the assault. A loud squeak of metal on linoleum shot through the store. The front door! Austin bolted out from his hiding position and threw himself at the blockade. A group on the other side was pushing it in. Garbarino joined him, wanting nothing more than to shoot a few rounds into the group outside, but worrying that would attract even more attention. Right now there were ten people outside, but in the distance he could see hundreds more shuffling through the flattened ghost town.

Paul joined them a moment later. "What's the plan?"

Austin grunted, pushing against the heavy barricade. "Find the back door. Be ready to run."

Paul nodded and returned to the back of the store.

"What about the roof?" Garbarino asked.

"They'd starve us out," Austin said. "We need to move."

"We could pick them off one at a time."

"Not enough ammo," Austin said. A jolt pushed them both back a few inches. They were losing the fight. "Besides, they come back to life after what, sixty seconds?"

Garbarino placed his feet against the checkout counter and shoved hard. "Good point."

"Paul found the back door," Mia said from behind the isle. "Didn't hear anyone back there, but he hasn't opened it yet, either."

"Don't open it!" Austin shouted. If just one person made it in the back, they'd be screwed. "Get everyone ready. When you hear the gun-shots, open the door and run. We'll be right behind you."

"What about Dwight?" Mia asked.

"The man's a serial killer," Austin said.

Garbarino nodded. They were thinking the same thing. "Fuck 'im."

Mia nodded and slid back behind the aisle, coordinating with the others and moving them toward the back of the store.

"So that's the plan, eh?" Garbarino said. "Pop a few of them in the face and make for the hills?"

"That's about it," Austin said.

Garbarino offered a nervous smile. "Works for me. On three?"

Austin nodded. "One."

"Two."

A roar blasted through the store like a fog horn. The muscles in Austin's and Garbarino's arms and legs turned to Jell-O. But the door didn't budge. The sound had effects on the mob too. For a moment. Both sides regained control of their bodies at the same time.

The people at the door pushed.

Austin and Garbarino stayed focused. "Three!"

Both men launched to their feet, took aim and just as quickly drop-ped back down. Not a shot fired.

"Did you see it?" Garbarino asked.

Austin nodded. They were in serious trouble.

"What the fuck is it?"

He had no reply for the question. What could he say? The thing outside was all muscle and stood several feet taller than anyone in the horde. A tattoo of an eagle, wings outstretched covered the chest. A banner, clutched in the eagle's talons read: PEACE.

If Austin had to guess, he would say the monster was a man because of the build—thick torso, broad shoulders—but it had no hair and from what he saw of the naked beast, no sexual organs. But the girth and power of the man-thing wasn't its most offensive feature. That had been reserved for its face. The eyes were small and sunken beneath a brutish brow. There was no nose or ears, just four jagged holes. A lack of lips and cheeks exposed its thick, brown teeth. Drool hung from the side of its open mouth, spraying with each hard breath.

Austin chanced a second glance as the pressure on the barricade eased up. The thing was headed straight for them, drawn by the noise of those trying to get in. It sniffed at the air like a two legged dog. The horde in front of it parted like the Red Sea before Moses. One woman wasn't quick enough and it lifted her by one leg, took hold of the other and tore it away. A tearing of skin was followed by a slick pop as the joints separated. With pieces of the woman in both hands, it tossed them to the sides, discarding them like old rags.

The woman didn't scream. After hitting the ground on either side of the monster, she pulled herself away, while her severed limb kicked in the road, spinning in circles.

The thing continued toward the store. It had no real interest in the woman. She just got in the way at the wrong time.

It stopped in front of the store. Each breath the thing took sounded like an engine revving.

Austin held a finger to his lips.

Garbarino nodded. He knew the score. The slightest sound might set it off and neither doubted its ability to smash through the storefront.

They heard a deep inhalation of breath and then the thing roared again. At point blank range, the deep rumbling sound made both men vomit, consuming their bodies with fear. But the creature's own voice kept it from hearing them. When it began sniffing at the air again, Austin realized it wasn't trying to hear them, it was trying to smell them.

It could smell their fear.

Austin held his gun up for Garbarino to see. The man nodded. The giant knew they were there, but it didn't know they were packing. The plan might still work. He held up his fingers in a silent countdown.

One.

Two.

Screaming. Mad screaming.

After hearing the giant turn away, Austin looked up. Dwight was outside, running away in clear view of the horde, his panic blinding his good sense. As the horde turned toward him, so had the giant. Then it charged.

Austin and Garbarino stood and watched. The thing charged on all fours, smashing through anyone in its way. Bodies flew through the air, trailing streams of blood. The thing roared again and everything outside fell to the ground. It crushed several more people before reaching Dwight. And when it did...

The attack was unlike anything either man had seen before. One hand took hold of Dwight's head and squeezed. It burst like overripe fruit. Holding him by the legs, the monster swung him up and then slammed him into the ground. Over and over. Arches of blood sprayed through the air. It threw him on the ground, limp and shattered, and stomped on him. Crushing his body into the earth, pulverizing him. Liquefying him.

Garbarino vomited again.

Austin would have, too, if he hadn't remembered the others.

A fresh roar turned him back to the monster. It stood above what little remained of Dwight the Delight.

Austin took Garbarino's arm. "Let's go."

The thing raised its head and sniffed the air.

"Now!" Austin led the way to the back of the store. They didn't have long to get everyone out of the store and on the move. The trouble was, everyone else was already gone.

27

Austin found the rear door of the convenience store wide open. It exited into a small employee parking lot surrounded by a now flattened chain link fence. Beyond that a grid of streets led into the distance. Ruins lined the streets for a mile before buildings far enough away from the blast still stood. Beyond that, the forest began again, rising up a steep grade that had kept developers away. But what stood out most about the view down the long straight street was the group of running people.

Nine of them.

Mia, Liz, Chang, Paul, Mark and Collins had a short lead. Three others, one clothed, two naked, an assortment of races, all screaming, gave chase.

"They're not going to make it," Garbarino said as he exited the store and saw the group up ahead.

In reply, Austin broke into a sprint.

But as fast as he ran, he could only watch as the three killers gained on the group slowed by age, gear and fatigue. The killers suffered from none of these things. In fact, the only thing that seemed to affect them at all was an overwhelming desire to not do what they were about to do.

C'mon, Austin thought. Do something!

Realizing the group—armed with handguns, an MP5 and two shotguns—might simply be too afraid to stand their ground and fight, Austin took aim and prepared to fire three rounds. He didn't think any of the shots would find a target, but hoped the sound would remind the others that they weren't defenseless.

"No!" Garbarino shouted, catching up to Austin. "Don't fire!"

"Why not?"

Garbarino thrust his thumb over his shoulder. "He will hear you!"

Shit. He was right. Using their weapons might temporarily stop the three killers, but the noise might also attract the monster that pulverized Dwight. And he wasn't sure how many bullets it would take to stop him. He hoped to never see the giant again, not only because the term "killing machine" best described it, but also because he recognized it, or at least the tattoo on its chest. And that was one reality he couldn't deal with yet.

Austin ran as fast as he could.

Garbarino ran faster.

Neither were fast enough.

Mia could hear the screams getting closer. There would be no outrunning them. Not while carrying their gear. Not while holding Elizabeth. "We need to fight them! But quietly! Don't use your guns!" she shouted. When she remembered who she was talking to, it seemed a ridiculous thing. Chang was an out of shape young woman. Collins was an aging man with a heart problem. Mark was no spring chicken and as a priest had probably not been in a fight in a very long time, if ever.

And Paul, the only one of them with the experience they needed, was the oldest of them. He was also the bravest. "Keep going," he shouted before stopping.

The move caught everyone off guard, including the killers. He managed to clothesline the first, who turned out to be an older woman. She flipped into the air, grasping at her ruined throat. The impact spun Paul around and sent a stab of pain up his arm. The second killer, a naked man with long black hair and tan skin, leapt at him. But Paul was ready and caught the man by the throat, using the killer's momentum to lift him off the ground and pound him onto the pavement.

But there was nothing Paul could do to stop the third killer, a young woman with blood stains covering most of her white-skinned naked body.

Arms outstretched, the woman dove at Paul's back, screeching, "I don't want to!" in a thick British accent.

The impact that followed was bone crushing, but Paul remained untouched.

Mark tackled the woman by the waist and the pair slammed into a telephone pole before falling to the pavement. The woman clawed at Mark while he rained down punches. "You can't have him yet!" Mark screamed, sounding as mad as the woman beneath him.

With the first two killers writhing on the ground Paul stood and ran to Mark's aid. Seeing the woman unconscious beneath Mark's continued barrage, he took his brother by the waist and pulled him away.

"You can't have him yet!" Mark kept shouting. "You can't have him!"

"Mark," Paul said, holding his brother tight, as he struggled to get back at the woman. "She's down, Mark. She's done."

Mark began to relax.

"She's done."

As Paul loosened his grip, Mark leaned forward, breathing hard, tears streaking down his cheeks.

Austin and Garbarino arrived a moment later.

"Everyone okay?" Austin asked.

Paul gave a nod and placed a hand on Mark's back. "You okay?"

After a taking a deep breath, Mark stood upright. He was about to answer. Pain throbbed through his chest, face and fists—none of it life threatening. But the look of horror on Paul's face had him asking, "What's wrong?" instead.

Mark looked down at himself. His fists and body were covered in blood. He wiped at his face with his clean palm and it came away bloody. He turned to the naked woman, covered in a fresh coat of her own blood. The reality of what he'd just done set in. "Get it off," he said. "Get it off! Get it off!"

Paul quickly found his water bottle and doused Mark's face. "Hold still."

Mark took off his outer shirt and threw it away. The white t-shirt beneath had a red ring around the collar, but was otherwise clean.

With much of the blood gone, Paul got his first look at Mark's clean face. "You're hurt," he said.

Mark touched his face gently. The woman had clawed both his cheeks, leaving seven long gashes that had somehow already stopped bleeding. His hand flinched away from the wounds.

A roar sounded in the distance.

"We can look at it later," Austin said.

Garbarino drew a long knife and stabbed each of the killers in the back of the neck. Their bodies twitched and then lay still. When he finished, he looked back at the others who stared at him in shock. "What?" he said. "It's not like I'm killing them. I just wanted a head start."

Mia picked up Liz. "Good idea," she said.

Garbarino smiled. "Thanks."

A second roar, this one louder, set them moving.

"We'll stop in the woods," Austin said, leading the way. "Don't use your weapons unless there's no alternative. We need to get as far from here as possible, as quietly as possible, before night falls."

"Bad things happen when the sun goes down," Liz said, as she looked over Mia's shoulder.

"Not tonight," Mia replied. She hated lying to Liz, but couldn't bring herself to tell her niece turned daughter what she really thought. False hope was better than no hope.

As they exited the city and entered the woods on the other side from where they'd entered, Liz saw something rise up on the horizon of the long straight road that led to the forest. A line of dark specs bobbed up and down, like people walking.

As the dark forest swallowed them, Liz whispered, "Bad things."

28

Mark pitched forward, clutching his side.

Paul caught him. "You okay?"

"Got a cramp," Mark said with a grimace.

They had been moving quickly for nearly three hours. The woods had thinned into new growth—now dead—but the forest floor was mostly clear of debris, because the smaller branches had yet to fall. The bare branches above gave them a clear view of the sky, glowing from rapid-fire heat lightning. The open forest allowed them to move faster, but not everyone could sustain the pace set by Austin who drove them north like an unstoppable freight train.

"Hey boss," Paul said to Austin, who was nearly forty feet ahead.

Austin turned and saw Paul standing next to Mark, who was still doubled over. Everyone else had stopped already, too.

"We need a rest," Paul said.

Austin gave a thumbs up and began walking slowly back toward the others. His gut told him to keep moving, but he felt impressed with how well the group was holding up. As he walked past Garbarino, he said, "Keep watch south and east. I'll watch north and west." After Garbarino nodded, he took up a position at the group's rear behind a granite boulder.

Mia sat with Liz and Chang, silently sharing pieces of what little remained of their food supplies. No one had taken any food from the convenience store, so they were left with the dwindling number of protein bars and water bottles in their packs. Mia rationed it as best she could, but exerting so much energy left their stomachs craving more.

After taking two bites and a drink of water, Liz, who had been walking for two hours, quickly fell asleep. Chang and Mia followed the girl's lead, laying down in the crunchy leaf litter and closing their eyes.

After sitting Mark down, Paul began pacing. His nervous energy kept him moving. He hadn't felt like this in a long time—the adrenaline of battle, the heightened awareness that comes with knowing death could arrive at any moment. In Vietnam he sometimes went days without sleeping. It seemed, even in his old age, his body hadn't forgotten the lessons it learned during the war.

Collins emerged from behind a tree, zipping up his fly, and took a seat next to Mark. He took a protein bar from his pocket and unwrapped it. He broke off a chunk and offered it to Mark. "Something to eat?"

Mark held up his hand. "No. Thanks, though."

Collins took a large bite and slowly chewed the thick bar. It took three chugs of water to wash it down. "Ugh. Disgusting."

Mark kept his eyes on the ground below him, his side still clutched by the occasional cramp.

"So," Collins said, "where'd you learn to fight like that."

"She was a woman," Mark said.

"She was certifiable," Collins replied. "Would have torn your brother apart if not for you. But you took it to her. Boy, you took it to her."

Mark shook his head. "Wasn't always a priest."

Collins waited for more, but Mark stayed quiet. "That's it? You weren't always a priest?"

Mark looked at him."Drugs. I sold drugs. Pot. Coke. Heroin. I was young and stupid. Didn't think about what I was doing to other people, the lives I helped destroy."

"What turned you around?"

"You ever done drugs?" Mark asked.

"Smoked a lot of pot," Collins replied. There was no reason to lie about it now.

"Nothing harder?"

Collins shook his head, no.

"Consider yourself lucky. Guy I sold some coke to took his first snort right then and there. Didn't know how to do it and I wasn't paying attention. He took too much, too fast. Died at my feet. I found forgiveness in the Church. And rehabilitation. Dedicated my life to the God that saved me."

"Forgiveness, huh?"

"Yessir."

"You buy all that Bible crap?"

Mark laughed, but the motion caused a spasm of cramping. He grunted. "Look around you. Any of this seem more outlandish than what's in the Bible?"

Collins thought for a moment. "Suppose not." He took another drink of water, then asked, "And what about the woman? You need to be forgiven for that now, too, or are you in the clear on account of her trying to kill your brother?"

"You really haven't figured this out yet?" Mark asked.

Collins stared at him. "Figured what out?"

Mark swung his hands out around him, meaning everything. "This."

"What's to figure out?" Collins asked. "Nuclear war changed things in ways no one could have guessed. The survivors mutated. Went mad. I don't know."

Mark chuckled again, but kept it to a minimum. "You know it's more than that."

"What makes you think that?"

Mark looked him in the eyes. "Because you're talking to me about it."

Collins held his gaze for a moment. He opened his mouth to reply, but his nose crinkled instead. "You smell that?"

"What?"

"Smells like rotten meat." Collins sniffed, leaned closer to Mark and sniffed again. He winced back. "God, it's you. Your face."

Mark put his hand on the wound. There was no pain. "Feels okay."

"Smells like death," Collins said.

Mia sat up upon hearing the word 'death'. She saw Collins inspecting Mark's face and moved over to them. "You okay?" she asked Mark.

"His wounds stink," Collins said.

Mia looked at them. The wounds were full of dark dry blood. The skin around them had turned black. She tried to keep any hint of fear out of her voice when she spoke. "Could be infected. Maybe we have antibiotics in our packs. I'll check with Austin."

Mark offered a half-hearted smile. "Thanks."

Crunching leaves announced Mia's approach. "How are they holding up?" Austin asked without looking back.

Mia stopped behind him. "How'd you know it was me?"

He turned around and showed her a small, handheld mirror.

"Still watching everyone, huh? The world's last voyeur."

He grinned. "Wanted to make sure Garbarino was keeping watch."

"And is he?"

"Actually, he's coming this way. Paul is keeping watch now."

Mia looked over her shoulder. Garbarino was indeed headed toward them.

"What's up?" Austin asked.

"Mark's in trouble."

"How so?"

"The skin around his wounds. It's rotting."

"Rotting?"

"Necrosis. Some spiders' bites do the same thing. His skin and the tissue beneath the wound are literally dying. And it will keep spreading unless..."

"What?"

"Unless we cut it away."

He glanced at Mark. Even from a distance he could see the dark gashes covering his face. His face. "We're just as likely to kill him."

"I know, but..." She could hear Garbarino approaching from behind. She didn't want to say this in front of him, so she spoke quickly. "His cramps haven't stopped. I think whatever this is...I think it's inside him."

Austin's eyes went wide. "You think it's killing him?"

She nodded.

"Give him morphine for the pain. Should be some in your first aid kit. But not so much he can't walk. If we don't move soon, we're all dead."

She gave a quick nod and turned around just as Garbarino arrived.

"Everything all right?" Garbarino asked.

"She was just harassing me about finding a place to hole up for the night," Austin said, as Mia walked away. "What's up?"

Garbarino took a seat next to him.

"Wanted to talk to you about our new friend. You know, the one that's built like a tank and has no face."

Austin made sure no one was close enough to hear him. As far as he knew, the two of them were the only ones to see the monster up close. "What about him?"

"Don't feed me any bullshit," Garbarino said. "You know exactly what about."

Austin had hoped Garbarino hadn't noticed. Seemed he had. "The tattoo," he said.

"Shit, yes, the tattoo. You and I both know we've seen it before."

Austin cracked his knuckles one at a time. He did recognize the tattoo. It belonged to Henry Masters, the leader of a peace protest movement that wanted all U.S. troops pulled out of the Middle East. He led the group, fifty thousand strong, toward the White House, where they were greeted by a wall of riot police, snipers and Secret Service agents. Austin had been in charge of the response. He and Garbarino hadn't been more than twenty feet from Masters when he tore his shirt off, chanting catch phrases. The tattoo of the eagle clutching a peace banner was etched in his memory when riot police tried to break up the crowd. Despite Masters's pleas for non-violence, the crowd responded first with stones, then with fists. When the tear gas flew and panic set in, people stampeded.

In the thick soup of tear gas, no one thought about what, or who they were stepping on to escape. Masters was trampled and killed by his own people.

Austin pushed on his index finger until it popped. "What I can't figure out, is how it's possible."

"He was dead. Already dead—in the dirt dead—when the bombs dropped."

A nod was all Austin had to offer.

"So how's he alive now?"

"Wish I knew."

Garbarino sighed. "Ironic though, right?"

"How's that."

"Masters. Peace activist. Comes back to life as a killing machine. Became the thing he hated most. Like the rest of these poor schmucks.

Can't stop themselves from killing no matter how bad they don't want to do it. Merciful thing would be to find a way to keep them dead."

Austin stood. He didn't want to think about how fucked up the world had become. "We need to find someplace to hide tonight."

"It's already night, boss." He held up his wrist. "Took a watch from the man-cave house. Wind-up. Still works." He looked at the watch. "It's eleven PM. We can still see because of all the heat lightning."

Austin looked up at the shimmering clouds above. Silent lightning flowed through them, glowing orange. The sky was alive. And it seemed, would never grow dark. "Then we'll stop sooner than later." He headed back toward the others.

Garbarino gave a chuckle and followed after him. "Man, nothing fazes you, Austin."

Austin let the comment go because the truth was, he wondered if surviving the end of the world was actually a worse fate than death, even if the dead didn't stay dead. They were all going to die eventually. It couldn't be avoided. And then they would be just like Vanderwarf and White. "Let's go, people," he said. "Won't be light out forever."

He started ahead of the others as they packed up and followed. Even though part of him longed for death, he wouldn't give in to it. He looked back at Mia and Liz. Not while there was still someone who thought life was worth living.

29

"This will do," Austin said to Mia.

They stood over a dry riverbed of smooth round stones and patches of sand. Brown brush and tall dead grass lined the banks. The air smelled of dust and carried a slight odor of dead fish, though none could be seen. The river had been eight feet deep at its deepest, so even standing they couldn't be seen from a distance. A ready-made trench.

Mia climbed down and sat Liz on a rock. She and Austin helped Paul lower Mark into the dried out river. His skin fell cold and clammy, and he shook when she touched him. The man didn't have long. When she looked into Paul's eyes, she could see he knew it, too. He seemed weaker. Less resolved. The hero in him faded along with his brother's life.

As Garbarino, Chang and Collins slid into the riverbed, Mia, Austin and Paul laid Mark down on a soft patch of sand. He grunted, semi-conscious, and said, "You're not ready yet."

"Who are you talking to, Mark?" Mia asked.

"Him," Mark said.

"Me," Paul said.

"You."

"Not ready for what?" he asked. But Mark had fallen asleep.

Mia and Austin stepped away, pretending to scout out what lay ahead around the river bend. "They're in a bad place," she said.

"They?"

"Mark is dying and Paul is losing his brother."

"Seems like a strong guy. He lost men in the war."

"Not his brother who saved his life. And not after everyone else in the world died. I think Paul pictured things the other way around. Him dying to save Mark. Not him being the one left behind."

Austin picked up a stone.

It felt cool and smooth in his hand.

"We'll stay here until it happens."

"Won't be long," Mia said. Mark's condition was deteriorating rapidly. Rotting flesh covered most of his face now, and his abdomen felt firm, like his insides were solidifying.

Austin wanted to throw the rock, to watch it bounce off the larger stones down river. But there was no way to know if something would hear the sound or see the stone's flight through the air. He gripped the stone tight, pushing his frustration into it.

"You need one of those stress dolls," Mia said as Austin's fist shook. "You know, the rubber kind with the eyes that pop out."

Austin's tension broke and he smiled. "Had one of those when I was a kid. Cut its head off with a table saw."

"Morbid."

"It was, actually. The liquid inside was red."

"Probably toxic."

"Doesn't matter much now. Seems the whole world is toxic."

"Is it the whole world?"

"Mark is rotting."

"From gouges inflicted by that woman."

"Do you have any open wounds?"

Mia looked at herself. She didn't have a scratch on her. "No."

"Neither do I," he said. "But I can tell you right now, I don't want to get a splinter and find out any open wound sets a body to rotting."

Mia knelt down and found a smooth, flat stone, the kind perfect for skipping. She looked at the sparkles of mica embedded in it. There was a little beauty still hidden in the world. But not much. "Plan still to head north?"

"Got a better one?"

"Nope," she said, standing back up. "Way I see it, we keep moving until we find someplace safe. Any direction is as good as the other, so long as we're not walking in circles."

When Austin stayed quiet, she asked, "We're not walking in circles, are we?"

"Not yet," he said. "But I haven't seen the sun since those clouds rolled in."

They both looked up at the shimmering clouds.

"It's like the sky is on fire," she said.

"Mmm," Austin dropped his stone. "Remember the way the world looked from orbit? The dark clouds? Flashes of orange lightning?"

She nodded.

"I think we were seeing this from above," he said.

"You think the whole world is covered again?"

"No way to know for sure."

Mia threw her stone up in the air and caught it. She tossed it and caught it five more times before pocketing the stone and turning back to the group. "I'm going to have a conversation with the president."

"'Bout what?" he asked.

"Truck convoys in Afghanistan."

"You sure that's a good idea?"

"Going to come to his rescue?" she asked with a smirk.

"Not my job anymore."

Her smile widened. "Could have fooled me."

Mia approached Collins and took the stone out of her pocket. She tossed it up and caught it, repeating the action as she stopped in front of Collins, Garbarino and Chang. She met Collins's eyes. "Mind if I have a word?"

"Be my guest," Collins said.

"Wasn't talking to you," she said, glancing at Chang and Garbarino. They both understood and got to their feet. As he left, Garbarino gave her a pat on the shoulder. He knew what this was about.

She sat down across from Collins, elbows propped on knees, the stone bouncing back and forth between her hands. "Truck convoys don't run in Northern Afghanistan."

If Collins was surprised by the statement, he didn't show it. But she knew he had years of practice.

"If you say so," he said. "Specific troop movements are up to the generals I assign to the task. I'm sorry that you think your husband—"

"Fiancé."

"—Fiancé was responsible for all this, but—"

"He was responsible."

This caught Collins off guard. His defenses lowered for a moment. "What?"

"Just like you are responsible."

"Now hold on a minute. I—"

"Ordered the assassination of the Russian President. Instigated a war you thought wouldn't go as far as it did. And for what?"

He stared at her, his eyes brimming with anger.

She leaned in close to him, matching his anger with her own. "For. What?"

He shifted away from her, suddenly uncomfortable under her glare. "The Arctic Ocean."

She nearly slipped off the stone she sat on. "This—this was about oil?"

"Most modern conflicts are," he said with a shrug. "The Russians claimed large areas of the Arctic as their own. The Russian president wouldn't budge. We knew his successor would."

"And Matt?"

"Not a truck driver."

"A sniper."

"The best."

Mia's insides twitched with rage, both at Collins and at Matthew Brenton. The man she'd shared a bed with, the man she had planned to marry, had lied to her about everything. At home he acted gentle. Creative. Compassionate. But he was really a killer. An assassin. The betrayal cut deep. But then, she thought, I'm not better than him. He betrayed me in service to his country. Something he had been doing before we even met. Probably had no choice in the matter. I betrayed him when I should have been most faithful.

She looked up at Collins again and found him staring at the stone in her hands. She tossed it aside and saw some of the fear in his eyes slide away. "I wasn't going to hit you," she said.

"But you wanted to, just like I wanted to hit the Russians back. You have to understand, I couldn't let them get away with it. I couldn't let them."

She stood. "Don't push it."

"Or what?"

She motioned to the others. "Or I'll tell them the truth. I'm sure one of them would be happy to kill the man who killed everyone they love." She picked up the stone she'd thrown. "Going to hang on to this, just in case I change my mind."

Mia stormed away, heading for Paul, who was sitting with Liz near where Mark slept. Collins watched her go. His instincts told him to respond in anger. But he knew better, now. He stood and put his hands in his pockets, ready to start pacing, but felt something that wasn't there before. Felt like a small book. He took it out and discovered Mark's small Bible. Must have slipped it into my pocket when I was helping him along, he thought.

Collins looked at Mark, lying in the sand. He was dying. Of that there was no doubt.

Unsure of what to do with the book, Collins flipped through the pages. The text was tiny, but some of it stood out in red text. He paused on one of these pages and read. He returned to his seat and turned the page. He read to the end of the chapter in twenty minutes.

That's when Mark began screaming.

30

"You're not ready!" Mark's voice cut through the air like a Navy warning klaxon. "None of you are ready. It's too soon. Too soon!"

Paul dove to Mark's side, propping him up. Mark's eyes were rolled back, white orbs. "Mark!"

Garbarino leapt toward them, eyes wide. "Shut him up!"

"How?" Paul asked, an uncharacteristic panic filling his voice.

"Knock him out!" Garbarino shouted, drawing his weapon and preparing to pistol whip Mark.

"He's already unconscious!" Paul shouted.

Garbarino shoved him aside. "Then I'll make him more unconscious." But when he stood over Mark, saw his face, black and sunken like an old pumpkin, he froze. When he caught a whiff of the thick rot slowly consuming Mark's body, he staggered back.

"Not ready, not ready, not ready!" Mark continued.

Mia arrived a moment later, a syringe in her hand. She shoved the needle into Mark's arm and pushed the plunger down. A moment later, Mark stopped shouting. Stopped moving.

"Did it work?" Chang asked as the others arrived.

"No," Austin said. "Morphine doesn't work that fast."

As Paul began to weep, the rest finally noticed that Mark's chest had stopped moving. He was dead.

Then, as though sharing a consciousness, they all took a step back. Austin and Garbarino raised their weapons at Mark.

"Get your gear together. Follow the river downstream." Realizing there was no downstream, he pointed in the direction he meant. "That way."

Collins and Chang, who led Elizabeth away, obeyed dutifully. Mia stood still, watching.

"What are you doing?" Austin asked her. "Move!"

Mia jumped at the sound of his voice, but didn't leave. She just stared at Mark, waiting.

Paul slowly pulled himself together and stood. His eyes were dark and tired. He drew his weapon, letting it hang by his side. "My brother..."

"How long's it been?" Garbarino asked.

"At least a minute," Austin said, focusing his aim on Mark's head. Once the man moved, he would take a single shot and give them time to run before Mark came back again. But one minute became two. And then three.

Chang returned carrying several packs, short of breath from rushing and fear. "We've packed...everyone's...bags. We can go."

Austin lowered his aim.

Garbarino did as well, and said with a quiet voice, "He's not coming back." He looked at the others and repeated the sentence louder. "He's not coming back."

"Could be the way he died," Collins said. "Made his insides harden. Maybe so he can't come back?"

Paul knelt by Mark's head. "My brother..."

"Doesn't matter why he's not coming back," Austin said. "Just be glad he didn't. But we still need to leave, just in case he does. Maybe it's different for everyone. Maybe he'll come back in ten minutes. Maybe an hour. Maybe tomorrow. But we're not going to be here if and when he does."

"Don't cry, Mr. Byers," Liz said.

Mia started at the girl's voice. She hadn't spoken in almost a day.

Paul looked up, his eyes pink from the intensity of his emotions, his face wet, his teeth gritted together.

"I'm sorry about it, Mr. Byers," Liz said.

"Me too," Paul said. His face suddenly softened and he looked beyond them. "Look," he said. "A bird."

Every single one of them turned to look.

A bird would give them hope.

If something other than psychotic humans had survived, maybe they had a future.

As Mia scanned the shimmering clouds for some sign of the bird, she heard a metallic click. Her eyes widened as she realized that Paul's last act of heroism on this planet was to turn Liz's attention away while he followed his brother into the afterlife. She covered Liz's ears just in time to block out the thunderous boom of Paul's handgun. With her ears ringing, Mia didn't hear the pieces of Paul's skull clatter against the rocks, or his body slump and fall. But she didn't need to. She knew what had happened just as surely as the rest of them did.

No one turned around right away. No one jumped. They just kept on watching the sky, hoping to see that bird, hoping that Paul's distraction hadn't been a ruse.

But there was no bird.

There was no hope.

Paul confirmed it when just thirty seconds after taking his own life, he stood up and apologized for it. "Sorry," he said, taking a step forward and then lunging.

If not for the uneven footing, he would have caught Chang by the throat, but the stone beneath his foot rolled and he fell early, catching her leg instead.

Liz began screaming hysterically. Mia picked her up and put her hand over the girl's mouth, muffling her voice.

Paul reached out with his open mouth, aiming for Chang's calf. But his head snapped back as Chang kicked out with her free foot. Unaffected by the pain, the impact only delayed him. As he lunged for a second attack, he was struck again, this time from the side, and much harder.

Blood splattered as Garbarino's boot sent Paul rolling away. Garbarino drew his handgun.

"No weapons!" Austin hissed.

"Fuck!" Garbarino said as he holstered the weapon and drew his knife.

"Don't let him scratch you," Mia shouted back to them as she ran with Liz, hand still clapped over the girl's mouth.

Paul lurched to his feet. "Run," he said. "Please, run!"

"Not likely," Garbarino said.

"Please, I don't want—" Paul's voice was replaced by an inhuman roar as he charged toward Garbarino.

Reaching out with one hand and side stepping, Garbarino intended to catch Paul around the neck and stab him in the back, severing his spine. But he made several incorrect assumptions about Paul's attack.

That he would be slowed by age.

That he would lack fighting skills.

That he would be weak.

None of these things were true. In fact, Paul seemed faster and stronger than he had been in life and all of the dirty fighting tricks he'd picked up in the jungles of Vietnam could still be put to use by his reanimated body.

Paul caught Garbarino's arm and twisted. Garbarino could feel the bones reaching their breaking point and screamed. But Paul's grip loosened as he spun around and kicked out, catching Austin in the midsection.

As Austin went down, Garbarino used the distraction to swing down with his knife, burying the blade halfway into Paul's forearm. The grip on his arm loosened, not from Paul reacting to the pain, but because the tendons in his arm had been severed.

Garbarino yanked free and fell back, losing the knife as he reached out to break the fall. Even with both hands free, the river bed was too uneven. His uncontrolled fall ended with him slamming into a large stone. The impact didn't knock him unconscious, but it did leave him bloodied and stunned.

Paul stormed toward him, the fingers of his injured arm flapping uselessly. But then, as though a part had been snapped back into place, his fingers regained mobility. They clenched like a hawk's talons as Paul reached out for Garbarino, who had yet to come to his senses.

"Joe!" Austin shouted, just now getting to his feet.

Garbarino saw Paul coming and screamed. Just before Paul reached him, a massive explosion ripped through the air, and knocked Paul back. A shotgun blast.

Garbarino sat up quickly and turned around. Mia was there, shotgun in hand, Liz on the ground by her feet, crying hard.

There was no time for thanks. They all knew Paul would return. And others, if the shotgun blast had been heard. But the shotgun didn't get a response. It was Liz. The little girl, wracked by sobs that shook her whole body, turned her eyes to the sky and screamed.

And then, in the distance, Henry Masters roared back.

31

Chang fell with a shout and skinned her elbow on a jagged stone at the bottom of the dry riverbed. "Shit."

Garbarino helped her up. "Watch your step."

"I can't run down here. We'd be faster up there," she said, pointing to the riverbank a foot over her head.

The group stopped to catch their breath. Austin turned to Chang. "Forest has thinned out even more. Might be visible from a mile away. Maybe more."

"We don't even know if they're back there," Chang said. "It's not like the river runs in a straight line or even if we're still heading north."

She was right, of course. But Austin's next words silenced the argument. "You want to go up there and take a look, be my guest."

Mia picked up Elizabeth, who had been walking on her own for some time. The girl clung to her like a monkey to its mother. "What about Paul? White followed us through the woods because he knew which direction we were heading. Paul knew we were following the river."

Austin looked upstream. As far as he could see, no one was coming. But Mia was right. Paul would be following them as long as they stayed on the river. "First road we come across, we'll follow. Until then, we need to keep moving. Doesn't matter if Paul knows which way we're going if we stay ahead of him."

"What if he tells the others?" Collins asked and then yawned.

Garbarino and Austin hadn't told the others that it was actually the middle of the night. The combination of constant light from the heat lightning filling sky and the distraction of running for their lives made keeping track of time impossible without a watch. Better to let them think the sun still shown above the clouds and rest when they found someplace safe.

"I don't think they talk, really," Garbarino said. "More like a pack mentality. Might be following Masters now, too."

"Who?" Mia asked.

Austin shot Garbarino an angry glance and sighed. "Henry Masters. Peace activist."

"I remember that guy," Collins said. "Tore his shirt off over the war and got trampled by his own people."

"After we gassed them," Austin said.

Collins shrugged. "You saw him?"

"The big one," Garbarino said.

"The one that roars?" Chang asked.

"Yes," Austin said. "You can't tell by looking at his face—"

"Because there isn't much of one to speak of," Garbarino added.

"But his tattoo—"

"The eagle with the peace banner," Collins added, remembering the press photos.

"—is easy to identify."

"But he died," Chang said. "Before."

"I know," Austin said. "Doesn't make sense to me, either, but—"

A voice rolled down the river, faint but carrying the weight of white water rapids behind it. "I don't want to hurt you!"

Paul.

Though panicked and distant, they all recognized his voice, and ran. No orders issued. No questions asked. They just ran.

They stopped two miles downstream.

Paul's voice persisted behind them, not gaining, not fading, but pacing them. The trouble was, he wouldn't tire. And the group was exhausted. But the old stone bridge in front of them offered some hope. A small dirt path, probably made by kids seeking the perfect fishing hole, rose up the bank next to the bridge.

"Let's go," Austin said, motioning everyone up. "Hurry! We can't let him see us."

Elizabeth and Mia climbed up first, clawing at the dirt, clinging to exposed roots. Chang followed, shoved up from below by Garbarino. Collins came next and then Austin.

"Get down!" Austin hissed, diving behind the low stone wall at the top of the bridge. Paul's voice was loud now.

Just as everyone lay down on the bridge, Paul's voice grew louder. He mostly grunted, or whimpered, but occasionally would shout. "No, no, no!" he screamed as he neared the bridge.

Elizabeth jumped at the sound, but Mia held her tight and kept a hand over the girl's mouth, just in case.

"Run!" he screamed.

Elizabeth began squirming.

"Run!" Louder this time. Right beneath them. Had he stopped?

Mia and Austin locked eyes. He glanced down at his hand gun. The message was clear. He wouldn't let Paul get them, but the chase would begin anew as the gun's report attracted attention from Henry Masters and the horde of killers following him.

The silence that followed tore at them. Was Paul climbing the bank? Was he standing beneath them, listening for a sound? Smelling the air?

Elizabeth struggled for freedom, but Mia just held on tight, afraid to even shush the girl.

Paul screamed again. But this time, when his voice reached them, everyone relaxed. He'd already moved further downstream. Mia eased up on Elizabeth. "It's okay," she said, trying to soothe the girl, who was now crying lightly. "It's okay, baby."

Garbarino stood slowly, looking over the wall. "He's gone."

When Mia got up, she saw Elizabeth holding her wrist. She knelt down and looked at it. The skin was red and bruising slightly. Mia gasped. "Did I do that?"

Elizabeth gave a subtle nod.

"Oh my God, I'm sorry," she said, hugging the girl tight. Consumed by panic, she hadn't thought about how hard she was holding Liz. The girl hadn't been trying to get away from Paul, she'd been hurt by Mia's crushing grasp.

"It's not your fault," Liz said. "I was scared, too."

Mia pulled back and looked into her eyes. "I'm so sorry."

"It's okay," Elizabeth insisted, placing a hand on Mia's face. "You're doing your best."

At this, Mia's eyes grew wet with tears. She nodded, sniffed, wiped the tears away and stood. "Let's keep moving."

Twenty minutes later, the group stopped in the middle of the street. Tall leafless maples rose up on the right. On the left was the largest church any of them had ever seen. Its modern, beige art-deco exterior made it look more like a wealthy college than a house of God, but the sign out front read: Trinity Non-Denominational Church. The parking lot, covering nearly an acre, was empty save for one car, a black Mercedes-Benz.

"Good a place as any to settle in for a rest," Garbarino said.

Austin looked the building over. "Not very defensible. Too many entry points."

"Lots of hiding places," Chang said.

"Which can work in our favor or against us," Collins added.

"We're stopping," Mia said, heading for the building's front entrance, a series of six, large hardwood doors.

"Hey," Austin protested.

"You're the one who put me in charge," she said over her shoulder. "Besides, it's nearly three in the morning."

"It is?" said Chang, now following Mia.

"Ask Garbarino. His watch works."

Garbarino looked at the watch, then at Austin. He shrugged. "She must've seen it."

Mia found the doors unlocked and let herself in.

The others followed.

Mia put Liz down as she entered the massive, three story foyer. Stained glass windows featuring scenes from the Bible surrounded them, filling the room with shimmering colors projected by the heat lightning flashing in the sky outside. A sign reading "sanctuary" hung over three sets of double doors at the other end of the foyer. Several other doors lined the sides, as well as a long hallway on either side.

She whispered to the others. "Lock the doors."

Austin and Garbarino quickly and quietly locked all six front doors and then rejoined the group in the middle of the foyer.

"What's the plan?" Garbarino asked Mia.

"Find someplace dark with locks on the doors and sleep." She led the way into one of the long hallways. She stopped at a thick wooden door. She drew her handgun and motioned for the others to wait. Austin ignored her and joined her at the door.

"You open. I'll go in first."

She took hold of the doorknob. He gave her a nod. With a quick twist of the doorknob, Mia opened the door and pushed.

Austin surged into the room, swinging his weapon back and forth. But the space was empty except for several small tables, twenty miniature chairs and boxes of toys. "It's a nursery."

"Sunday school," Mia corrected, following him in. She motioned for the others to follow.

Chang quickly found a stack of nap mats and laid them out on the floor.

Liz, who still remembered the kindergarten routine, wasted no time in claiming hers and lying down. She fell asleep in seconds.

Austin slowly approached the two large windows on the other side of the room. Each four foot by eight foot window offered views of the large parking lot wrapping around the building, the woods beyond, and the shimmering clouds above.

"We'll see anyone coming," Garbarino said.

Austin shook his head, no. "We won't see them and they won't see us." He drew the shades. The room would have been pitch black if not for the light streaming in on the sides of the shades. Austin moved back to the door, closed it and locked it.

"Who's keeping watch?" Mia asked.

"Nobody," Austin said. "I don't think there is one of us who could stay awake. The doors are locked. If we need a quick exit, we'll shoot out the windows. No lights. No shouting. No leaving this room without a partner."

No one responded. No one needed to. Anything that might reveal their location could get them killed. One by one, they staked their claims on the floor mats and lay down to sleep.

Within ten minutes, they were all asleep, totally unaware of the faint shouting voice echoing in the church's massive sanctuary.

32

Mia woke. The ceiling above her was white. As was the down comforter covering her body. She sat up. The old mattress bent beneath her, compressing to half its thickness. She bounced on it twice. The frame squeaked.

She was home—the home of her childhood. She couldn't remember why she was there, only that it felt right. She stood, already in her slippers.

As she descended the staircase, a loud chopping sound filled the air.

"Hungry?" her mother called out.

"Starving," she replied as she walked through the dining room. It looked just how she remembered it, red carpet, white lace curtains, and ornate crystals dangling from the shades that created little rainbows around the room when the sun came in at the end of the day.

She entered the kitchen, but it wasn't her mother standing there, it was Matt. He stood over a cutting board, working a knife up and down on a carrot. "Hungry?" he asked.

"Starving," she said.

The chopping came louder now, drawing her attention back to the cutting board. Matt's fingers were now under the blade. He cut through them, making little diced finger bits—red on the outside with a small circle of bone in the middle. There was no blood. He looked back at her and gave her a wink.

"Hungry?" he asked.

"Starving," she replied. "Feed me, please."

"Here," he said, turning around with a platter in his hand. The platter held his heart, resting on a bed of bloody veins. She couldn't see an opening in his chest, but she knew the heart was his.

"I'm hungry," she said.

"Eat this," he replied. He lifted the knife up, pulled it back and threw it straight at her face.

Mia sat up. She breathed deep twice and the dream was gone except for one lingering element that had been rooted in reality: hunger.

"Pssst."

Mia searched the darkness and found Garbarino sitting in the corner peeking through a slit in the window. She stood slowly and crossed the Sunday school room, careful not to step on Liz or Collins as she stepped over them.

"How long?" Mia asked. "How long did we sleep?"

"Three hours for me." He looked at his watch. "Four and a half for you. Bad dream?"

"I think so."

"You were kicking around."

"I'm hungry."

He nodded. "Starving."

The phrase pulled back parts of her dream. The knife flying at her face. She closed her eyes and blocked out the image.

He took an unopened protein bar from his pocket. "We could split it. My last one."

Mia looked at the bar. She'd eaten so many of the foul, dry, sugar-filled bars that she couldn't stand the sight of it. "I'm not that hungry yet."

"How about we go raid the kitchen for some grape juice and Jesus wafers?"

"Jesus wafers?"

"You know. What they eat for communion."

"That's Catholics. This is a non-denominational church. I think they use bread."

"Well, then maybe they have some Wonder Bread. That shit could survive a nuclear war, right?"

Mia nearly laughed. She motioned to Austin. "We can't leave without telling him."

Garbarino abandoned his post. He opened a cupboard and took out some paper and crayons. When he did, a piece of paper fell away. Mia picked it up and found a child's drawing. The crayon sketch featured smiling parents, a little girl, a large house, a dog and what appeared to be a convertible car. The innocence of the image got to her and she found herself staring at it until Garbarino snatched it from her.

"No time to go soft," he said, and then held up his quickly scribbled note. It read, "Went to raid the pantry. Be back soon. G and M."

They slid into the hallway a moment later. Garbarino locked the door from the inside before closing it.

"We won't be able to get back in," Mia said.

"We'll knock."

"Austin's liable to shoot us."

"We'll knock gently." He drew his weapon and motioned for her to follow him and they searched further down the hallway.

They found two more classrooms, identical to the first, but with slightly larger furniture. At the end of the hall were a set of bathrooms, men's and women's. "Gotta go?" he asked.

She did. "We should check the bathroom together. Take turns."

"After you," he said.

They entered together and after finding the bathroom empty, and very clean, they took turns using two different stalls, Garbarino first, Mia second. When she exited, Garbarino was standing in an open door leading to a stairwell on the other side of the hallway. He entered the stairwell and held the door open for her. For some reason, she wanted to explore every inch of this building. Maybe because it looked so pristine, so untouched by the events outside. Maybe because she wanted to be sure there were no killers lurking in the darkness. She wasn't sure. So she followed him down the stairs.

Garbarino opened a door at the bottom of the stairwell. The smell of oil and metal spilled over them. "It's a garage," he said.

Two small windows provided enough light to see by. The three car garage held two bright green riding mowers and a red car. Garbarino moved past the mowers and looked at the car. "It's a Porsche. What kind of a church has a Porsche in the garage?"

Mia shrugged, looking around the rest of the space. Giant peg boards at the back of the garage held an assortment of gardening tools. Shelving along the side wall held fertilizer, pots and six large red tanks of gasoline. "We could take the car," she said.

"Uh-uh," he replied. "EMP would have killed the starter."

"Damn." She looked around one last time and returned to the stairwell. "C'mon. I'm still hungry."

They returned to the hallway and headed toward the oversized foyer. On the way, they paused at the Sunday school door, listening for voices or any sign of someone else being awake. Hearing nothing, they continued on. Multicolored heat lightning continued to flash through stained glass windows. The sight was beautiful, but the silence made it eerie.

They continued through, heading down the hallway on the opposite side of the building. Boxes of orange light flickered on the hallway floor, cast down through skylights in the ceiling. They found two more classrooms, a large nursery, a storage closet and finally a kitchen. Garbarino stood in the doorway. "Shit. Have you ever seen a nicer kitchen?"

Mia shook her head. The kitchen was gourmet, complete with three ovens, and an island covered in burners and a grill. An array of shiny, stainless steel pots hung above it all. Mia approached the two massive, stainless steel refrigerators.

"Don't even bother with those," Garbarino said.

"Right," she replied, moving to the cupboards, which were surprisingly barren. "They must stock up only for events."

"Found the bread," Garbarino said. He stood aside revealing a tall cupboard filled with blackened, rotting loaves of bread.

The crusty black rot reminded her of Mark's face. She turned away quickly and leaned her head down on the counter. When she did, she saw two small bags of Cheez-It crackers. She took both bags and tossed one to Garbarino. "Bingo."

"He opened his and dug in. "So good," he said, but stopped chewing when he saw she wasn't eating. "You don't think they're radioactive or something?"

"Saving mine for Liz."

He shook his bag at her. "Take some of mine, then."

They quickly ate the bag of Cheez-Its, did one more pass of the kitchen and found a package of one-hundred calorie cookies, which they saved for the others. As they walked back down the hall toward the foyer, Garbarino took a pamphlet from one of many dispensers attached to the walls. He read through it quickly.

"Well this explains a lot," he said, handing the green, tri-fold pamphlet to her.

"Get right with God, give to His Church," she read aloud. She opened it and read from the inside. "God's grace is bestowed upon those who have faith. Faith is expressed through tithing. Those who tithe the minimum ten percent will experience God's grace as promised, but those who give more, who express their faith in miraculous ways will inherit the Kingdom of Heaven." She turned to Garbarino. "I've been to church on Christmas and Easter for most of my life and even I know this is bullshit."

Garbarino motioned to the massive stained glass windows as they entered the foyer again. "God will bless you if you give him your money. Looks like people were buying it."

Mia looked at the back of the pamphlet.

There was a picture of a middle-aged man in a suit coat. His teeth sparkled. His hair had been slicked back. His eyes were such a pale hazel they looked almost yellow. And the hands clasped on his raised knee were covered in large rings. Beneath the photo was the name: Pastor Billy Jackson M.D. Beneath the pastor was an image of a small vial of yellow oil attached to a cheap looking chain. She read the text beneath the vial and scoffed. "Blessed oil," she said. "With your gracious donation, one hundred dollars minimum, Pastor Billy will send you one ounce of oil anointed by the Holy Spirit."

"Snake oil's more like it," he said, but as he looked back he stumbled over his own foot and fell to the hardwood floor. His weapon hit the floor and clattered away.

The noise echoed in the foyer.

Mia tensed.

Garbarino lay still.

Mia didn't think the noise would have been loud enough to hear outside and she didn't see anyone through the small windows on the outside doors. But it turned out the listening ears were already inside.

"Hello?" said a raspy voice that belonged to no one in their crew, living or dead. "Who's there?"

Garbarino scrambled for his gun, picked it up and took aim in the direction of the voice.

It came from the sanctuary.

"Please," said the voice. "I'm starving."

33

Mia and Garbarino held their weapons at the ready and crept toward the center set of double doors. They stood to either side of the two one foot tall, six inch wide windows above the handles. "Recognize the voice?" Garbarino whispered.

"No," Mia replied, her voice barely audible.

"What are you two doing?" Austin's voice, an angry hiss, made them both jump. As Mia quickly shifted toward him, her body bumped the door.

"Hello?" the voice shouted. "I can hear you out there."

Austin's eyes widened at the voice. He ducked down and moved toward the double doors nearest to him. He stood, like them, beside the window. He quickly took a peek inside. The odd facial expression he made after looking pushed Mia's curiosity over the edge and she took a look. Garbarino followed her lead next, peering around the door.

The sanctuary was massive, like a theater in the round, complete with balconies. The stadium seating was plush and upholstered in royal red velvet. The stage was gaudy, decorated in gold and silver and surrounded by golden cherub statues. At the center of the stage, around which was seating for two thousand people, sat a gilded throne, upholstered in purple satin. Fit for a king.

But there was no king on this throne. Instead it held a brittle looking man, more bones than anything. His distended belly looked like he'd swallowed a basketball. It seemed impossible that this man could still be alive. But then he spoke again.

"Food," he said. "Please. Give me something to eat."

Mia moved to enter, but Austin's hand took hold of her arm. "What are you doing?"

"He's not one of them," she replied. "One of the killers."

"How do you know?"

"Because," she said, "He's not telling us to run away."

"While you're right about that," Garbarino said, "him being hungry doesn't exactly inspire a lot of confidence. He might eat people."

"Did you get a good look at him?" she asked. "I doubt the man can move."

"What are you going to do?" Austin asked.

Mia reached into Garbarino's pocket and took out his protein bar. "I'm going to feed the man. And then, I'm going to see what he knows. If he witnessed everything change, maybe he can point us in the right direction, or a safer direction."

"I can hear you!" the man shouted.

Mia tucked her handgun into the back of her pants and shoved open the door. She put on her best smile, forcing it over the revulsion she felt at seeing the man in detail, and said, "I'm coming. I have food."

The man tried to move, but only managed to jiggle himself lower on the throne. As Mia walked down the carpeted walkway that led to the stage, she got a closer look at the opulent sanctuary. The sides of the balcony were covered in carvings of angels, some holding banners stretched out between them. Each banner held a single word. Faith. Service. Blessings. Anointment. The words reminded her of the pamphlet selling snake-oil to the financially faithful.

Could this whole place be built on that message? she thought. What kind of person could sell that kind of garbage and pawn it off as God?

Her questions were answered when she got a closer look at the man on the throne. The slicked back hair was gray and messy. The sparkling white teeth had rotted brown and were now crooked. The rings, gold and encrusted with an assortment of jewels, hung loose on his bony fingers. But the eyes, they were still just as yellow. Like a snake, she thought, walking more slowly now.

"You have food!" he said. "Give it to me!"

She no longer saw desperation in the man's eyes. It had been replaced by entitlement. She started up the stage stairs.

"Keep your distance," Austin warned.

She looked back and found Austin and Garbarino ten feet back, weapons ready.

"Patience is a virtue, Pastor Billy." She held the still wrapped bar up for him to see.

The pastor convulsed as though shocked. "Give it here!"

"Answer some questions first."

His yellow eyes went wide. "Look at me!" he shouted.

She did, and saw a shirtless man wearing pants that hung on him like curtains. Whose skin had been shrink-wrapped around his ribs and shoulders. Whose perfectly manicured face had become a hideous thing. But the same man wore precious stones and gold the likes of which she had never seen. He wore a cape made of fine fabric and clasped around his neck by a chain of pearls. And he sat on a genuine throne. The amount of precious metals and jewels on the throne alone could have fed a starving nation for a year.

"I am looking at you," she said, her body tensing with disgust, not just for what the man had become, but also for what he'd been before.

"What happened here?" she asked.

"What does it look like?" the man spat. "My flock has abandoned me!" He licked his dry lips and eyed the protein bar.

"What about the rest of the world?" she asked. "Do you remember the bombs? There was a nuclear war."

"War?" he said. "I am hungry!"

"You don't remember?"

"Give me that food, you bitch!" The man leaned forward, reaching out with surprising quickness.

Mia jumped back out of reach while Austin raised his weapon.

"That's far enough, buddy," Austin said.

The pastor regarded Austin for the first time, his eyes seething with hatred. "You and your descendants will be a curse on the ground! You will find no mercy in the pits of hell! No lenience or quarter given to those who will not repent of their sins and give to the Lord what is His. Give to the Lord what is His! Give it to me and I will bless you! Give me what I want and I will anoint you with blessings! For I am the Lord God and I command you to give Me that fucking food!"

Austin lowered his weapon. The man had attempted to stand twice during his tirade, but couldn't. As long as Mia stayed clear, she would be safe.

"And you thought I was off my rocker on the EEP," Garbarino said. "This guy needs a padded cell."

Pastor Billy seemed not to notice. "Tithe," he said. "Tithe what you have and I will forgive you. I will shower you with anointing oils."

"Olive oil," Garbarino said.

"Joe..." Mia said, but he had a look in his eyes that said he needed to see this conversation through, if only to expel the anger gnawing at him.

"Anointed by the Holy Spirit."

"But still, olive oil."

Pastor Billy grinned wickedly. "Canola. Bought in bulk. Worthless, but made priceless by my spirit. I will heal the sick. Make the poor wealthy. Clean the unclean. We were made to prosper and God will prosper us if we first show our faith by giving of ourselves. Give up your worldly possessions and follow me."

"And give everything to you, right?" Garbarino said, motioning to the opulent sanctuary.

The pastor licked his lips. "What better way to continue God's work than to fund it?"

"I wonder how many lives you have destroyed."

"Lives are more easily remade after hitting rock bottom."

"Looks like you're ready to be remade then, huh?" Garbarino shook his head in disgust and stepped back. "You look like you could use a bucket of snake oil yourself."

The pastor lurched forward, hissing. Austin, Mia and Garbarino took one big collective step back.

"We should get back to the others," Austin said. "He doesn't know anything."

"Don't know anything?" Pastor Billy said. "Don't know anything? I know that you, all three of you, will taste the eternal fires of God's holy vengeance. You will gnash your teeth and beg for mercy. You will ask for drink and none will be giv—"

Billy Jackson shook.

His eyes looked down at his trembling hands, then at the protein bar in Mia's hands. "God, no."

Mia realized what the man was thinking. "You're wrong," she said.

He looked at her. "No, no, no. You will not be spared." He glanced toward the sanctuary doors, and then pointed. "Only the child will be spared!"

Mia looked back and saw Chang, Collins and Elizabeth staring down at them. At the man.

"The child," he said. "The child is innocent. Not yet tainted by the world. Not yet able to understand the choice...the choice..."

"You're wrong," Mia said again, unwrapping the protein bar. The man's eyes locked on it. "There is still mercy in the world." She tossed the bar to him. He caught it in his bony hands, losing some rings as he did, but he paid no attention to them. He gnawed on the bar like a wolf does a deer's bones.

She turned to Austin and Garbarino. "Let's go."

As they moved up the aisle, the frightened faces of Chang, Collins and Elizabeth were easy to see. But the pastor's condition wouldn't account for the horrified looks on their faces. Something else was wrong.

Austin broke into a jog. "What is it?"

"Outside," Chang said. "There's a lot of them."

"They arrived just a few minutes ago," Collins said. "I think they know we're in here, but haven't figured out a way in yet."

Austin looked at the six doors on the far end of the foyer. He could see bodies outside, moving around, occasionally banging on the door, but nothing more.

"We can make a run for it," Garbarino said. "There are plenty of other doors."

"They might have the whole place surrounded," Collins said.

"He's right," Austin said.

Garbarino pushed his way through. "Then we'll get them to come here. Attract and distract while we—" He pointed to the far end of the sanctuary where a red exit sign hung over a single metal door, "—make a run for it."

"What are we going to distract them with?" Austin asked.

Mia realized Garbarino's plan. "A fire," she said.

"There are six gas cans in the garage," Garbarino added.

Austin looked displeased. "Garage?"

"We've been up for a while," Mia said.

Austin looked at the doors again. It seemed like they had some time. "Collins, go with them to the garage. Get all the gas you can carry in one trip. Chang, find a way up onto the balcony. Liz honey, you stay with me and watch the doors, okay?"

Liz nodded.

Before they left the sanctuary, Pastor Billy's loud devouring of the protein bar drew their attention. He swallowed the final bite, moaning in ecstasy. He laughed for a moment before his face screwed with pain. Then he pitched forward and vomited. Chunks of the chocolate protein bar spilled from his mouth mixed with an impossible amount bloody fluid.

He sucked in a loud breath and then vomited a second time, more violently than the first. "No!" he shouted and emptied his stomach a third time. He looked skinnier and frailer than he had before. "No!" he shouted again, and threw himself to the floor. He landed with a wet splat and thrashed around in his own bile.

He hissed again and pulled himself to one of the disgorged protein chunks, picked it off the floor and ate it again. He vomited so hard in response that his back cracked when it arched. He fell again, his cape absorbing bloody liquid while he cried out, "I'm starving! I need food!"

Leaving Pastor Billy behind, the group set about their work, preparing for what might be their last stand.

34

"Here!" Garbarino shouted as he burst into the garage and headed for the gasoline containers. He picked up two and handed them Collins. The next two went to Mia. He picked up the last two and found one of them empty.

"Shit," he mumbled. No one heard him. Mia and Collins had already gone back up the stairs. As he headed for the door, he saw a set of car keys hanging next to the door. He picked them up and inspected the Mercedes Benz logo keychain.

When it came to cars, he was something of a safety freak. He wore his seatbelt. But he also kept a flashlight strapped beneath his seat. The flashlight had a small razor blade function that could cut through the seatbelt should it become stuck. Beyond that, he kept a small first aid kit, survival pack, orange cones, roadside flares and a full-sized spare tire. He'd supplied all of this for his own vehicle, but new, a lot of luxury car dealerships threw in safety packages as perks.

So when he opened the trunk he wasn't surprised to see a neatly packaged emergency kit inside. He tore into it, looking for one specific item. He smiled when he found two of them—roadside flares. They were small, but lasted a long time, and best of all, would set fire to gasoline a hell of a lot easier than trying to make a spark with a bullet.

He pocketed the flares and reached up to close the trunk. When he did, he saw a black leather briefcase. Curious, he picked up the case and opened in. On top of the case was an issue of Playboy. But what lay beneath the magazine really held his attention. Money. More than he could count.

Garbarino picked up a stack of hundred dollar bills and flipped through it. He shook his head. Nothing but worthless paper, now, he thought. He took the Playboy, rolled it up and stuffed it in his pocket. He threw the briefcase back inside the trunk and left, running to catch up with the others.

Upstairs, Austin watched the front doors with Liz by his side. He'd seen the number of people outside increase steadily to the point where they blocked out all the door windows. Exactly how many people were out there, he had no way to know. But there were enough.

"Are we going to be okay?" Elizabeth asked him.

"We'll be fine," he said.

"I don't want Auntie Mia to get hurt."

He looked down at her large blue eyes. "I won't let anything happen to her."

"Why do you help people?" she asked. "Your job is to save people, right? Maybe to die for them. Why?"

He smiled. "It's what I'm good at. And most of the time no one else will do it."

"We're in a church," she said. "Maybe God will do it?"

He sniffed out a laugh. "Sorry kiddo. In my experience, if God exists, He doesn't give a shit. People kill people. People save people. Simple as that."

"Simple as that," she repeated. "What about him?"

Austin followed her little pointed arm to a statue of Jesus surrounded by children. "If Jesus Christ walks through those doors with a cache of weapons I'll greet him with open arms. Until then, he's just a curse word."

Elizabeth frowned. She wanted to say more, but the others all returned at the same time.

"There are four staircases leading up to the balcony," Chang said. "One on each side of these doors. Two on the far side of the sanctuary. One of them isn't far from the exit. There's a few windows back there. I could see outside. A few of them are back there, but not as many as out front. And that dude hasn't stopped puking yet. Freaking me out."

A bang on the front doors made them all jump.

Muffled voices from outside could be heard now. They couldn't make out the words, but no one needed to hear them to know what was being said: Run. I'm sorry. I don't want to. The mantra of the mournful killers.

Garbarino slid to a stop and put down his gas tank. "Five tanks. Maybe twenty-five gallons." He took out the flares. "We can use these to set the fire."

"What about him?" Chang asked, motioning to the sanctuary when pastor Billy wailed in anguish before searching for bits of protein bar.

"Way I see it," Austin said. "If he's like the others, he'll come back. No harm done. If he's like us, and stays dead, well, I think it'd be the merciful thing to do."

When no one argued, he said, "Everyone take a tank. Pour the gas around the perimeter, then down the aisles. Leave the area around the back door clear. Keep a full tank in the center aisle."

"What are you going to do?" Mia asked.

"The foyer," he said, taking the flares from Garbarino. "I want you all to take up positions on the balcony. When I come running, shoot anything you think is too close."

"What do you mean, come running?" Mia asked, crossing her arms.

He stood and took her by the shoulders, looking in her eyes. "Someone has to get their attention. Traps only work with something inside."

She regarded him for a moment. Out of all of them, he was the best. If he died, they'd be lost. But the truth couldn't be denied. Someone needed to be the bait. And if any of them was ready to die, as much as she hated to think that way, it was him, the man born to die for others. She picked up one of the gas cans and pushed into the sanctuary. "Let's move."

The group quickly broke up, dousing the sanctuary and the foyer in gasoline. Once finished, Chang took up a position on the balcony nearest the front entrance. Collins stood near the back, keeping watch out one of the windows. Mia, Liz and Garbarino stood opposite Chang, ready to cover Austin. "We're ready!" Mia shouted.

"All right," Austin replied. "No matter what you hear, do not leave the balcony. Do not come down."

"Copy that, boss," Garbarino shouted in reply, his words punctuated by pastor Billy's continuous vomiting.

In the foyer, Austin looked at his handy work. The large open space was covered in two large puddles of gasoline. The hardwood floor beneath would keep the flames burning long after the gasoline was consumed. A single dry patch of floor ran down the center of the foyer toward the sanctuary doors.

Austin chambered a round in his weapon as he approached the door. He had thirteen rounds and a single spare clip left. When they'd run from Paul in the dry riverbed he'd left behind his other gun. They'd also lost all three MP5s—which would have come in very handy now—and one of the shotguns. Between them they had four handguns, two shotguns and a shit-load of gasoline.

Against an army, Austin thought. An army that can't die.

He took a deep breath, let it out slowly and placed his hands against the doors. He shook the door hard and shouted, "I'm in here you sons-a-bitches!" He pounded on the wood and shook the door again.

But there was no response.

He shifted to the side and looked out the window. Just inches from his face, staring back at him, was Paul Byers. "I'm sorry," Paul shouted back through the door. Then the shaking began. All six doors shook.

Collins's voice echoed out of the sanctuary. "They're leaving the back door! It's working!"

The banging intensified.

"C'mon!" Austin shouted, but was starting to wonder if the horde of killers could break through the sturdy doors.

When the banging stopped, he wondered if he'd have to actually unlock the doors for them. He looked out the window again. Paul was gone, but a body, back to the door, blocked his view.

He pounded on the door. "What are you waiting for!"

A roar like a fog horn struck him and sent him down to one knee. Recovering quickly, he stood just as the man outside stepped to the side.

Henry Masters rocketed toward the door like a cruise missile. His chest shook as he ran; making the Eagle tattoo flap its wings. His cheekless mouth hung open, trailing drool.

Austin dove away from the door and sprinted down the landing strip of dry floor. Three seconds later Henry Masters hit the front doors.

35

"Get under him!" Tom Austin shouted to his ten year old brother.

"I am!"

Austin slipped beneath the pool water, the weight of his unconscious, naked father pulling him deeper. At eight years old, Austin had never rescued a drowning victim before. But it wasn't just inexperience fighting against him. While his father weighed barely over one fifty, his dead weight made slick from the water seemed determined to slide to the pool's bottom.

Austin saw his older brother, John, on the other side of their father, struggling to get a grip. Though John was two years older, and much stronger, his will was the weaker of the two. So when their father had passed out by the pool and slid over the side, his twelfth beer rolling away on the deck, John had screamed frantically for help while Austin leapt in after him. It wasn't until Austin had ordered him in the pool that John had thought to help.

It was night, and the faint spotlight outside the house didn't provide much visibility under the water. But when they reached the bottom, John saw Austin's outstretched fingers counting down from three and knew what he intended.

Three.

The boys took hold of their father's shoulders, gripping so tight that the bruises wouldn't fade for weeks.

Two.

Tom planted his feet firm against the bottom of the pool, ignoring the burn in his small chest.

One.

The door exploded.

The force of the impact sent a portion of the hard door flying into Tom's back. He spilled forward and slid to a stop within the strip of foyer floor that wasn't covered in gasoline. He struggled to his knees and looked back over his shoulder, wondering why Masters hadn't yet pummeled him into oblivion.

The giant man stood there, rubbing at his eyes, irritated and confused. Some part of the door, or part of the now missing wall above it, had gotten in his eyes.

Austin wasn't sure what made him think about his father's near drowning—the event that propelled him on a career of life-saving—in those seconds before Masters struck the door, but the memory of it, the feeling of absolute desperation and fear did for him now what it had done for him as a child. He acted fast, without thought, but with utter clarity. He jumped to his feet and ran for the sanctuary.

The sound of his feet slamming on the hard wood snapped Masters's attention back to Austin. He let out a roar and charged. With his body no longer blocking the opening to the outside, the horde flooded into the sanctuary, screaming apologies and the words of the horrified. Many of the first to arrive slipped on the gasoline and fell. Those that followed tripped over their bodies. But the flow never stopped, and for every one slowed by the slick floor, five continued in pursuit of Austin, hot on the heels of Masters.

Austin flew through the sanctuary door. The scent of gasoline rose up from the floor. The rug squished beneath every step. Seeing the full gas can ahead, he raised his weapon and fired a single shot into it. Gasoline began to chug from the side of the tank. He leapt over the tank, unlit flare in hand.

"Hit him with everything you've got!" Austin shouted. He hadn't looked to see where everyone was, but he knew they were there, waiting. And when Masters crashed through the sanctuary doors, gunfire ripped through the air.

Austin slid to a stop at the bottom of the ramp, just before the stairs to the stage.

"How dare you! This is a house of God!" Pastor Billy shrieked from his spot on the floor. His stomach convulsed, but he held a building retch down.

Masters raised his large hands in front of his ruined face and staggered back for a moment. The gas tank lay five feet in front of him.

Close enough, Austin decided. "You were right about the flames of hell," he said, looking back at Pastor Billy. "But you were wrong about who was going to burn." He struck the flare on his thigh. Red sparks burst from its top.

"No!" shouted the emaciated pastor.

Austin threw the flare. It spun through the air, leaving a twirling trail of smoke behind it. After striking Masters square in the chest, the flare fell to his feet. Flames followed, shooting out to either side, following the gasoline soaked perimeter of the sanctuary and straight down the center aisle toward the stage.

The blaze followed the gasoline to the tank with the bullet hole in it, but the tank didn't explode. It simply continued chugged out flaming liquid. In that moment, Austin knew the distraction might not be enough to stop Masters. The horde, on the other hand, found themselves engulfed as the fire reached the foyer. But they never stopped moving, even as their bodies were reduced to ash. New waves of killers filled the foyer, screeching in agony as their bodies fueled the flames that would devour the next surge.

Masters roared, sending everyone in the room to their knees. Trapped inside the sanctuary, which had been designed to amplify sound, the roar was as painful as the flames licking up Masters's legs.

"Get out of this house!" Pastor Billy shouted. "You have violated sacred ground!"

The voice drew Masters's attention. The giant man saw the pastor, and then Austin. He took one step toward them when a shotgun opened fire from the balcony. The shots were wild and mostly ineffective, but one solid shot to Masters's shoulder stole his attention long enough for Austin to make a dash toward the exit just as the blaze reached his feet.

Austin looked up and saw Chang leaning over the balcony railing, unloading all eight shots in her shotgun.

She pumped it twice after running out of ammo, and then dropped it.

"Get out of there, Chang!" Austin shouted. If the girl didn't start for the exit now, she might not make it before Masters. The flames were slowing and distracting him for sure, but the giant had followed them this far. Austin doubted he would give up.

As Chang turned to run, Austin saw Masters duck down into the fire for a moment. When he came back up, his whole arm was on fire. He had picked up the fiery gas tank. Austin guessed what was coming next and opened his mouth to shout a warning, but Masters roared again.

Austin fell to his knees, but managed to keep an eye on Chang as he fell. A moment later, the gas can shot through the air, a massive Molotov cocktail.

"Chang!" Mia shouted as she reached the door with Elizabeth. "Get do—"

The gas can struck the railing in front of Chang and burst. Gasoline sprayed out from the impact and ignited. Chang's body was drenched in cold liquid one second and then an inferno the next. A single scream shot from the flames and then she dropped to the floor.

Masters roared again as they reached the exit, sending them all down. The giant strode down the aisle, his body on fire and twitching in pain. But not stopping.

Pastor Billy, surrounded by fire, saw him coming like a demon from hell and somehow managed to get to his feet. The man's cape had started to burn, but he paid no attention to it as he faced down the giant.

"Abomination!" Pastor Billy shouted at Masters. "You dare enter this house! The house of J—" The pastor seemed unable to speak. Masters climbed onto the stage and stood over Billy, looking down at him, oblivious to the crackling of his burning flesh.

"This is the house of the Lord J—"

Again, the pastor found himself unable to speak.

"I cast you out in the name of J—"

Masters raised his fists.

The stage succumbed to the flames and burst into fire.

Pastor Billy screamed.

The giant fists descended together like a wrecking ball. The pastor's body crumpled beneath the impact. But Masters didn't stop there. He picked up the ruined body and began pulling it apart, smashing it on the burning floor, stomping it into sludge.

Austin urged the others out the back door, watching the scene as they fled into the woods. The grassy space behind the church was free of killers, but Austin could still hear them screaming in the foyer. He didn't know if they could survive the flames, but he doubted all of them would die before realizing the group had slipped out the back. When that happened, the hunt would continue.

Masters turned toward him. Their eyes met. The monstrous man stopped, ignoring the crackle of his burning flesh and pointed at Austin. "Peace," the man said, his voice a growl. He took one step toward Austin and the stage collapsed beneath him. He howled as he dropped through the floor, flames and sparks launching clear up to the high ceiling above.

Austin turned to the exit and stepped outside. The ninety-degree heat outside felt cool compared to the church turned furnace. He saw the others disappear into the forest, but a voice turned him around.

"I'm sorry!"

Austin stepped back inside. "Chang?"

He saw Chang then, still burning, but oblivious to her charred condition. She charged around the balcony, headed for the staircase that led to the exit. Flames covered her body, but her lungs and voice, somehow still worked.

But she was no longer Chang.

She was one of them.

"Run!" Chang shouted. "I don't want to hurt you!"

And Austin ran, as fast as he could, before the human torch previously known as Stephanie Chang embraced him or Masters found a way out of the fiery pit.

36

The woods behind the burning church were thick, but the combination of the heat lightning-filled sky and the immense burning church behind them lit the area like the sun. The light on their backs as they hopped over fallen trees and large rocks made them easy to see. The cracking of dry branches beneath their feet and the sounds of their panicked shouting voices made them easy to hear, even over the roar of the blaze.

The fiery form of Chang, racing into the woods behind them, drew the attention of the killers still outside the church. She was a beacon. Impossible to miss. The horde swarmed behind her.

Like a school of fish changing direction as one, the mass of screaming people gathered at the side of the church, turned and followed. The shift made its way around to the front of the building until even those burning inside the foyer reversed direction and gave chase, still smoldering.

Garbarino ran ahead of the others, his feet carrying him swiftly down the wooded hillside. As a boy he had called it bunny hopping—the ability to sprint through the woods, avoiding obstacles with ease and never slowing down. After he and his friends set several traps along the walking paths, which older and meaner kids sometimes fell victim to, bunny hopping became an art form. It helped him escape several beatings as a kid. His skills took him fifty feet ahead of the others before he realized he was leaving them behind.

But Austin noticed. "Give us some cover, Garbarino!" he shouted down the hill.

The horde of killers behind them did nothing to conceal their pursuit.

They crashed through dead trees.

They screamed and hollered in horror. And several of them were on fire, including Chang, who still led the pack.

Garbarino stopped at the bottom of the hill and looked back, and then forward again, as though debating whether or not he should leave them behind.

"I don't want to do it!" Chang shouted.

She wasn't far behind now. Collins and Elizabeth slowed them down and Austin wasn't about to leave them behind.

"Garbarino!" Austin shouted again, but then Garbarino did the unthinkable.

He left.

I'll kill the son-of-a-bitch! Austin thought. "Faster!" he shouted at Collins, giving him a shove before stopping, wheeling around and firing two shots. The first round found Chang's chest. She pitched forward, but didn't stop. Her head snapped back as the second round struck and she fell to the ground. Her flaming form hit the dry foliage of the forest floor. The fire spread fast, reaching out in all directions. The dried trees went up like torches. Thick gray smoke rose up like a curtain, blocking Austin's view of the approaching swarm.

Beyond the wall of fire and smoke, a roar exploded into the air. Henry Masters was free. A thunderous cracking followed as the church finally imploded. A cloud of orange glowing embers danced into the sky, hauntingly beautiful with the heat-lightning backdrop.

Austin turned and ran again.

Mia saw Garbarino leave and was as confused as Austin was angry. After all they'd been through, she didn't think he would leave them to die, but what they'd just seen could put anyone over the edge.

"What happened to Stephanie?" Liz asked, her eyes vacant of emotion.

For a moment, Mia wondered who Stephanie was, but then remembered that it was Chang's first name. "She's dead, honey." Mia surprised herself with her honesty. It was such a cold thing to say, but Liz deserved the truth.

She'd come to realize that anything less in this new world could get her killed.

"But I can still hear her," the girl said.

That was one truth Mia wished she could ignore. "I know." As she reached the bottom of the hill, she searched for Garbarino. At first she couldn't see him, but then he rose up in the distance, across a field, waving his arms.

His voice barely reached her. "Follow the path!"

She didn't know how she'd missed it, but a slender path cut through the tall, brittle grass. The sky lit up with a burst of heat lighting and she saw it reflected on the ground beyond Garbarino. Not ground, she thought, water.

Collins reached them, sucking hard, clutching his chest. But there was no time to ask him if he felt okay. She pointed at the path and said, "Follow that to Garbarino."

As Collins ran, Mia looked back up the hill. Austin ran toward her, a wall of fire spread out in the forest behind him. She wasn't sure how Austin had done it, but the fire seemed to have stopped the murderous crowd.

That's when the first body ran through the flames and ignited. She couldn't tell if it was a man or woman. Didn't really matter. The fire didn't stop it. Or the next fiery person to emerge. Or the next. A flaming army followed, glowing as they ran, screaming in pain, and in sorrow.

Mia didn't wait for Austin. She followed the path. The tall grass clung to her legs, slowing her steps. Her arms burned from holding Liz. Her legs ached. She slowed, suddenly weary.

She put Liz down on her feet.

"Auntie Mia?"

"Run," Mia said. "Go!"

Elizabeth shook her head quickly and raised her arms up to her.

"I can't," Mia said, bending over to catch her breath. "Run!"

A crashing in the grass spun her around, raising her gun.

A hand reached out, took hold of the weapon and pushed it aside. Austin moved in a blur. He had Elizabeth over his shoulder one second and a tight grip on Mia's arm the next, dragging her forward. She looked back and saw bodies that should be dead, burning bright, running through the grass behind them and setting the whole field ablaze. The dead trees at the bottom of the hill snapped and fell away, crushing several killers.

A fiery Henry Masters emerged.

Mia found her feet and ran hard without Austin's help.

They reached the end of the field and hit sand. The loose earth beneath them sunk. All three fell.

Austin was up first, pulling Mia and Liz to their feet.

"Over here!" Garbarino shouted.

They turned to find him standing knee deep in water, a canoe beside him. Collins was already inside, sitting on the floor of the boat. They rushed to the boat. Austin put Liz in first. Mia went in next, sitting behind Liz.

"Get in the front," Austin said to Garbarino.

Garbarino slid deeper into the water. "Lean the other way," he said, "so my weight doesn't tip us."

Collins and Mia understood and leaned away from Garbarino.

"Fuck!" Garbarino shouted as he leaped up. He lost his grip on the side of the boat and fell forward, striking his head on the side. But something had him spooked and frantic and he scrambled inside the canoe.

"What happened?" Mia asked.

"Something grabbed my foot," he said, pulling himself into the seat and keeping an eye on the water.

A roar pitched them all forward in the canoe.

Masters charged out of the blazing field, his body burning.

"Go!" Austin said, pushing the canoe deeper and leaping into the back. He and Garbarino picked up the paddles and stabbed them into the dark water. The old white canoe was dirty and held a disconcerting number of patches, but it cut through the placid water with ease.

They were twenty feet from shore when Masters reached the water. He rushed in, steam hissing off his burning body as flame met water. If the water had been shallow, he would have reached them, but the lake deepened quickly and the water rose to his chest ten feet from shore. He pounded his fists at the water in frustration. The burning horde entered the water behind them, a cloud of steam rising as the flames were extinguished. They watched in silence until a single shouting voice said, "Go! Run!"

It was Chang.

Unlike the other voices that shouted apologies and urges to run, Chang's sounded genuine. She remembered who they were and honestly wanted them to escape, not just from her, but from the horrors of this new world.

Mia stood in the boat and met Chang's eyes. She watched as the charred flesh around Chang's eyes flaked off and fell away, replaced by new skin.

"Go!" Chang said.

Masters must have heard the slight difference in Chang's tone because he roared again, picked her up and tossed her into the air like a football. Her now limp body sailed over the water, toward the canoe, but landed twenty feet short. The small wave created by Chang's body hit the canoe's side and the sudden motion knocked Mia off balance.

Garbarino's hands locked on to her hips from behind, holding her steady. "Sit down," he urged.

Mia turned her eyes down, but instead of watching where she sat, she caught a glimpse of something in the water. She froze, looking over the side of the boat. Something white shifted beneath them.

Austin saw her attention on the water. "What is it?"

"I'm not su—" Heat lightning ripped across the sky above, lighting the lake in dazzling orange light. The bright burst cut through the water and revealed the faces below. Dozens of pale, swollen faces with white eyes and open mouths stared back at her.

Mia dropped into the canoe, clutching Liz close, more for her comfort than the girl's. "Paddle," she said, looking up into Austin's eyes. "Paddle!"

The boat shuddered as something thudded against the hull.

Mia's eyes grew wide and wet. They were too late.

37

"What's down there?" Garbarino asked. "What is it?"

A second bump against the hull answered his question. He put his paddle down and drew his weapon. Before he could ask again, the sounds of splashing reached them.

A man rose to the surface, floating face down. Dead. The gases of decomposition had finally made his body buoyant and returned him to the surface. His skin was wrinkly and pasty white.

A second body emerged, bobbing to the surface like a buoy that had been cut loose. This was a woman, her slight body hanging on the surface, her long black hair flowing like stringy seaweed.

"Are they dead?" Collins asked.

A third body bobbed to the surface. Austin reached out with his paddle and pushed it away. "Dead."

Mia shook her head. "I don't think so."

"What do you mean?" Collins asked, motioning to the three bodies. "Look at them."

She shook her head again and held Elizabeth close, doing her best to cover the girl's eyes. She didn't want to look. Not again. The lifeless faces she saw would haunt her for the rest of her life, not because they were dead, but because she somehow knew they weren't. Not really.

A fourth body came up. Then a fifth, this one far away.

A sudden splashing and gasp for breath startled all of them. The first man to rise thrashed in the water. He coughed and sputtered. Water poured from his mouth. He breathed in loudly, twice, and then shouted. "Help!"

The group froze. His request was simple.

Save him.

But he had been dead and the sight of the now revived man shocked them so much that all they could do was watch him struggle.

More bodies rose up. Hundreds. They filled the center of the lake. And one by one, they returned to the world, panicked and desperate.

The man who awakened first grappled with a woman next to him, each trying to hold onto the other. "Help me!" the man cried.

But there would be no help for him. As more bodies returned to life and began their own struggle in the water, the mass of hands reaching, grabbing, scratching and pulling became overwhelming. The man went under. His hand reached up and caught the woman's hair, pulling her down, while he returned for a breath. But others were waiting for him, hoping to keep themselves above the water and they pushed him down again. Still sucking in air as he went under, water rushed into his lungs. He fought for the surface, but was pushed deeper. His body twitched and then sank, lifeless once more.

"Oh God," Collins said. "God no."

A heavy thud on the side of the canoe tore them away from the sea of struggling bodies. White hands clung to the side of the canoe. A woman with wide open, milky white eyes pulled herself up. "Help me," she whispered, her voice shaky and wet.

Everyone stared at her, the living dead, and not one of them moved to help. She wasn't violent or trying to kill them, but she wasn't one of them, one of the living, anymore. Not really. The sight of her repulsed them.

A second set of hands rose up behind the woman and latched onto her face. A man pulled himself up, desperate for air. For rescue. His eyes went wide when he saw the boat. He reached for the side, but the woman, who he was pushing down, fought against him. Their combined weight and struggle tipped the boat, dunking both of their heads underwater. They both let go and fought to reach the surface again, pushing and pulling at each other.

The boat tipped the other direction.

More hands reached up.

"A boat!" someone shouted.

"Help!" shouted another.

A mass of writhing bodies struggled toward them, some pushing others down, sliding over the drowning bodies of men and women who had just reached the surface. More hands reached out.

"We're going to tip!" Collins shouted, hugging his still unfired shotgun like a life preserver.

A gunshot ripped through the air.

Mia flinched and Elizabeth screamed.

A second shot. Then a third, each coming faster than the last and from two directions. Austin and Garbarino quickly shot everyone clinging to the canoe and then worked their way out to those still en route. After reloading and firing several more shots, they stopped.

All around the lake, the recently revived were drowning again, either pulled down by other victims or too tired to hold themselves above water. But the group around the canoe hadn't drowned. They'd been shot. A large red plume of blood encircled the canoe.

Austin and Garbarino searched the red water, looking for anyone else who might try to latch onto their small lifeboat. But no one emerged. The lake had gone silent again.

Mia looked up. The water, placid once again, smelled like copper. She looked in both directions, searching for white bodies, sure that one would rise up and try to snatch Elizabeth from her arms. If one of them had fallen in... She pushed the thought from her mind as it threatened to start her down a spiral of anxiety.

Motion on the distant shore, perhaps a mile away, caught her attention. Movement. She looked back to the shoreline they had launched from. The burning church glowed like a massive lighthouse on the hill above the lake. The forest beneath it and the field beyond burned brightly. But the shore, where Henry Masters and the crowd of killers had nearly caught them, was now empty.

She looked back at the distant shore. Between dead trees and brush she saw people. Running. And at the front, an unmistakable hulking man. She looked to the other far shore and saw more of them there.

"They're circling in both directions," she said.

"What?" Austin asked as he set his paddle to the water and said, "Let's go," to Garbarino.

With both men paddling again, they moved quickly over the water, but Mia wasn't sure it would be fast enough. "Masters," she said, "and the others. They're circling around the lake!"

Austin glanced to the far shore and caught a glimpse of movement. He looked the other direction and saw the same thing. He put all his weight into the next paddle. "Garbarino!" he shouted. "Faster!"

Both men fought against the water, pushing as hard as they could while keeping them on a straight course for the shoreline opposite the burning church. They would reach shore long before the horde circuiting the lake did, but once on foot again, their advantage was lost. And staying in the water wasn't an option. If the drowning victims didn't pull them under, the killers and Henry Masters could just encircle the lake and wait them out.

It was now or never. Run or die.

38

"Start running as soon as we hit the sand," Austin said, digging his paddle deep into the lake water. A few times he thought he'd struck one of the bodies below, but he paid little attention to what lay beneath now. He needed to focus more on what was ahead, and to the sides.

They could hear the voices of the horde growing closer. As disturbing as the shouts of horror were, Austin was thankful for them. If the killers were silent, he had no doubt they would have been caught long ago.

"Run where?" Mia asked.

Her hands had gone tingly and her legs felt heavy. She noticed her breaths coming quick and shallow. She forced herself to take a deep breath, hold it, and let it out slowly.

"Straight ahead," Austin replied. "Any other direction will take us closer to them."

"Right," she said, looking at the beach ahead. The sandy shore rose up slowly for twenty feet, most of it sand. The beach and woods beyond were separated by a small dirt road. Beyond that, a series of paths, picnic tables and mobile homes were scattered throughout the tall pine trees. The campground would have been an inviting sight under different circumstances and Mia could imagine children enjoying the beach, family picnics and lines of people fishing along the shore.

When Garbarino's paddle struck bottom, he stood and prepared to jump.

A voice called out behind them.

"Help!"

"It's happening again!" Collins shouted, pointing back behind them. White bodies bobbed on the surface of the lake, many of them reviving already.

Ten feet from shore, Austin gave one final paddle and prepared to leap from the boat. "Do not slow down. Do not stop to catch your breath. If you do, I won't—"

A loud splash followed by a hoarse intake of air burst out behind the canoe. Mia turned around in time to see white arms wrap around Austin and pull him over the back. He disappeared into the water. They struck shore a moment later.

"Austin!" she shouted, standing and moving to the back of the boat.

"Mia, move!" Garbarino shouted.

She turned and saw Collins already running up the beach.

Garbarino plucked Liz from the boat.

Shrieking voices grew louder all around them.

"Now!" Garbarino shouted and then ran up the beach with Liz in his arms.

Beneath the water, Austin fought against the hands gripping his clothes. For a moment, he became a child again, struggling to save his father in the pool. He took hold of the arm around his chest and felt the same cool, slippery skin. He felt the same desperation. But the man holding him down couldn't be saved. He was already dead. He just didn't know it.

Austin pulled the man's arms away and slipped down, out of his grasp. His feet struck bottom.

He looked for his brother, ready to count to three. Instead he saw corpses. Dozens of them, glowing white beneath the water. He pushed off the bottom, aiming at an angle while desperate hands reached out for his feet.

Mia stood knee deep in the water, torn between diving in after Austin and fleeing up the beach. The choice was made for her a moment later when a body rose from the waters and reached out for her. Hands wrapped around her shoulders. Deep breathing filled her ears. She nearly fell over under his weight, but managed to keep herself, and Austin, upright.

Austin shoved her toward the shore. "Go!"

She ran. The lake water clung to her as though trying to pull her back, but she reached the shore a moment later, and with a surge of adrenaline, she pounded up the beach. Collins, Garbarino and Liz were already across the road, climbing the hill into the maze of camper trailers and brown pine trees.

"Shit," Austin shouted.

She looked back at him as they crossed the road. "What?"

He lunged up the hill next to her. "Lost my weapons underwater."

As they reached the first camper, a voice shot out of the woods to their side. "I don't want to!"

"Austin," Mia shouted. When he turned to her, she tossed him her handgun. Having it made her feel safer, but Austin would put every round in the gun to good use while she might miss every shot.

He caught the weapon and pulled the trigger once. The shot clapped loud in Mia's ears. A man stumbled out of the woods and fell.

The hill's grade grew less steep as they neared the top, allowing them to run faster. But as they crested the hill, they found Garbarino facing them with a gun raised. He pulled the trigger three times. Bullets buzzed between them. A thud followed. Neither looked back. They knew he'd dropped at least one of the killers.

Atop the hill was a field of short brown grass. A paved road cut through the middle of the field, leading downhill to a chained exit. Beyond the exit, the hill continued down, further down than anyone could see.

Henry Masters roared from somewhere behind them.

"We're not...going to...make it," Collins said, out of breath.

Austin ran past him, toward a large RV parked on the side of the road, pointed downhill. The giant vehicle was dirty, but looked new enough and sported a turquoise swipe of paint along its side.

"Get in!" Austin shouted.

"What are we going to do," Garbarino said, "push it?"

Mia and Liz entered, followed by Collins.

"Won't need to," Austin said, pointing to the hillcrest. Henry Masters rose up, scanned the area and upon seeing them, charged.

Garbarino climbed into the RV's passenger seat. "Hold on!" he shouted back to Mia, Liz and Collins, who were sitting around the small dining area, clutching the small table.

Austin jumped inside and threw himself into the driver's seat.

He grabbed the shift and threw the RV into neutral. "Brace yourself!"

The impact felt like a large truck had struck them from behind. Mia fell to the floor, striking her head hard on the side of the mini-fridge. She shook her head, stunned, and looked toward the back of the RV. The rear end beneath the large window was dented in.

"We're moving!" Garbarino shouted from the front. The impact coupled with their downward pointing front end pushed them onto the smooth road and gravity took care of the rest.

Mia felt a tug on her shoulder and turned to find Liz standing above her. "Auntie Mia?"

Movement behind them caught Mia's attention. Henry Masters was charging again. "Liz, get—"

The force of Masters's fresh assault dwarfed that of the first. The back end imploded. Glass and fragments of metal shot toward the front of the RV like confetti from a compressed air popper.

Liz dropped down, silent. She hit the floor at Mia's feet.

Mia reached for her. "Liz!" But the sudden increase in speed kept her pinned to the floor.

The back shook again, drawing Mia's attention. A gaping hole in the back was filled with Masters's body. His stripped face and evil eyes stared at her. The "peace" tattoo wept blood from several lacerations.

"Help!" Mia shouted. "Someone help!"

Masters took hold of the ruined rear wall and pulled, tearing a larger opening to accommodate his body. In a moment he would be inside with them.

"I need a gun!" Mia shouted.

Collins slid out of the dining area and pumped his shotgun. He stepped over Mia and just as Master's opened his mouth to roar, he pulled the trigger. Masters's head snapped back. But the injury didn't stop him. A portion of his skull was missing, but the monster didn't seem to notice. He simply shook his head, scattering blood, and turned his ruined face back toward them.

Mia expected Masters to let out a roar now, but Collins screamed a battle cry and ran toward the back, pulling the trigger seven more times until the weapon was empty and Masters had no head.

The headless body fell limp and dropped backwards onto the road. It tumbled off the road and snapped to a stop against the side of a thick tree.

Looking beyond Masters, Collins and Mia could see that they'd already broken through the chain-locked campground exit. But then the view changed. One moment they were looking back at the campground behind them, the next, they saw the turbulent, heat lightning-filled sky.

"Oh shit!" Garbarino shouted.

Austin's voice came next, full of dread. "Hold on!"

Mia glanced forward and saw a steep, curvy hill dropping down before them. The RV accelerated rapidly, once again pinning Mia to the floor. She reached out for Liz and found the girl's hand.

It felt slick with warm, thick liquid. Mia drew her hand back and looked at it, hoping to see anything other than what she saw.

Blood.

39

"Auntie!" Elizabeth shouted before running across the front yard and leaping into Mia's arms. The first warm air of spring filled them with energy as the pair spun and fell onto the damp lawn. Mia had just announced her engagement to Matt and the six year old Elizabeth, who had always dreamed of being a flower girl, was overjoyed.

"I'm so proud of you, Auntie Mia," Elizabeth whispered into her ear.

At first Mia laughed, surprised by the girl's mature reply. But after the words sunk in, Mia found herself tearing up. Her sister had somehow raised an intelligent and sensitive daughter—two attributes she wouldn't have used to describe her sister—and the girl had said exactly what Mia needed to hear. Mia's parents never expressed pride in their daughters. Not for graduating college, nor landing a good job, nor getting married. Instead they critiqued and questioned the legitimacy of things. They were glass-half-empty naysayers. Anything good in life was probably too good to be true.

So when Elizabeth said those few words, Mia found the girl had cut deep and exposed a potent mixture of pain and longing.

They lay in the damp grass, ignoring the wetness and looking up at the sky.

"What's it like?" Elizabeth asked. "To love someone not in our family?"

Mia smiled. "He'll be in our family soon."

"I know, but...he wasn't always. Some people you love because they're there when you're born. But even then, not all the time."

Mia saw what the little girl was getting at. Her father was an asshole. The girl adored Matt, but was probably confused about how he differed from her deadbeat dad. "I think that some people were made to be together."

"Like made by God? We're all puzzle pieces that fit together?"

"Something like that, sure." She turned toward Elizabeth, their faces inches apart. "Like you and me."

"Puzzle pieces."

Their hands linked as they smiled at each other.

"We fit together," Mia said.

"And no one can pull us apart," Elizabeth added.

"Never."

"Elizabeth!" Mia screamed. "Elizabeth!" She struggled to reach the girl, but the steep angle of the RV kept her leaning back. If she sat up, she'd fall forward. "God dammit!"

Pushing against the side wall of the center aisle, Mia was able to brace her body and turn to face Liz. She saw her hand first, covered in liquid red. The amount of blood made Mia nauseous. Blood didn't normally bother her, but the large amount she saw indicated a severe injury.

Each breath came harder than the last as panic constricted her neck. She put her hand down to turn herself the rest of the way around and slipped on the blood soaked rug, hitting her head a second time.

The RV suddenly lurched to the right, slamming her against the opposite side, further dazing her. But through it all, she could smell the blood of her niece turned daughter.

At the front of the vehicle, Garbarino buckled himself in and clutched the handle above his door. "Watch out, watch out!"

"I see it!" Austin shouted, swerving around a fallen tree. The quick turn tilted the large vehicle toward its left side. Austin felt the RV tip. He yanked the wheel in the other direction, leveling them out.

The trees on either side of the road became a blur of brown. Dead leaves covering the road billowed behind the heavy vehicle as it barreled downhill.

"Shit," Austin said. Several small trees had fallen across the road just before it turned hard to the left. "Hang on!" he shouted just before striking the first tree.

The RV shook with each impact.

Each jolt slammed Mia against the floor, pounding the fight out of her. Consciousness began to slip away. "Liz," she said, fighting to stay awake, struggling to move. But then they reached the left turn. Tires squealed, two of them coming off the ground for a moment, and Mia slammed into the hallway wall, hitting the back of her head. Her beaten body finally succumbed. She fell to the floor and would have no memory of the next five minutes.

Austin looked down at the speedometer. Fifty miles per hour, and climbing.

"Sharp right!" Garbarino shouted.

Austin drifted to the left then cut across the road like a race car driver so that the angle of the sharp turn was reduced. They came out on the other side, skimming the side of the road, kicking up a cloud of dead pine needles and leaves.

"Left!"

"I see it."

Austin performed the same maneuver and pulled them through the turn, but this time he heard a thump behind him that made him cringe. He couldn't chance a look back, but he recognized the sound of unconscious bodies thudding and rolling. He instinctively slammed on the brake pedal several times, but without power behind the pump, it was useless. And slamming on the emergency break at this speed could get them all killed. The only way through this was to reach the bottom.

After clearing the left turn, the angle of the road dropped even further—a straight shot to the bottom. The RV hit sixty five and began to shake.

"I think one of the tires is losing air," Garbarino shouted over the shaking, which had become violent.

The front right of the vehicle dipped forward slowly. Austin gritted his teeth and fought with the RV, keeping it on the road as the ruined tire tugged to the right. They reached the bottom of the hill and started up an incline. The RV quickly slowed and when its momentum finally stopped and began to reverse, Austin threw the vehicle into park.

He and Garbarino leaned back in their seats, exhausted from the rollercoaster ride, but elated to be alive.

"Holy shit," Garbarino said.

Austin chuckled. "I didn't think we were going to make it." He smiled and sighed, unbuckling his seatbelt. Then he remembered the thumping and turned around. The first thing he saw was the hole in the back. He could see the road descending behind them. Then he saw Collins, sitting up in the hallway, but unconscious. In front of him was Mia, twisted at an odd angle, but breathing. He saw the blood next, tracing it from Mia's hand to Elizabeth's.

"Oh my God," he said when he saw her small body. "Elizabeth."

Garbarino saw her, too. "Fuck!" he shouted, unbuckling himself and launching over the seat.

"It's too late," Austin said quietly.

"Fuck it is!" Garbarino said as he knelt down beside the girl, ignoring the blood that soaked into his pants. But when he inspected her body, he saw Austin was right. A large chunk of shrapnel was buried in the girl's neck. Several smaller pieces dotted her body. "How long?"

"What?"

"How long do you think she's been dead?"

Austin understood the real question. Is she coming back? "If the initial impact didn't kill her, it looks like she would have bled out in under a minute. Maybe less."

It had been at least two since Henry Masters tore a hole in the back of the RV. Garbarino's body sagged as he sighed. "Then she's not coming back," he said. "Thank God."

Austin moved past Garbarino. "Let's get these two outside and wake them up. We need to move."

Garbarino looked down at Elizabeth's pale body. "What about her?"

"We left the others," Austin replied. "And we don't have time."

"She's a kid."

Austin gripped Mia beneath the arms and hoisted her up. "She's dead." He dragged Mia to the door, kicked it open and pulled her outside.

Garbarino looked back down to Liz. He brushed her hair away from her face. "You're in a better place," he said in a hushed voice. He thought about the effect her death would have on the others. Austin seemed unfazed, focused on the living as usual. Collins might not care at all. That she didn't come back gave Garbarino hope, because it meant the things he'd been thinking about, the hope he now clung to, might be real. But Mia...it would tear her apart. "Be seeing you, kid."

Garbarino pulled Collins from the RV and sat him down, leaning his body against the back tire. He woke when his head leaned back. "We made it?"

"Not all of us," Garbarino replied.

Collins held his head and looked around. There were trees, dead like the rest. A paved, double yellow-lined road. Austin knelt over Mia a few feet away. She had blood on her hand and a small wound on her head. He saw her chest rising and falling, which left, "The girl?"

Garbarino offered a grim nod.

"How?"

"Shrapnel. Bled out."

"Is she—"

"One of them? No."

Collins struggled to his feet. Garbarino helped him.

"You sure?" Collins asked.

"Let me ask you a question, pres, you seen any other kids around? This whole time, since we dropped from the heavens, have you seen a single child?"

Collins leaned against the RV, replaying the past few days in his head. Garbarino was right. They hadn't come across any children. Not one.

Before he could answer, Mia woke with a scream. She thrashed, reaching out as though still in the RV.

Austin held her arms. "Mia. Mia! You're safe. We're stopped."

She fought against him, kicking and pulling her arms. He pinned her arms against her body and straddled her kicking legs. "Mia! We're okay!" Her fighting slowed. She looked Austin in the eyes. "We're okay," he repeated.

He lied.

She saw it in his eyes as soon as her senses returned. "Where's Elizabeth?"

Austin's grip loosened. He rolled away and sat beside her. She looked to Garbarino, then to Collins. "Where is she!"

For all the bravery, training and public speaking experience shared between the three men, none of them could bring themselves to tell her. But their silence spoke for them.

Mia's bottom lip quivered. Tears rolled down her cheeks. "She's dead?"

Garbarino gave her a slight nod. The small gesture unstopped the dam and Mia's emotions flooded out of her. She groaned like a woman in labor, curling in on herself. The last thing she held precious in this world was gone. And she had died without saying goodbye. Without the comfort of looking into her aunt's eyes as life faded. She had died violently. And alone. Mia's body shook as she wept.

Garbarino, moved to tears by Mia's anguish, knelt beside her and pulled her to him. She cried into his chest while he held her.

When Mia's sobs abated, Austin said, "We need to go."

"Her niece just died, man," Garbarino said. "Give her some time."

Austin stared at him, unsympathetic. "And we'll be next if we don't move. It won't be long before they catch up again. We'll stop to rest, and mourn, when we find a defensible position."

Mia sniffed and sat up. Red splotches covered the skin around her bloodshot eyes. "He's right."

"You sure?" Garbarino asked.

Mia stood. "I just need to see her first."

Garbarino caught her arm as she headed for the RV door. He didn't need to say what he thought.

"I can handle it," she said. She pulled her arm away, opened the door and climbed inside.

A fresh wave of grief surged over Mia when she saw Elizabeth's small body, covered in wounds and blood. "I'm sorry," she whispered. "I failed you."

"You didn't," Garbarino said softly as he entered.

Mia wiped her arm across her nose.

"How do you figure that?"

"She didn't come back."

Mia sniffed, fighting back tears. "That's a good thing?"

"Seems to be the only real escape," he said. "Better than being here."

Mia's lips twitched, a fraction of a smile, grateful for the comforting words. "Thanks."

He reached his hand out to her. "C'mon," he said. "We better go before Austin leaves us here."

She knelt down and kissed Elizabeth's forehead. "Love you, Lizard." She returned to her feet and stepped toward the door. Her anguish had been replaced by something else, something Garbarino didn't recognize until it was too late.

"Just one more thing," she said. "Then we can go."

40

"Mia, wait!" Garbarino said when he saw her fist clench.

But she was already in motion—an unstoppable force of rage directed at a single person—former president Collins. Her fist collided with his cheek and sent him reeling to the side.

"This is your fault, you son-of-a-bitch!"

He covered his face, feeling blood.

She kicked him next, a solid shot to the stomach. He coughed and held his stomach.

"You did this!" Mia shouted and then hammered him with a second shot to the face.

"Wait," Collins said, staggering. "Please."

"Elizabeth is dead!"

"I'm sorry," he said.

This slowed her assault, but she wasn't done. As she stepped toward him, he backed away. He glanced to Garbarino and Austin, his former protectors, but they seemed to understand this had to happen. They knew the same thing he did. The state of the world was his fault. He had ordered the assassination. He had denied the problem. Dodged diplomatic solutions. He had driven the world to the brink.

"I did it, okay?"

She shoved him. He fell back into the brush on the side of the road. He stood again.

"This is all my fault. Everything! I destroyed the world. The blood of billions is on my hands. I know that!"

"You killed her," Mia said.

"I know."

She grabbed hold of his shirt and shook him.

He had more than fifty pounds on her and despite being older, probably out-muscled her, too. He could have broken free. Could have fought back. But he didn't.

"How can you live with yourself?" she asked. "How can you stand the sight of your own face, the sound of your own voice?"

"I wanted to live long enough," he said.

"For what?"

He looked into her eyes. They burned with hatred. Nothing he said would change her heart or bring the girl back to life. So he was honest. "Redemption."

Mia glared at him as the word permeated her anger. When it did, she cocked her fist back and brought it into his soft stomach. Collins doubled over with a wheeze. He struggled to catch a breath.

"Get up!" she shouted, kicking dirt at him. "Get up." She positioned herself to kick him in the gut, when she saw him clutching at his chest instead of his stomach. Her eyes went wide with realization. She shoved him onto his back.

Collins's face was twisted with pain. His body rigid. He took a frantic breath and whispered, "Forgive me." His voice trailed off with a moan as the last air in his lungs seeped out. The President of the United States was dead.

"No!" Mia shouted. She turned to Austin. "He can't get off this easy! Bring him back!"

Austin just watched.

She punched his chest twice. "Come back!"

Garbarino stepped forward. "Mia."

"Bring him back, Joe," she said. "He can't. He doesn't deserve this."

Garbarino drew his weapon. "You might yet get your chance."

Mia stood and jumped away from Collins's body.

Visions of White, Vanderwarf, Paul and Chang filled her thoughts. She reached out to Garbarino, "Give me your gun."

He did, and drew a second. "You can hang on to that. Five rounds left. Use them well."

She took aim at Collins's head, waiting for him to return so she could kill him again, and again, and again. "I intend to," she said.

"Thirty seconds," Austin said, standing to his feet. He walked up next to them, waiting for Collins to come back. "One shot."

"What?" Mia asked.

"I'll give you one shot."

"He deserves worse."

Austin's voice was grim. "If you insist on ringing the dinner bell, we're not going to wait around and see who comes running."

They stared at each other, each waiting for the other's will to break.

"Forty-five," Garbarino said.

Austin's stare intensified. "One shot."

"Fine," Mia said. "One shot."

"Sixty seconds," Garbarino said, taking another step back. He had no idea how fast Collins would be able to move once he came back.

But Mia stood rooted over his body, gun aimed at his face. Collins's eyes were wide open. The lifeless orbs stared straight up at her. She waited, finger on the trigger, for some hint of life to return.

As the seconds ticked past, her hands began to shake, subtly at first, but then so violently that if she took a shot, she was likely to miss. She wasn't counting, but she sensed the truth. Collins wasn't coming back.

Garbarino confirmed it when he lowered his weapon and said, "Two minutes."

"No," Mia said. "No!" She kicked Collins hard in the leg. She repeated the attack while screaming in newborn rage. "You don't deserve it! You don't fucking deserve it!" A final kick sent something flying out of his pants pocket. She cocked her head toward it.

She instantly recognized the small black book with gold lettering on the front. Mark Byers's Bible. The sight of the book and the memory of Mark deflated her anger. She stepped away, wiping her eyes. "We can go now."

Garbarino bent down, picked up the book and brushed it off.

Austin snatched it from his hand.

"Hey," Garbarino said in protest, but Austin had already wound up and he threw the book deep into the woods.

Mia watched the book sail into the trees and disappear. She didn't care what Austin did with it. She felt numb to everything. Cold. All that remained was the journey. The instinct to run. To survive. Nothing else mattered, and if she died, so be it. Her life held little meaning now. She started up the hill without looking back.

"What did you do that for?" Garbarino asked.

"That book has already caused enough problems for us," Austin said, starting up the hill.

Garbarino looked in the direction Austin had thrown the book. For a moment, he thought about going to get it, if only just to piss Austin off. But a roar from atop the mountain they had careened down signaled the return of Henry Masters to the world. Garbarino set off after the others.

They walked into the woods.

Then they ran.

41

Leaves crackled underfoot. They heard nothing else for an hour. No one spoke and nothing seemed to be following them. Mia walked between Austin, who had the lead, and Garbarino, who kept watch behind them. Her body was sore, more from the RV ride than walking, but she hardly noticed.

Her mind was still on Collins, replaying what he'd said. Redemption. How could a man like Collins, who'd doomed billions of people to horrible deaths and turned the world into a living graveyard even begin to think he could be redeemed? And yet, he hadn't come back.

Mia clenched her fist around a long branch she had picked up and used as a walking stick, anger tensing her body.

She felt a pang of guilt for dwelling on Collins, but if she didn't her thoughts would turn to Liz, and that wound still hurt too much. So she focused on Collins, on how much she wanted him to come back so she could kill him again.

A wave of sadness swept through her. Kill him? What the hell have I become? she wondered. She wasn't just thinking about killing a man, she wanted nothing more in the world than to put a bullet in Collins's face. And despite her rising guilt over the desire, she'd do it now just the same. He deserved it. He deserved worse.

Without thinking, Mia swung her walking stick at a tree, grunting with anger and exertion. The thick stick cracked loudly, breaking into two pieces. "Fucker," she muttered, picturing the tree as Collins.

Austin looked back at her, neither upset nor amused. "Probably not a good idea."

She nearly snapped at him for stating the obvious, but held her tongue. He had acted selflessly and thought of nothing but preserving the lives of others. Mia felt guilty for losing Elizabeth. She imagined Austin felt the same about the six others who had died under his watch.

"Austin," she said, intending to thank him.

He looked back again as he passed through a stand of dried out ferns. "Yeah?"

"I wanted to—"

"Hey," Garbarino said, his voice filled with urgency. "Do you smell that?"

They stopped at the base of a forty foot hill. Mia tested the air with her nose. She hadn't noticed the subtle change, but now that she focused on it, the scent of rot made her nose crinkle in disgust. A breeze carried a fresh waft of the scent. She put her hand to her mouth. "Something died near here."

"That's what doesn't make sense," Garbarino said. "People don't stay dead here. There are no animals. The trees and plants are crispy dry. What could be rotting?"

"Survivors," Austin said. He looked at Mia with sad eyes. "If they stayed dead."

The image made Mia cringe, but Austin was right. Rot would consume the dead until only dust remained.

"I don't know," Garbarino said. "The air here is dry. And there are no insects. The dead might be—" He saw the discomfort Mia had with the subject. She spared him by finishing the thought.

"Mummified," she said. That made sense too, which validated his initial question. What could be rotting? "We should check it out," she said.

Austin shifted. "I don't know."

"If there's even a small chance it could be other survivors, we should risk it." Garbarino lifted some dry leaves and let them fall. The wind carried them downhill. "Whatever it is, it's probably just over this rise."

Austin scanned the woods around them, looking for any hint of danger. He sighed. "Quickly. Quietly. If there is even a hint of danger, we leave. If we find someone alive, we take them. I doubt the killers or Masters have given up."

Garbarino agreed with a nod. He started up the hill. Using his hands to help distribute his weight, he carefully picked each step. Mia and

Austin followed. The leaves crackled under their weight, but made little more sound than a gentle breeze.

Mia tensed as they neared the top of the hill. Most of her worry had been eradicated by Elizabeth's death. The fear of Liz getting hurt or killed had been her primary concern. And now that she was gone, all that remained was the fear of death. Of pain. And in comparison to losing the only person left on Earth she loved, pain and death seemed less significant, though not entirely irrelevant. Anything could be on the other side of this hill. The horde could lay in wait. Or maybe just Masters. Or an army of monsters just like him. Or a vomit eating preacher. The world had been unpredictable before. It was beyond comprehension now.

Garbarino paused at the top of the hill. The scent had grown stronger and if there was something dangerous, something that needed to be shot, he wanted all guns on hand when the time came.

Austin and Mia slid up next to him.

"Quick peeks," Austin whispered to Mia. "Poke your head up, see what you can and then drop back down. If we see nothing dangerous, we'll get a little closer."

She didn't respond. She just waited for the go ahead.

"Now," Austin said.

All three pushed up, looking over the crest of the hill. But not one of them dropped back down.

"Oh my God," Mia said.

Garbarino smiled. "Pay dirt!"

The other side of the hill dropped more than one hundred feet. The valley below, now full of shattered pine trees, had concealed the gleaming white surface of an EEP. The backside of the large Earth Escape Pod faced them, hiding the front hatch.

"It's the third escape pod," Mia said. "It'll have food and water."

"And guns," Garbarino said. "Lots of guns."

Austin stood.

"Let's take this slow. Something down there stinks."

They followed him down the hill, weapons drawn and eyes wary.

"Could an EEP stand up to the horde?" Mia asked. "To Henry Masters?"

"You mean if we have to hide inside?" Garbarino asked. "The things were designed to take the impact of multiple nuclear shockwaves. So, yeah."

"I'm not talking about hiding inside," she said.

Austin looked at Garbarino. "She's talking about living inside."

"There's only three of us now. The food and water would last a long time. If there are vents anywhere, air wouldn't be an issue. Maybe we could outlast them?"

"Or live as long as possible without being torn apart," Garbarino said.

As they approached the bottom of the EEP, the smell grew stronger. "Don't get your hopes up," Austin said as he stopped, looking down at the ground. A streak of wet, black goop cut through the carpet of brown leaves, arcing around toward the front side of the EEP.

Austin squatted down next to the streak, picked up a stick and dunked it in. A wad of dark ooze clung to the stick as he lifted it up. He sniffed and winced. "This is what smells."

The tip of the stick bent and then dropped away.

Mia winced. "It rotted."

The dark rot spread up the stick, turning the next few inches to black ooze before dropping away, too. Austin tossed what was left of the stick into the trail of goop and it sank in, rotting as though captured by a time-lapse camera. In ten seconds, the whole stick was gone.

Austin stood. "Try not to step in it."

One by one, they carefully stepped over the rotted earth and continued moving around the EEP. Several more streaks crisscrossed around them. The area of rot grew dense and then became impassible up close to the EEP. Austin led them back, and then circled around further away.

They stopped when the hatch came into view. It stood open, the interior beyond beckoning them closer. Someone had left, and that meant someone had survived. But the black rot covered more than a hundred square feet of earth around the hatch and criss-crossed even further out.

"We'll never make it to the hatch," Garbarino said.

Austin turned away. "We should go."

But Mia had seen something else.

Someone else. "Who's that?"

Garbarino and Austin followed Mia's pointed finger. A body lay on the far side of the rotted patch. The deeply tanned skin of the naked man made him hard to see in the brown leaves that surrounded him. His hair was slick and pulled back. His eyes were closed and his mouth wide open, as though singing opera.

"Vicano," Austin said. "Robert Vicano. Secret Service."

"I'm sorry," Mia said.

Garbarino tossed a stick into the black tar-like ooze. He watched it sink. "Don't be. The man was an ass. So in love with himself that he hardly noticed anyone else. Probably closed the EEP door behind him without letting anyone else in."

Mia looked at Vicano's swollen body. Aside from the tan, he looked like the average American couch potato. "He doesn't look like the type."

"She's right," Austin said. "Something's wrong with his body. If he wasn't on duty, he was working out. Now he looks...not swollen...fat."

The heat lightning above increased in violence for a moment, casting them all in brighter light. The light reflected off of Vicano's body.

"And wet," Mia said. "He looks like he's covered in—"

The man's eyes opened. His mouth snapped shut.

Mia, Austin and Garbarino took a quick step back.

Vicano's eyes darted around. Then he saw them, looking each one of them in the eyes. He stopped on Austin. "Austin? Is that you?"

"Vicano," Austin said in greeting. "Are there any other survivors with you?"

The man looked around, feigning a search. "Ah, no. Just me. Just me."

"He's not moving," Garbarino whispered.

Mia had noticed it too. Vicano was stark naked. But if he was as vain as they said, maybe he really didn't care.

"Are you injured?" Austin asked.

"No. No. Just, ah, just lying down." He looked them up and down, licking his lips. "You know what, I am having a hard time getting up. Can you come over here and help me?"

Austin looked down at the black goop. "The black rot," he said. "It's dangerous."

Vicano looked disappointed, but the expression lacked the desperation of someone in need of help. He looked more like a spoiled child who didn't get what he wanted for Christmas.

"What happened to the others on board?" Austin asked.

Vicano glanced at the EEP. "I was alone."

"Why didn't you get in touch with the other EEPs in orbit? You were trained to—"

"I...didn't make it. I barely got into the EEP before the launch started. I don't think—I don't remember getting strapped in. I was standing, I think, when the first Orion burst hit. After that...I was here. Maybe that's what happened to my legs? Maybe that's why I'm like this?" His voice was pleading. Desperate.

Austin thought, like what? Sensing something was off, Austin thought they should leave, but the weapons and supplies inside the EEP offered a temptation nearly impossible to resist. Feeling a little like Hansel before the candy house, Austin stayed rooted in place, eyeing the EEP's open hatch, hoping to find a way inside. "How did you get outside? Past the rot?"

Vicano looked at the streaks of black. "I hadn't noticed them before. I don't recall it bothering me."

Garbarino placed a hand on Austin's shoulder. "I think we're just going to take a look around." He stepped away and was glad to see Austin follow his lead. Something was very wrong with Vicano and they needed to leave before that something tried to kill them. "We'll come back soon."

"No, wait!" Vicano shouted, lifting his head. The sudden motion made him roll onto his stomach. He slid down a small rise leaving a trail of clear slime behind him. His arms and legs stayed limp, as though boneless. The leaves beneath the slime rotted, turning black and wet, then became just another trail of ooze.

Austin and Garbarino took aim. Mia held her gun ready, but didn't raise it.

"Don't move, Vicano," Austin said.

But the man didn't listen. Instead, he slithered forward through the muck, unaffected by its ability to rot.

"He's the source of the rot," Mia said. "Some kind of slime is covering his body."

Vicano's fatty exterior slid forward, as though moving over his bones, pushed down, and then pulled. Each undulation moved him further through the muck.

"Like a slug," Garbarino said.

"Shut up!" Vicano shouted, scooting forward another foot. "You'll never look as good as me."

"He's not a survivor," Mia said.

"Shut up!" Vicano shouted.

Mia stepped back again, this time stepping over a trail of rot. "He died during the launch and came back, as this."

When they reached the edge of the rot and backed up the hill, Vicano grew furious. "Get back here!" he screamed. "I'm better than all of you! I'm going to fucking eat you!" When Vicano reached the edge of the rot, he opened his mouth and bit the dry leaves in front of them. As he chewed, they could see the leaves rot in his mouth. He swallowed and a moment later, the rot oozed from his anus.

Mia covered her mouth. "Oh my God."

"Fuck," Garbarino said, staggering back. Austin caught him and pulled him up.

Vicano quickly ate, shat and slithered his way toward them, but was far too slow to ever catch them. Between mouthfuls, he shouted, "Get... back...here! You don't deserve to walk! You're not good enough!"

They left him there, chewing a new trail of muck, rotting the earth with his touch, and they never once regretted not gaining access to the supplies inside the EEP. Despite the food, weapons and shelter just a stone's throw away, despite being hunted by a horde of killers and Henry Masters, and despite losing everyone they cared about, they did not share Robert Vicano's fate.

And that counted for something.

42

They walked in silence for nearly an hour after leaving Vicano behind, each digesting what they'd seen in their own way. But not one of them wanted to talk about it. Finally, Mia broke the silence. "Maybe he'll slow them down?"

Austin, who was still in the lead, looked back. "Who?"

"Vicano," she said. "Maybe the killers, or Masters, will walk into the rot and be eaten by it." It was the only silver lining she could think of—the only way her mind could come to terms with what she'd seen. If Vicano's fate somehow saved them, she might be able to live with it.

"Maybe," he said.

"Somehow I doubt we'll get that lucky," Garbarino said.

"I know. I just—"

A loud snap interrupted her. Austin disappeared, falling from view with a shout.

Mia dashed after him, but Garbarino caught her arm. "Joe, let me—" She looked down and saw an eight foot drop. Austin lay at the bottom, rolling onto his back and catching his breath. She looked back at Garbarino.

"Thanks."

"Don't mention it, he said.

Although Austin had been the group's champion, Garbarino continued to surprise her. She and Austin had him pegged as trouble from the beginning. He'd nearly shot Paul while they were in orbit and had seemed to be on the verge of a nervous breakdown. But his hopelessness-fueled breakdown had slowly reversed as things got worse. Not only had he saved her life on one occasion, and cared for Elizabeth, but they had somehow become friends. She couldn't say that for Austin, with whom she'd connected initially—as things got harder for the group, his skin got thicker, his personality more abrasive.

Garbarino knelt by the hole in the ground and peeked in. Austin lay on a cement floor. A sagging wooden framework hung above him. "Looks like an unfinished foundation," he said. "Branches and leaves collected on top. As good a place to rest as we're going to find."

Austin looked around the dim space. Tiny shafts of light filtered through the foliage cover, illuminating the cement floor, which held its own leafy carpet. Dry organic dust filled the air and tickled his nose, but it was safe. They couldn't be seen from the outside, even from a few feet away, and he doubted they could be smelled with the heavy scent of earth concealing their scent. As long as someone didn't fall in like he had, they would be safe. "We'll sleep for a few hours and then keep moving."

Garbarino helped Mia into the hole created by Austin's fall. After plucking a bushel of dead ferns, he slid inside and used the ferns to cover the hole. "There," he said. "Home sweet home."

After arranging some leaves into a poor excuse for a bed, Mia lay down. Austin sat, head against the cool stone wall. Garbarino lay down on his stomach, arms under his head. Each one of them was lost in thought, Austin about their next move, Garbarino about the book Austin had thrown away, and Mia about the fate that Collins deserved. But none of them lasted longer than thirty seconds before falling asleep.

Six hours later, Mia stirred. Not asleep, but not quite awake, her thoughts drifted in that vivid place between dreams and reality. Memories came and went, unhindered by mental filters.

"Do you, Mia Durante, take Matthew Brenton to be your lawfully wedded husband?" Elizabeth smiled. It had taken her five tries to make it all the way through the questions without stumbling.

"I'll think about it," Mia replied.

"Auntie Mia!" Liz shouted. "That's not what you're supposed to say."

Mia slipped off the shoes she had just tried on and handed them back to the saleswoman. They had been shopping all day, picking out the bridesmaids dresses and the flower girl's dress, and they had a second fitting for the wedding dress. They'd just had lunch and had moved onto her post-wedding outfit, the one her sister Margo insisted brides wear between after the reception and before the actual honeymoon began. No bride actually wears her honeymoon night lingerie under the wedding dress. "Too much sweat, make-up and aching feet," she'd said. "You'll probably shower and sleep before even thinking about getting nasty."

Mia had conceded the point. She and Matt had been living together for a while and "getting nasty" was a regular occurrence. A shower and nap wouldn't be out of the question, for sure. So she'd gone along with the notion of picking out an outfit only to discover that she'd either gained a few pounds, all in her feet, or the Thai she'd had for lunch was making her feet swell.

She smiled at Liz. "Hey, you're the flower girl. You don't have to ask any questions."

"But I want to make sure you know the answers."

"Which are?"

Liz stomped her foot on the floor and made a face that showed one part smile and one part wide-eyed snarling animal. "Aunt-tee!"

Mia laughed. "Okay, okay."

"Do you," Elizabeth started again, her voice proper. "Mia Durante, take Matthew Brenton to be your lawfully wedded husband?"

Mia said, "I do," as the memory faded, replaced by a new one.

Her hair hung over her face so she couldn't see his. But she could feel him beneath her. She gripped his chest as she rolled her hips over him. Her back tensed as she moaned and pushed harder. He responded by holding her hips and adding the strength of his arms to each thrust. She arched back with a release of energy, lost in the moment.

When the feeling faded, she leaned forward again, hands on the bed sheets. She put an arm under her sweat dampened hair and flung it back, looking into his eyes.

The wrong eyes.

Matt's were brown. Those eyes were blue.

But he didn't see the look of horror in her eyes as he laid her back and satiated his own desires. Each thrust was like a stab wound. When he finished, she ached, physically and emotionally. She had betrayed the man she loved and though they weren't yet married in the eyes of the law, she'd always felt that the bond they shared was equal. She would wear a scarlet A for the rest of her life. No one but her would see it. Some would even applaud it. But she would never forgive herself for it.

Recent memories blotted out her betrayal. Violence and death overshadowed her carnal act. The dead, but not dead, faces of White, Vanderwarf, Paul and Chang stared at her. Then the dead who stayed dead; Mark the priest, Collins the president and Elizabeth the child.

Mark's last words echoed in her mind. ""You're not ready! None of you are ready. It's too soon. Too soon!"

Not ready, she thought. For what?

But the other implication of his statement sought to control her thoughts. Mark wasn't worried about himself because he felt ready? Or was he just being selfless, worrying about his brother? But Mark didn't come back. And Paul did.

And what about Elizabeth? She was just a child. How could she have figured things out and gotten ready for something the rest of them missed?

"Only the child will be spared!" The memory of Pastor Billy Jackson's screeching voice nearly snapped her wide awake. "The child," he had said. "The child is innocent. Not yet tainted by the world. Not yet able to understand the choice...the choice..."

What choice? She thought. Were he and Mark talking about the same thing? And if so, why had Mark stayed dead while the Pastor lived on? It's a choice, she reminded herself. Knowing the options isn't enough. You have to choose the right one.

But what are the options? How can you choose if you don't know?

Images of Collins filtered into her thoughts. How did he know? No single person before him could claim to have killed so many. He caused a world-wide genocide that resulted in this twisted new Earth where people are tortured and killed only to be brought back repeatedly. Murderers are prey to former average Joes, who are now horrified by their awful deeds. Peace activists are killing machines. A pastor living the high-life by putting God up for sale is dressed as a king and is incapable of eating. And what about the people in the lake, drowning again and again? What had they been before?

It didn't matter. The question that needed to be answered wasn't what all those tormented people chose that led them here, it was what the few who didn't come back chose that let them escape.

What did Collins say before he died?

"Redemption."

She remembered wondering how he could expect such a thing. The idea was ludicrous. But then he hadn't come back. Renewed anger pumped adrenaline into her system. Her eyes fluttered as she came out of her near-sleep.

But then she remembered something. The last thing Collins said wasn't, "Redemption," it was, "Forgive me."

The memory became crystal clear as she woke. "Forgive me," he had said as she clutched his shirt. But there was something odd about the statement she hadn't placed at the time. He wasn't looking at her. He wasn't talking to her.

"You're not ready," Mark's voice repeated. "None of you are ready!"

"The child is innocent," Pastor Billy said. "Not yet able to understand the choice."

Not ready.

Mia sat up fast, sucking in a deep breath. "I'm not ready!"

The dim world came into focus around her. Shimmering light from the heat lightning above danced on the floor where it shone past the leafy covering. Garbarino and Austin leaned against the wall to her side. Austin's eyes were wide, an index finger to his lips. Both men held their weapons.

A cracking of dry foliage above confirmed her fears. Someone was out there.

"Hello?" came a woman's voice.

Mia slowly drew her handgun.

"Hello-o." The woman's sing-song voice sounded friendly enough, but here, in this place, nothing was what it seemed.

The woman giggled. "Come out, come out, wherever you are."

The light above Garbarino and Austin was blocked out.

Mia looked up and saw a shadow. She followed the shape up, seeing bits and pieces of the woman's body, and then her face. Their eyes met through a grapefruit-sized hole in the cover. The woman's eyes widened with a smile. "Aha! There you are."

43

"Now where'd you go off to, hon?" the woman said after Mia ducked away and joined Austin and Garbarino against the wall. Her voice was sweet and tinged with a southern drawl. Mia imagined she'd been a waitress in some cute diner before the world went to shit.

When dust fell from above and scattered on top of Mia, she realized that if the woman got any closer she might fall on top of them.

Austin realized this too and crouch-walked to the covering of dead ferns. He pointed to Garbarino, locked his fingers together and made a heaving motion. Garbarino nodded, locked his fingers together and held his hands down low.

As Austin put a foot in Garbarino's locked hands, Mia figured out the plan. "Don't shoot her if you don't have to," she whispered.

"Hello-o," the woman sang.

Gun in hand, Austin nodded to Garbarino. Faster than Mia thought possible, Austin launched up, exploded through the ferns and rolled onto the forest floor. He came up fast, gun raised, and he drew a bead on the woman's forehead. If Austin wanted to, he could have killed her and been done with it.

But he didn't.

"Oh!" the woman said. "You gave me such a start."

Austin stared at the woman. She stood stark naked and would have been beautiful if she wasn't covered in blood and filth. She stood a little over five feet tall, had wavy blond hair and a voluptuous body. Despite the grime, Austin found himself staring. Since returning to earth, she was the only pleasant thing he'd seen.

She smiled at him, oblivious to the weapon pointed at her. "Don't just stand there, come and give me a hug."

The strangeness of the request snapped Austin back to reality. As she took a step toward him, he said, "Stop! Stay right there."

The woman complied. "Whatever you say."

Mia rose out of the concealed foundation and took Austin's offered hand. Garbarino leapt up and pulled himself out. They saw the woman at the same time.

"Whoa," Garbarino said.

"She's beautiful," Mia added.

Austin nodded, but pointed out what her beauty concealed. "And covered in dry blood."

"Aren't you all as sweet as apple pie," she said. "I do try to look my best."

"Is she one of them?" Garbarino asked in a hushed tone.

Austin shook his head. "Don't think so."

"How do you know?"

Mia stepped toward the woman. "She hasn't tried to kill us yet."

"Then what's her deal?

"What's your name?" Mia asked the woman.

"How rude of me. Not introducing myself." She stomped forward, breasts swaying, hand extended in greeting. "Melissa. Melissa Rose."

As Mia reached out and took the woman's hand, she heard the hammer of Austin's weapon click into place. If the woman attacked, it would be the last thing she did. But she just shook Mia's hand. "Pleasure to meet you, Miss...?"

"Durante," Mia said. "Mia Durante." The greeting was as pleasant as any Mia had experienced except that, given the circumstances and her nakedness, it felt totally inappropriate. "Do you want some clothes?"

Melissa looked down at herself. She seemed oblivious to her nude body and the blood covering it. "I don't know."

Garbarino unbuttoned his outer shirt and took it off. It wasn't much cleaner than the woman's body, but the extra-large shirt would hang to her thighs. He handed it to Mia, who gave it to the woman.

"Put this on," Mia said.

The woman took the shirt, put it on and buttoned it up. "Aren't you all polite."

With Melissa clothed, her strangeness diminished a little and the group relaxed. Austin lowered his weapon, but didn't holster it.

"What are you doing here?" Mia asked.

Melissa looked around as though seeing the woods for the first time. She shrugged. "Out for a walk, I guess."

"How did you survive?" Austin asked.

"Survive what?"

Austin's grip on his weapon tightened.

Mia placed a hand on his arm. "Maybe she's in shock."

"What do you do for work?" Mia asked.

"Department store. I run the register. We just got some of them new color TVs in."

"Color TVs?" Garbarino said.

The woman's eyes widened. "Don't tell me you haven't seen them yet."

Austin pointed beyond the woman. "Can you go wait over there while we talk?"

"Sure thing," the woman said. She turned and walked away.

"Wait," Mia said.

The woman stopped.

Austin gave her a look that asked what she was doing.

"Why don't you sit right there," Mia said.

The woman sat. "Whatever you say."

Mia drew her gun and walked toward her.

"What are you doing?" Garbarino asked, his voice full of concern.

"She's not like the others," Mia said. "But she's one of them."

As Mia stopped behind the woman, Austin asked. "How do you know?"

Mia raised the gun and placed the barrel of it against the woman's head. "Do you know what I'm holding?"

"A gun," the woman replied.

"You know what it can do?"

The woman's head bumped against the barrel as she nodded. If Mia had her finger on the trigger it might have gone off.

"It doesn't concern you? Me having a gun against your head?"

The woman turned around, all smiles, so that the gun was now against your forehead. "Course not, darling. I trust you."

"You just met me," Mia said.

"You seem nice enough."

"I have a gun to your head."

"You have kind eyes."

"I'm going to fucking blow your brains out."

Without a moment's pause, the woman said, "I trust you."

Mia stepped back and put her weapon away.

"Weird," Garbarino said. "She's cursed with blind trust?"

"The world being how it is," Austin said, "that's probably not a good thing. Given the dry blood on her body, I'd say she's already trusted the wrong people more than once already."

A question snuck into Mia's thoughts. Pastor Billy, Henry Masters and the serial killer had all become the extreme opposite of what they had been before, perhaps even what they had detested. What could make a woman trust complete strangers, or even people that wanted to tear her to pieces? "What's the worst thing you've ever done?" Mia asked.

Melissa looked at her. "What do you mean?"

"You're greatest...sin. What is it?"

"That's simple, hon." The woman shifted, getting comfortable as she stared off into the distance, remembering her previous life. "I was thirty two. My husband was fifty five. He robbed the cradle. Everyone said so, even though I was a grown woman. But I was really the one robbing him."

"You're a thief?" Garbarino asked.

"Heaven's no. He was rich. And I spent his money on whatever tickled my fancy. But he got what he wanted, too. She motioned to her body. I was his whenever he wanted. I did whatever he wanted. Even pretended to like it. But I'm a woman, you know? Despite his voracious appetite for sex, he wasn't fulfilling my needs."

Mia tensed. She didn't like the story's direction.

"Our staff was mostly women, but there was a young man—well, my age. He worked in the kitchen." Her body shivered at the memory. "My husband found us in the pantry. I was leaned over a hutch, dress hiked up. He'd come home early. Heard me shouting and thought I was being hurt. We never heard him come into the kitchen and I'm not sure how long he watched. But when I...you know...he took a knife, placed it over his heart and shoved it in. Turns out the old man actually loved me."

Mia took a step back and sat down. Her head spun and her stomach twisted. This is my fate, she thought. This is what I'll become if I die... when I die.

A hand on her shoulder drew her wet eyes up. "You okay?" Garbarino asked.

Mia barely heard the question as she fought the urge to vomit. Her body shook.

Melissa stood up, excited, and unfazed by her story or Mia's reaction to it. "Do you hear that?"

The group fell silent. Distinct voices reached them, despairing, horrified voices. The horde was closing in.

Melissa hopped up and down, clapping her hands. "More friends!" she said and then shouted, "Over here! We're over here!"

44

"Quiet!" Austin hissed.

Melissa smiled and said, "Okey-doke, artichoke."

But it was too late. The voices had grown louder in response to the woman's shout. They were coming.

A woman's voice reached them from the distance. "I'm so sorry!"

Melissa waved her hand toward the voice. "Pish! Get on up here and—"

Austin clapped his hand around the woman's mouth. She laughed. "We're going to play hide and seek," he said.

Melissa gave a vigorous nod.

"You know how to play right?"

She continued nodding.

"Stay as quiet as possible. Our friends are going to try to find us. But we have to stay quiet. Okay?"

She nodded six more times and then stopped. Austin removed his hand. The voices grew louder.

"We gotta go," Garbarino said.

"Is there a place we can hide?" Austin asked Melissa.

She pointed to the concealed foundation. "Down there worked great!"

"Someplace further away," Austin said. He'd considered returning to the hidden foundation, but if they were found, they'd be trapped. And while Melissa trusted all of them implicitly, he couldn't trust that she'd stay quiet. Besides, with so many people tracking them, one of them would surely stumble across their hiding spot. "Someplace with lots of hiding spots."

"Oh, yes," she said. "I grew up near here. In a city. Lots of places to hide."

The voices were getting loud, fast. Henry Masters hadn't announced his presence yet, but none of them doubted he was out there, hunting them.

"Good enough," Austin said. "Can you take us there?"

"This way." To Austin's relief she headed away from the voices. He followed her.

Garbarino took Mia's arm and tried pulling her up. But she didn't want to stand. Her will to live had been decimated by Elizabeth's death. She'd been acting on survival instincts since then. But now, knowing what she would become upon her death, all hope had left her. Her betrayal of Matt had cursed her to a life of perpetual violence. She saw herself wandering the woods naked, trusting everyone she came across, murdered, mutilated and raped for eternity.

Her body sagged in defeat, resigned to let the violence begin shortly. She deserved it.

"Get up," Garbarino said. "They're coming."

"Let them come," Mia said.

Garbarino got down close to Mia's ear. "Look, I get it. You fucked around on somebody and think you're going to end up like her. But we've all done bad things in our lives. Collins sure as shit did. Even the priest. Right now we're still alive and from where I'm sitting that means we have a chance to turn things around."

"I don't deserve it."

"None of us do," he said. "But some of us, for some reason, escape from this place and don't come back."

"Get moving!" Austin whispered back to them. Melissa wasn't stopping and he wasn't about to lose track of her.

"The way I see it," Garbarino said, "is that the people who don't come back go someplace else. If that's true, we'll see the people we lost."

"How can you be sure? My sister is probably here. My parents. Matt. What if they're all here?"

He took her chin and turned her face toward his. "There's no way to know about any of them, but I can say for certain that Elizabeth is not here. And wherever she is, she wants you to join her."

"What if you're wrong?"

"Then we die and stay dead. Cease to exist. That's still better than living here."

"Mark knew," she said.

The voices grew louder still. Garbarino looked into the woods. He couldn't see anyone yet, but he knew they were out there. He looked for Austin and found him nearly one hundred yards away, waving them on. He'd be out of view soon. "Knew what?" he asked.

"That we weren't ready. That we would stay here." She looked at the ground. "And that he wouldn't. He knew where we were. I figured it out this morning. Before I woke up."

Garbarino actually smiled. "I thought you were smarter than that."

"What?" she looked up at him, confusion in her eyes.

"I figured it out two days ago." He picked her up and was relieved to find Mia helping this time. "We're in Hell."

"On Earth. But still alive."

He looked beyond her for any sign of the killers. He still couldn't see anyone, but heard the crack of branches beneath their feet. "And for some reason, we've been given a second chance to make things right."

"I'm not sure that's possible. Not after what I did."

"A question to be answered another day," Garbarino said. He ducked low and pulled her down. The top of someone's head was moving beyond a distant ridge. "And to answer it, we need to live. Are you with me?"

"Let's go," she said.

The pair hurried away, keeping low to the ground. But Austin was no longer in sight. Garbarino led them toward where he'd last seen Austin, but there was no way to know if Melissa had kept the same course. Once they were positive they were out of sight of the mob, they sprinted through the woods.

Three hundred feet later, they stopped. There was no sign of Austin or Melissa. "Dammit," Garbarino said.

"I'm sorry," Mia said.

Garbarino shot her a stern look. "Don't say that."

"But it's my—"

"I know it's your fault, but it makes you sound like one of them." He motioned behind them, toward the voices. "Scared the shit out of me."

An aberration on one of the trees caught her attention. "Over here," she said. The dead bark had been pulled away and dropped on the ground. Knowing what to look for, she searched the area and found a second tree in the same condition, leading away from the voice. Then a third. "He left a trail."

"Let's hope we're the only ones smart enough to follow it," he said before following the trail himself.

They moved swiftly, doing their best to stay quiet while increasing the distance between themselves and the wall of voices. The woods ended abruptly and opened up into a patch of dirt on a rise where the trees had recently been cleared. Austin and Melissa were there, laying on their stomachs, looking over the edge of the rise.

Austin rolled onto his back at their approach and thrust his handgun in their direction. Once he saw their faces, he relaxed and motioned for them to get down.

Mia and Garbarino crawled up to the edge of the rise and lay on their stomachs. The view below them made them wish they'd taken their chances in the abandoned foundation. A city stretched out before them. Tall buildings now in ruins stood in the middle. A line of old, red brick mills lined a river filled with yellow, stagnant water that no longer flowed. Inner city buildings mixed with malls surrounded that. Suburbs lay beyond. A construction site sand pit lay directly below, and that, thankfully was devoid of movement.

The rest, however, was hell.

45

A piercing scream turned Mia's gaze to the street that crossed the far end of the construction site. A woman ran across the pavement, one way, and then the next—a frantic retreat. "She's like Dwight Cortland. A runner."

"But what's she running from?" Garbarino asked.

"More friends," Melissa answered, pointing further down the road where a crowd of killers streamed into the road and gave chase.

The runner went into convulsive fits as the apologetic shouts of the killers reached her. She started in one direction, but a loud shout startled her and she turned around. This happened twice until she had become so blinded by raw panic that she ran into the arms of the killers.

"They're not your friends," Garbarino said to Melissa.

She waved a hand at him. "Pish. Look, they're hugging her."

The runner disappeared beneath the mass of clawing, horrified killers. Mia was thankful for the distance between, not just because they were hidden from the mob, but because they couldn't hear the tearing of skin or smell the fresh blood. "Did they somehow get past us?" she asked.

"Those are the same people that have been tracking us," Austin said. Before she could ask him how he knew, Austin pointed deeper into the city. "Watch the streets. And listen."

Mia focused on the city beyond. Then she saw it.

There were hordes of killers everywhere, their screams creating a high-pitched white noise in the background she hadn't noticed before. Running in front of most crowds was a single person, sometimes a pair. More runners. A wail cut through the background noise. Mia saw nothing, but recognized the roar as being similar to that of the hunter, Henry Masters. A second cry answered the first from the other side of the city.

The mob below moved on, most of them now weeping in anguish for what they'd just done. They left a mangled body in their wake—torn limbs, a pool of blood and a trail of entrails. Mia was once again thankful for the distance that obscured the gruesome details. But when the body started moving, she longed to be closer, to see how it happened. From a distance she could only register the subtle movements below. Then the woman rolled over, coughing. She pushed herself to her hands and knees while looking all around her, the panic returning, perhaps with a fresh memory of how she'd just died. She got to her knees, gathering her trailed, eviscerated intestines and stuffing them back in her gut. Assembled once more, she stood and ran.

Straight toward them.

"She's going to lead them to us," Garbarino said.

Mia tensed.

She had as little desire to meet this runner as she did the killers

"Maybe she'll turn around."

"Hey friend!" Melissa shouted. While Mia, Austin and Garbarino were distracted, the woman had stood and cupped her hands to her mouth.

The runner below screamed and turned around, bolting back out of the construction site.

Melissa took a deep breath and opened her mouth to shout again. Austin rose up behind her, a large rock in his hand. He swung the stone around and cracked it against the side of her head. The woman dropped to the ground, silenced, but not unconscious. She stared at Austin with the eyes of a woman betrayed. Tears ran down her dirty cheeks, leaving clean streaks. Her jaw shuddered as she began to weep. "How could you?" she said, "Why did—"

Austin struck her again.

This time she fell silent as blood gushed from a dent in the side of her head. He crouched down again and looked at a shocked Mia and Garbarino. "Sometimes to save people you have to hurt other people, the latter of which I'm not sure she even qualifies as anymore."

When neither of them replied, he added, "Don't worry, she'll be back to her trusting self in no time."

That resonated with Mia and Garbarino.

Despite not being violent, she was one of them, one of the damned, destined to be betrayed for an eternity.

A scream turned their attention back to the road. The runner had been caught again. The horde did their work, tearing the runner apart. Thirty seconds. That's all it took. Then they were moving on again, leaving human road kill and a fresh stain of blood.

The whole world is going to be covered in blood soon, Mia thought. Then the female runner collected her body, waited for it to finish knitting together, stood and ran toward the city where several more killer mobs and at least two hunters waited.

"We can't go down there," Garbarino said.

Austin stared out at the hellish city. "No choice."

"The fuck there isn't," Garbarino said.

"He's right," Mia said.

Austin turned toward them, his face grim. "You both need to start listening to things or you're not going to last much longer."

Mia and Garbarino both held their breath and listened.

Tortured screams from panicked runners drifted out of the city first, mixing with the background noise of the thousands of killers. The occasional roar cut through the din. But there was something else. The voices of the killers grew steadily louder. But the noise wasn't coming from the city.

It came from behind them.

From the forest.

The horde of killers pursuing them since they'd dropped from the sky would soon be upon them.

Mia felt a sudden and rising panic and for a moment knew what it felt like to be a runner. She nearly got up and ran like a wild woman. Instead, she controlled her fear and asked, "Why are they still following us?"

"Dunno," Austin said and then pointed to the city.

"Maybe they can sense we're still alive?" Garbarino said. "Maybe it draws them toward us."

"Let's hope not." Austin motioned to the city. "Because we need to find a way through. If we can stay hidden long enough, and make it through the city, they'll get distracted by the other killers, or runners."

Garbarino nodded, but Mia wasn't so sure. The horde tracking them had killed Dwight the serial killer and Pastor Billy and hadn't looked back. The distraction was only momentary. This horde and Henry Masters had eyes for them and them alone. Maybe Garbarino was right. Maybe they were attracted to the living. Or maybe Masters remembered Austin and Garbarino from his former life as a war protester and was following them out of spite. It didn't really matter. They were all dead eventually.

What did matter was what happened post-death. Would she wake up like Melissa, become one of the mob and kill her friends? Or would she stay dead? I'm not ready, she thought.

"If forward is the only direction we have left, then let's start walking before we have to run. I don't know about you two, but I don't want to run head long into a mob of killers. Doesn't work out so well for the runners."

Mia moved into a crouch, looking for the best way down the ridge into the construction site. From there they would have to cross the road, a few neighborhoods, and the yellow river. Then they would have to pass through the core of the ruined city.

"Are we going somewhere," said a sugary sweet voice. Melissa had returned, all smiles and trust, Austin's betrayal forgotten.

Austin looked at the other two and made a face that said, "See!"

A shout from the woods behind them made everyone freeze. The horde was close.

Austin spoke fast. "Down the hill as fast as you can. Stay close to the sand piles in the construction site. We know there's a second group of killers close by so we'll need to scope out the road for cover, then stay close to the houses in the neighborhood."

A stick snapped in the woods.

"Melissa," Austin said.

She turned to him, smiling wide. "Yes, hon?"

"You have friends waiting for you in the woods. Go run and see them."

Mia and Melissa gasped in unison, Mia in shock, Melissa with excitement. Then the woman was up and running. As she disappeared into the woods, Austin slid over the edge and started down. Mia and Garbarino followed.

"That was messed up," Garbarino whispered to Mia.

She nodded in agreement, but when Melissa shouted, "Hey there, cutie-pie," a moment later, she knew the distraction Melissa would cause just might save them. Hopefully long enough for her to get right with whatever creator was sick enough to conceive a hell like this, but merciful enough to provide a way out.

"What are you doing?" Melissa said, her voice tinged with an uncharacteristic fear. "Why would you—that hurts!" The scream that came next chased them down the hill and haunted their thoughts as they entered the construction site.

46

Austin led the way through the mountains of sand, gravel and shattered stone strewn around the construction site. He did his best to keep their position concealed from the horde behind them, but he also had to worry about the killers stalking the road. He stopped at the bottom of a large mound of sand and crouched, waiting for Mia and Garbarino to catch up.

"We clear up ahead?" Garbarino asked, hiding behind a toppled over, rusty bulldozer. The road lay twenty feet away.

Austin hadn't seen nor heard any killers ahead and gave a nod. "How's our six?"

"Haven't seen anyone," Garbarino replied. "But the sand piles are blocking out the sound.

Austin listened. Garbarino was right.

The giant man-made sand dune was muting the shouts and screams of the killers behind them. "Once we hit the road, keep running until we reach the river."

"Banking on them not being able to swim?" Garbarino asked.

"And hoping there isn't a bridge nearby, yeah."

Mia frowned. She knew they didn't have a lot of options, but she wasn't keen on the river plan. "And if there are drowners?"

"We'll wait for them to drown."

A miniature avalanche of sand slid down the sand mound behind Austin. Mia traced its path with her eyes. "Look out!" she shouted before drawing her weapon and firing two rounds. The first missed the man running down the sand-hill, but the second caught him in the chest. He spun hard, fell and crashed onto the hard packed dirt next to a wide-eyed Austin.

"Two more!" Garbarino shouted before popping off two shots and dropping a man and woman rounding the sand pile.

Austin stood and shoved Mia ahead of him. "Run!"

As they cleared the cover of the construction site, each looked back and each saw a human waterfall pouring over the ridge that they'd come down. The three they'd just shot had been the front runners.

The group at the top was suddenly struck from behind. Three of them shot into the air and fell. Then Henry Masters stood at the top of the ridge, his eagle looking more like a fiery phoenix, shimmering in the light of the continuous heat lightning.

Masters roared, scaring Mia enough to trip when she reached the pavement. She fell to her hands and skinned her knees. Garbarino stopped, took her by the shoulders and hoisted her. As he did, he looked down the long, straight road and saw an army charging toward them, drawn by the gun fire.

"Go," he said. "Follow Austin!"

Mia listened without hesitation. Austin had just entered the woods and she stayed right behind him. Thirty seconds later she noticed there weren't any footsteps behind her. She stopped and turned around. "Garbarino?"

He wasn't there. She looked back to the road, but couldn't see it, or Garbarino.

Austin stopped and turned around. "What happened?"

"He's gone."

Two gunshots rang out from the road followed by, "Come and get me, you sons-a-bitches."

The voices of the condemned responded, shouting their sorrows in unison.

"No!" Mia took a step back the way they'd come.

Austin caught her arm. "Nothing you can do for him now."

"But—"

"When a man sacrifices his life to save someone, it's reprehensible to throw that life away." Austin looked into her eyes, locking her in a stare that would have made a bull elephant think twice.

She pulled her arm away. "Fine. Let's go."

The woods thinned as they approached the residential neighborhood. The houses were mostly vinyl sided capes sporting two car garages. Most of the buildings leaned toward the woods as a result of being at the outskirts of a nuclear explosion's blast radius.

Austin climbed over a small white picket fence and made his way into the backyard of the nearest house. A swing set lay on its side behind an above ground swimming pool that had burst. "Stay away from the houses," he said. "They look like they could fall if a butterfly lands on them."

Mia slid over the fence. "Good thing there aren't any butterflies left in the world."

Austin frowned at her, but said nothing. He led the way through five more backyards before stopping behind the second to last house on the street. He hugged the back wall and peeked around the corner. Mia knelt next to him.

He held a finger to his lips, pointed first at his eyes and then around the corner.

Mia took a peek and saw a man, skinny and frail looking. He leaned against the olive-green sidewall of the next house between the brick chimney and red bulkhead, catching his breath. It's a runner, she thought, and where there are runners, there are—

"I don't want to do it!" a shrill voice cried out. "Someone stop me. Please, God, someone stop me!"

The runner yelped at the sound of the voice, but remained stuck in place, shaking uncontrollably.

Austin swore under his breath. "He's going to lead them straight to us."

Hearing the question buried within the statement, she wondered the same thing, should we use him as a decoy? She nodded. Austin jumped from this hiding place and shouted at the man. "Gah!"

The man jumped up from his hiding place and ran into the road, making for the opposite side of the street. The response was instantaneous. A chorus of voices rose up and whatever horde was hunting on the opposite side of the neighborhood, between them and the river, gave chase. They'd catch and kill him, again, but it would clear the way for those still living.

As they ran past the last house on the street and headed for the stand of maple trees that concealed the river bank beyond, Mia wondered if agreeing to such a brutal distraction would make her escape from this place less likely. She was already an adulterer in her own eyes. Was she an accessory to murder now? No, she thought, he's already dead.

The man's scream ripped into her. Not dead, she told herself, damned. And if she didn't find time to stop and think things through, she would be one of them soon enough. The woods across from the neighborhood greeted her with thorns, scratching her exposed skin and tugging against her clothes. She fought against the clinging vines and pain, following Austin's broad back. The man moved like a tank, never slowing even through the thickest of the thorns. He just grunted and pushed forward.

She wondered how he kept going. She was the only one left for him to protect. When she died—she had no doubt Austin would outlast her— what would he do? With no one left to save, what would Austin have to live for?

Before she could dwell on the question, they emerged from the woods, standing above a strip of water-worn brown stones. Beyond the stones lay the stagnant yellow river. And beyond that, the opposite shore where a concrete staircase led up a steep slope to the back of a massive brick mill.

She could visualize the place in its heyday. Acrid smoke rising from the ten smokestacks. Laborers at work. The river thick with pollution. Maybe it had been a shoe factory. A tannery. A rubber plant. Whatever the bright red remnant of the industrial revolution had been before, it now promised refuge from the killing fields of the city streets. And she wanted nothing more than to find some dark corner inside where she could get herself right with God.

But it seemed God had other plans.

The surface of the yellow river rippled. A pale body bobbed to the surface. Then another. Hundreds more followed. The drowners. She sat down as the sea of people sputtered and screamed for help, tearing at each other, fighting for lives they couldn't possibly save.

Mia sat down on a large chunk of smooth granite and wept.

The desperation in the drowning voices struck a nerve. "What did they do?"

Austin looked at her. "What do you mean?"

"To deserve this?"

"Does it matter?"

"It does to me."

"The only thing that matters is the living. And I mean those of us that are really living. Not this." He pointed to the bodies as they sank back down beneath the water. "And right now, that's you and me. If we can lose the killers in the city and get clear, maybe we can—"

Mia laughed. "You don't really think we can survive this, do you? We're going to die. Sooner or later, probably sooner, we will both be killed. The only question is whether or not we'll come back, or stay dead."

Austin shook his head slowly. "I don't believe that. I can't give up on living. I won't let you die."

"This isn't living," Mia said. "And even if we aren't killed, we're not going to last much longer. When was the last time you ate? Or drank? We have no supplies, and I'm not about to touch that yellow piss of a river, are you?"

Austin stared at the water as the last of the bodies drifted back down.

"We have a day—maybe two—before we get dehydrated. It's time to face death, face God, and—"

"God," Austin said, his voice full of disdain. But he said nothing else. Instead he stepped toward the water. "They're back down. Now or never."

Mia contemplated staying. She still wasn't ready for death, and thought for sure the dead would rise up and drag her down again. But the horde might find her here, and surrounded by drowning victims wasn't exactly the best environment to sort out whether or not she deserved mercy. Because if she couldn't forgive herself for her betrayal, how could Matt. How could God?

If there even was a God. Maybe Austin was right? Maybe there were other survivors further north. If this was just the way the world had become and the dead simply ceased to exist, shouldn't she fight to live, like him, instead of accepting death like some sort of religious martyr?

Austin slipped into the water, pushed out and began swimming. When he wasn't instantly pulled under, Mia followed him into the ammonia scented liquid and began swimming, keenly aware that each downward kick of her feet struck a drowner's floating limb and that sometime in the next minute or two, those limbs would start grappling for the surface, and anything, or anyone, on it.

47

It's piss, Mia thought. I'm swimming in piss!

Her water-logged clothes made swimming laborious, and her muscles burned from the effort. Each breath, tinged with the smell and taste of ammonia, combined with the water pressure around her chest made breathing hard. And then the yellow liquid sloshed into her mouth. She gagged, spitting and coughing. Treading water, her legs tangled down into the brown depths.

"Don't stop!" Austin said from the far shore. He'd just pulled himself out of the water.

But Mia didn't hear him. She was lost in disgust at first, and then her leg struck a body below her. Fingers grazed over her thigh. She shouted and kicked, but the wild motion only slowed her down. She struggled only ten feet from shore, but it could have been a mile as far as she was concerned. I'm not going to make it. I'm not going to—I'm not ready!

"Help," she sputtered, dipping under the water for a moment. She opened her eyes and saw heat lightning in the sky above, tinged yellow by the water. When she surfaced, her eyes burned and rainbow halos bloomed in her vision.

"Swim!" Austin urged.

She turned her body toward the shore and reached out to begin a stroke, but a small splash to her side drew her attention. A stark white naked body—man or woman she couldn't tell—had surfaced just a few feet away.

A cry, like some kind of animal, rose from her chest and exploded out of her mouth. It repeated when a second body rose up. "I'm not ready!" she shouted.

She felt a tug on her leg, like a fish testing a lure.

She kicked away, frantically reaching for the shore, moving slowly.

As more bodies rose to the surface, the first few to arrive began coughing and hacking, clearing their lungs of the foul liquid. The drowning would start soon, and she'd be caught in the middle of it.

She clawed for shore. A body rose up next to her. A man. He was large and sported a yellow-stained handlebar mustache. His dead, white eyes stared at her for a moment. He returned to life with a scream. He reached for her, wrapping his arms around her and pulling down, fighting to stay up.

Mia went under. Her mouth filled. She felt her gun fall out of her pants. It would be impossible to retrieve. Then, just as quickly as she'd been pulled under, she broke the surface. She saw flashes of Austin pounding the mustached man's face and felt herself dragged to shore. The hard warm rocks on the shore felt more comfortable than any bed she'd ever slept on, and she longed to sleep and forget this horrible world. But Austin wouldn't allow it.

He nudged her. "We need to move."

A large part of keeping people alive had to do with keeping them aware and moving. A slow, injured or unconscious person was nearly impossible to save, especially while on the run. When she didn't reply, he shook her shoulder.

She moaned in response.

He hated what he did next, but there was no choice. Austin took careful aim and slapped Mia square across the cheek. Her eyes burst open and she sat bolt upright. Before she could realize what had caused the pain, he got right down in her face and said, "Get up and get moving now or you will die." He took hold of her arm and yanked her to her feet, his former gentleness gone.

Austin's rough approach snapped Mia awake. She could see fear and anger in his eyes, but also concern. She was the last survivor under his care, and she could see that he was terrified she would die. She realized he felt more afraid of losing her than he did about his own death.

She stood on wobbly legs, found her balance and took a step toward the remains of an old concrete stairway. She took hold of the rusted railing and hung on it. Water poured from her clothes and while the coolness felt good, the smell clung to her. She wondered if she would ever be free from the stink, but when Austin nudged her up the stairs she realized she wouldn't have much time to care.

Mia took the first step and her leg shook from the effort. Kicking through the water combined with nearly drowning had sapped the life from her legs. But a single sentence from Austin propelled her up the stairs.

"I can hear them," he said.

Them.

The killers.

If they could get up the stairs and into the mills then maybe there was a chance the horde would lose track of them.

Mia tripped on a landing halfway up, where the staircase turned ninety degrees. She fell to her knees, reopening the skinned wounds. The sharp sting energized her. She pushed off the concrete, and launched up the stairs.

"Keep it moving," Austin encouraged.

They reached the top of the stairs a moment later, crouching behind the last few steps and looking over the top. They couldn't see anyone, but they heard plenty of voices, in front, and behind.

Austin looked back. The killers pursuing them had yet to reach the river. But he knew it wouldn't be long.

He stood and ran across the parking lot to the back of the mill. Mia followed. The long brick mill was falling apart in places, the result of the nearby nuclear explosion, but it looked solid enough—a fact they confirmed a moment later when Austin attempted to open a green metal door at the top of a short stairway.

"Locked," he said.

Mia moved on without waiting. She dropped down into a loading bay where a large green garage door led into the mill's basement. "Here," she said. She gripped the door's handle and pulled. It opened with a loud metallic groan. The sound made her cringe. Someone must have heard it.

The door jammed a foot from the ground.

"Good enough," Austin said.

He lay on his back and wriggled beneath the door.

Halfway through, he stopped and braced the door with his arms. "Slide under."

Loud voices echoed around the back of the mill. The loud garage door had attracted some nearby killers.

Mia dove for the door, dragging herself into the darkened interior.

Austin rolled inside behind her. The door dropped, bouncing to a stop. The voices arrived a moment later. The thick metal door muffled the words, but the apologetic tone was impossible to mistake. The bottom of the door hovered an inch from the floor, leaving a crack through which they could see daylight, and feet. The killers outside were inspecting the door. Feet shuffled back and forth. Hands slid across the rough metal. One of the killers, against her will, lay down outside the door, peering beneath the crack.

Austin and Mia lay only five feet away, but darkness concealed them. They could see the woman in the bright light of the heat lightning. Her dark brown eye searched the darkness for them, but the eyebrows were turned up with worry. Despite the fervor with which her body hunted, she wanted nothing to do with it.

When the woman's head shifted away and she stood, Mia sighed with relief. But a moment later, she heard hands grip the handle outside.

Austin saw what was about to happen and knew he had to act. But what could he do? Killing the people outside would be a temporary solution. A minute later they would be back on the hunt again, and they would know he and Mia were hiding inside. If he used his gun, the sound would attract even more killers. As the door started noisily sliding up, he acted without thought.

In two quiet strides, he reached the door, took hold of the handle on the inside and held it tight. The door stopped moving only an inch higher than it had been before, simulating a jam. The door shook as the killers outside tried two more times to pull it up, but Austin held steady. As long as one of the killers didn't look under again and see his feet, the jam might be convincing enough to turn them away. But a sharp breath from Mia coupled with a shifting shadow below denied him an easy escape.

He let go of the door and took a leap away. He stood still, holding his breath. The woman's eye returned, scanning the darkness.

Austin moved a hand to his handgun. If they tried the door again, while the woman was looking, they'd be found. The woman stood again and after a moment, the shadows outside the door moved away. A distant scream started them running.

Mia and Austin let out long breaths and stayed there, silent, in the dark for fifteen minutes. They felt safe in the quiet dark. Alone. Without a word shared between them, they lay down and fell asleep, exhausted from the chase.

As the first hour of sleep passed, the scuffling of several hundred pairs of feet shifted past the garage door. By the time they woke up, three hours later, the mill was surrounded.

48

When Mia awoke on the floor of the subterranean loading dock, she wasn't sure if she was really awake, or if this was part of some dark dream. When she heard the shuffling feet and familiar apologies uttered just outside the large garage door, any doubt that she was dreaming crumbled. The nightmare had not yet ended.

With her eyes adjusted to the dim light provided by the slightly open door, she searched the room. Buckets of old paint hung from hooks on the ceiling. There were overturned wheelbarrows against the far wall and buckets of old pavement sealant. Half of the garage floor was taken up by a five foot stack of crumbling tar roofing sheets, possibly removed from the roof at some point long in the past. The floor beneath her was covered in oil stains from years of leaky trucks.

No wonder it smells so bad in here, she thought, and then remembered that as bad as all the tar, paint and oil smelled, the odor lingering since her dip in the ammonia-stinking water was far worse, and impossible to escape.

Just like them, she thought, looking at the shadows shifting outside the door. She turned around to where Austin had been and found the floor empty. She spun around, searching for him, too afraid to even whisper his name.

She stood and found that while her legs, and most of her body, ached, the severe energy drain from crossing the river had faded. But a strong thirst scratched at her throat. She tried swallowing some spit to moisten her stinging throat, but there wasn't much.

Fear overrode her hunger and thirst. She turned toward the loading ramp at the back of the garage. A large doorway led to darkness beyond. Only way out, she thought, and headed for the door, her breath shaky with fear. Her hand scraped against the rough, cool bricks as she balanced herself on the wall. She stopped next to the door, afraid to enter the darkness alone.

But she had no choice. She could stay and wait for Austin, but she didn't know where he'd gone or when he might return. Maybe he'd even gone scouting for something to eat and been killed. If she stayed here much longer, listening to the killers just outside the garage door, she'd go insane long before she died of dehydration.

Mustering her courage, she turned toward the dark opening just as a large hand reached out for her. A scream built in her throat, but a second hand covered her mouth. Austin's face came out of the gloom next, worry lines on his forehead. After Mia had caught her breath and calmed, he whispered, "You scared the shit out of me."

"Likewise," she replied.

Austin motioned to the dark hallway. "I found a way upstairs."

"Did you go up yet? Is it clear?"

"I've only been gone a few minutes. Didn't want to go too far without you."

Mia took a deep breath and let it out slowly. "Thanks." She looked at the shadows moving at the base of the garage door. "When did they come back?"

Austin shrugged. "They were there when I woke up. C'mon, let's put some distance between us and them."

He took her hand. The warmth of his skin sent a shiver up her back and covered her arms with goose bumps. His strength and confidence reassured her. If he was right about finding other survivors, about eking out some kind of life in the north woods, she felt glad it would be with him. She followed him into the dark without question.

She couldn't see anything in the hallway, but Austin held onto her hand, navigating them past unidentifiable debris that smelled like dry mold and rust. When he stopped, she walked into his back and nearly fell. But he turned and caught her. "Careful. The stairs are just ahead."

In that moment of closeness, Mia didn't want to move. She didn't want to find out what was above them. She didn't want to run anymore. She just wanted to stay inside that safe embrace and never leave.

Austin removed his arms and pulled her a few feet further. She heard the creak of a stair as Austin put his weight on it. She saw the staircase in the dim light seeping through the cracks around the closed door at the top.

Austin took another step. The stairs creaked again, making both of them cringe. Any noise felt like too much noise.

"Try stepping on the outside of the stairs," she whispered. "The wood won't bend near the joint."

He stepped again, this time in silence. "Good trick."

"I grew up in an old house. Came in handy as a teenager when I came home at three in the morning." Mentioning the old house she grew up in reminded her of the home she and Matt had bought. The stairs there squeaked even worse. Getting up them without making a noise had been impossible. She'd thought about that just before screwing Matt's best friend. If her mom or Margo had come to visit and let themselves in she'd have heard them long before they reached the top stair. She'd locked the bedroom door, too, just in case. But every second gained would give him time to slip out onto the back porch and into the backyard where he could continue doing the yard work he'd come over to do. The memory chased away her thoughts of a future with Austin. She followed him up the stairs.

Austin stopped at the door, listening. When he heard nothing, he twisted the rough metal handle and gave the door a push. It swung open with a light squeak. The space beyond was a short hallway that led to either side. The dropped ceiling above was brown with water stains and the white walls were peeling, but nothing else seemed out of the ordinary.

Light streamed into the hallway from both sides and a gentle, stale breeze tickled their noses.

"Which way?" Austin asked.

"Up," she said, pointing to the staircase to their left that led to the second floor.

They took the stairs quickly and repeated the process until they reached the fourth floor. Mia felt herself relax a little, knowing that four flights of squeaky stairs separated them from the killers.

After exiting the last flight of stairs, Austin turned right and moved slowly down the hall, pausing when it opened up into the next room. The space beyond was huge. The floor and ceiling were constructed of huge pieces of timber, the kind that were plentiful when the mill had been built, but that people had paid a fortune for before civilization came to an abrupt end.

Large holes covered the floor where bolts had once secured heavy machinery. Aside from random pieces of junk, the space stood empty. Twelve-foot tall windows lined the left side of the room. Most were shattered. Glass covered the floor beneath them.

"Watch where you step," he said.

For a moment, his concern moved her. Then she realized he wasn't worried about her cutting herself. He just didn't want her to make any noise. And neither did she. They took a circuitous route through the room, avoiding the windows and broken glass by hugging the back wall.

They found a large metal door on rollers at the other side of the room. It led to a small, twenty by twenty space, perhaps for storage. An identical sliding door was on the other side of the room, this one closed and locked by a large metal latch. After entering the room, Austin gave the open door a shove and it rolled quietly. When the door was closed, he twisted the lock into place.

"Seems like a good place to rest and figure out a game plan," he said.

She nodded. The brick walls looked sturdy and the she doubted the killers could break down the metal doors. Four stories separated them from the world and provided a modicum of safety.

She looked out the room's single, large window, watching the heat lightning silently cut through the orange clouds. "It's kind of beautiful."

He stood next to her. "I remember nights like this. In the summer. Seems like a dream now."

A sharp scream reached up to them from below. Mia took a step toward it.

"Get down," Austin urged, heading toward the window in a crouch before lowering himself to his stomach and sliding over the shards of broken glass. Mia followed his lead and slid across the floor, moving slowly in an effort to stay quiet.

At first all they could see was the red brick apartment buildings across the street and the ruins of a few pint sized skyscrapers beyond. But when they shifted closer to the edge and were able to see straight down, they froze.

Hundreds of killers stood around the building. They swayed and murmured, displaying a behavior neither Austin nor Mia had seen before—stillness. That might not normally have bothered them. The killers not killing made them look human again. The problem was that every single killer below stood facing the mill.

Hundreds of eyes scoured the building.

Mia slid away from the window, her chest rising and falling quickly. "They're looking for us."

Austin moved back. "But they're not coming in."

She turned to him. "They're waiting."

"For what?"

"For us to a make run for it."

He frowned. "Or for us to die."

Mia agreed. Without food or water, it wouldn't be long. Maybe another day at the most. If the horde lost its patience and stormed the building, probably a lot less.

49

"You still don't think this is Hell?" Mia asked. She and Austin had retreated to the back wall of the sealed room and sat on the floor.

"That what you and Garbarino decided?" He traced his finger through the thick dust on the floor. "That this was Hell?"

Mia stayed quiet. The tone of Austin's voice made her feel stupid for bringing it up.

"As a metaphor, sure, this is hell. But the Hell? Things don't add up." He rubbed a ball of dust between his index finger and thumb. "I went to Sunday school and I don't see a pit of fire. I don't see demons. People have changed, sure. Become monsters. But I'm sure there is a scientific explanation for it. We doused the world in radiation, exposed humanity to forces beyond our comprehension. This is the result."

Part of Mia agreed with him.

She'd never believed in God before and knew she'd only started considering the possibility because she felt afraid to die. That's not all, she told herself, remembering the fates of their fallen friends.

"What about Paul and Mark? What about Chang, and White, and Vanderwarf, and Collins?"

"And Elizabeth," he said, his voice full of regret for not saving them.

"And Liz," she said. "Why did some of them come back and some of them stay dead?" She leaned her head against the hard brick wall behind her. The grout dug into her skin, but the pain kept her alert. "Mark clearly believed. And he didn't come back. Elizabeth was a child. The pastor knew she wouldn't come back."

"And Collins? You really think the person responsible for turning the world to hell would get a jail pass? He ends up in hell, has a change of heart and is what, forgiven for bringing about Armageddon?"

She hit her head against the wall in frustration, hardly noticing the sting of splitting skin. "Then what? Why did some of them come back as...as one of them and the others not come back at all? And why aren't there any children?"

"I'm not sure. Maybe it has something to do with genetics. Some people are susceptible to whatever change has taken place. Something in the atmosphere. Something we're breathing. And maybe there are no children because of their size. Maybe whatever changed the adults, killed all the children?" He traced his finger along the floor, adding a curved line to his drawing in the dust. "Maybe the zombie movies are right and it's a mutated disease."

A thought struck Mia hard. "Or something we ate." She looked at Austin. "Elizabeth only ate the food we brought with us. I didn't see Mark eat anything local either. What about Collins?"

"I didn't notice," he said. "I haven't eaten anything but what we brought. You?"

Mia knew the answer to that question as soon as she'd thought about food. "Cheez-Its. At the church. I shared a pack with Garbarino. Took another for Liz, but she never got to eat it."

"Then maybe it's the food."

Mia stared at the floor.

He gave her a pat on the knee. "But I doubt it."

She smiled at his kindness. "It was worth it, anyway. They were so good."

Austin chuckled. "You see? I can't believe this is hell when we can still laugh. How could hope exist in hell?"

"I don't know," she said. "Hell seems the perfect place for false hope." She sighed and added, "You still think we can escape? Find survivors up north?"

"It's less likely now that we're surrounded, but yeah, I think there are other survivors out there. We just need to find them."

It seemed a fantasy to Mia. How could people survive in this world? But she and Austin had. And if they could figure out a way past the killers outside and leave the city behind, maybe they would find survivors. "Canadians," she said.

"What?"

"They'll probably be Canadians." She looked at him. "The other survivors."

He smiled. "French Canadians," he said with mock disdain.

She smiled. "My mom's parents were French Canadians."

"I'm sorry," he said.

Mia nearly let out a loud laugh, but contained it. Despite her fear, the hunger gnawing at her belly, and the still fresh sadness of losing Elizabeth, she thought Austin was right. There still was hope. And that was something, wasn't it? If this were Hell, how could hope exist? "Assuming this isn't the actual Hell, what about God?"

"What about God?"

"Does He exist?"

"If he does, he's a sadist. The world was bad enough before. Believe me. Collins trusted me. I heard a lot about what goes on in the world that the general public never knows. It was a sick, sick place. And now? What kind of creator lets his creation go to shit? I'm not perfect. I've done bad things in my life, but I couldn't let a perfect stranger die, let alone be tortured for eternity. We're supposed to be God's children, right? How can someone who lets this happen to their children be good? Never mind worthy of worship."

Garbarino's words came back to her. "It's a choice."

"What?"

The memory of Garbarino's sacrifice filled her thoughts. He had no fear of death when he sacrificed himself to save them. And she envied that confidence as much as she longed for Austin's hope. "That's what Garbarino thought. It's a choice."

"Free will?"

"I guess."

Austin stood and rubbed his hands on his pants, leaving streaks of dust. "That's an excuse that people who believe in God use to excuse the inaction of a creator who doesn't care enough to save his creation."

She looked to where Austin sat and saw a smiley face drawn in the dust. How could he be so optimistic in the face of death? After all the people they'd lost already?

Austin approached the window slowly, hugging the brick wall on the left side of the room. He appreciated the conversation. It provided a welcome distraction from the fact that they were surrounded by enemies. But they needed a plan and they needed one soon. If they were going to survive this, and he believed that they would, they would have to move before they got too weak from hunger and thirst. If they could navigate the city, maybe find an abandoned grocery store, he thought they could resupply and keep moving.

The killers below hadn't moved yet. They just stood still, staring at the building.

"What are they doing?" Mia asked.

Austin stepped away from the window and leaned against the brick sidewall. "Waiting, I think."

Mia started toward him, walking slowly, careful not to step on any glass. "Waiting," she said, stepping over a floor board that looked loose. "For what?"

The wall behind Austin shook from an impact and bent inward.

Mia scrambled further away from it. "Is the building coming down?"

Austin never got a chance to answer.

Before he could realize what was happening, the wall exploded. Austin raised his hands to block his face as bricks burst into the room.

One of the bricks struck Mia's shoulder and knocked her to the floor. She winced as she pulled herself back up. A jolt of pain shot down her arm, but she forgot it a moment later when she saw a large hand reach through the hole in the wall and wrap around Austin's head.

"Run!" he shouted, his voice muffled. "RU—"

His voice was replaced by a sudden crack.

Austin's head burst. Skull fragments and brain matter oozed from between the oversized fingers. Austin's body went limp as blood poured over it.

Mia screamed like never before, wrapped in a blanket of primal fear, her mind retreated and terror was all that remained. She screamed again, but was cut short by the half face of Henry Masters, leaning in through the hole, his perpetual grin sending chills through her body.

She stepped back, body shaking, voice trembling as she wept.

As Masters watched her, she noticed his eyebrows were turned up instead of down. Despite his horrific state, his eyes revealed something other than the pure hate his body radiated. Sadness.

"Peace," Masters said, his voice a deep growl. The few sinews that held Austin's body up finally snapped. His body dropped to the floor, oozing blood from his open neck. The thick red liquid drained into the cracks between the floor boards and rolled toward Mia like miniature rivers.

She backed away, her shaking body making little progress.

Masters watched her for a moment and then opened his clenched fist. A bloody chunk of flesh and bone fragments fell to the floor with a splat. He looked down at it. "Peace," he said again.

A small portion of Mia's mind returned during that pause. She scrambled to her feet, ran to the opposite door and unlocked it.

The loud metal clang of the lock snapped Masters's head toward her. Eyebrows still knit with despair, he opened his mouth and let out a roar.

Mia fell to her knees. The point blank range of the blast twisted her insides. She vomited hard. Over the sound of her retching she heard pounding and falling bricks. But she couldn't stop her body from convulsing. Before she could even look up, a tight pressure wrapped around her body and squeezed.

50

Mia wasn't crushed into oblivion. She felt no new pain as something lifted her off the ground and put onto her feet.

"This way," said a voice.

A hard tug yanked her through the door she'd unlocked. She spilled into a dim hallway and through a blur of tears saw a man running ahead of her. She followed after him as the violent shaking behind her intensified.

A second roar sent her to one knee, but her rescuer was there in an instant, pulling her back up and shoving her forward. "Keep moving!"

Mia ran down the hallway, drunk with fear, stumbling and slipping, but somehow staying on her feet. When she reached an open side door, the man took her arm and pushed her in. A thin staircase led up.

"It goes to the roof," the man said.

Mia climbed the stairs while the man waited below. She opened the door at the top and toppled onto the mill roof. Sheets of peeling, rough tar stretched to the edges. The roof's uneven surface looked like waves, gently rising and falling where water and time had warped portions of it.

She heard the door at the bottom of the stairs close. Footsteps pounded on the stairs as the man took them two at a time. Then her rescuer spilled into the light and fell to his hands and knees, catching his breath, head turned down. When he looked up at her, she was shocked into silence.

Garbarino stood and reached out his hand. "C'mon," he said. "I know a way out."

"Joe?" she said, climbing to her feet.

The roof shook as something rumbled on the floor below them.

"There isn't much time," he said.

Mia squeezed him in a tight embrace. He squeezed her back, then pulled away. "Are you ready yet?"

The question confused her, but then she remembered her earlier fears of death, Hell and eternity. With Austin, those concerns had been buried by hope, but now, with him dead, her confidence began to wane. "No," she answered.

"Then let's move!" He ran to the far end of the mill, pulling her by the hand.

"How did you escape?" she asked as they ran.

"They followed me for a little while, but were more interested in the two of you. I crossed the river using a pedestrian walkway that led to a park."

They stopped at the edge of the mill roof. The next mill building in line was ten feet away. Mia was about to point out that neither of them could make the jump, but Garbarino was already picking up a long thick floorboard from the roof.

He saw her looking at the board. "This is how I got here."

"How did you know how to find us?"

Garbarino lifted the board up and slowly lowered it so that it bridged the gap between buildings. "At first—" He grunted as the board's weight strained his arms. He placed the board down. "I noticed the mobs had stopped chasing the runners and had all headed in a single direction."

As Garbarino adjusted the board so that each side had a foot overhanging the edge of a roof, she asked. "You followed them?"

"Not at first. I thought I was home free. But then I figured out they were headed in your direction. I saw them focused on the mill and figured you were inside. When I saw Masters go in, I found a way around and came to get you out."

"But why didn't they chase you?" she asked.

He shrugged. "There were two of you." He motioned to the board. "Go ahead."

The roof beneath them shook. A muffled roar rose up from below. Henry Masters was looking for them.

Mia climbed onto the thick, eighteen inch wide board. It should have been easy to cross, but the height was dizzying. And she could see killers below, still focused on the walls and windows of the building. If they looked up...

Mia pulled her arms and legs in close and crawled across the board. She moved quickly, holding her breath, and when she reached the other side, she stood and turned around. Garbarino was already half way across.

The doorway at the center of the mill they'd fled exploded. Henry Masters stepped onto the roof. He looked away from them, searching, and then turned toward them. With Garbarino only a few feet from the roof, Masters howled.

Mia dropped to one knee, clutching her stomach, which still reeled from the point blank roar she'd endured just a few minutes before. Garbarino slipped and fell. His stomach struck the board and he slid to the side. But as he rolled, he latched onto the board with his arms and legs. The board began to tip.

Masters charged across the roof, his heavy feet leaving dents in the tar behind him.

Mia saw the board tipping up and knew that if Garbarino hung from it, there was no way he'd get up in time. She jumped up and put her weight on the board. It slapped back down.

Garbarino pushed himself back up and crawl-sprinted the rest of the way across even as it shook from Masters's approach. When he jumped onto the far roof, Mia began running. When Garbarino didn't follow, she shouted back to him, "What are you doing?"

He yanked the board toward him and it fell between the buildings. "We need it!" He grunted as he hung onto it and pulled it up.

Masters was twenty feet away.

Mia returned and helped Garbarino lift the board. Just as it fell onto the roof between them, Masters reached the edge and jumped. His massive body rose up into the air, arching toward them, silhouetted by the heat lightning-filled sky.

They fell back, raising their hands as if to fend off the blow. But Masters dropped out of sight. The roof shook as his body struck the sidewall of the building.

Garbarino stood and took a step toward the edge.

A hand reached up and grabbed the brick overhang. The old wall shifted under the weight, but held. Masters was climbing up. When his other hand took hold of the ledge, Garbarino dropped onto his back, turned his feet toward the wall and kicked.

Mia saw what he was doing and sat next to him. They kicked the wall together, and each blow shifted it a little bit more.

Masters's head rose up over the small ledge and looked down at them. He let go with one hand and reached out for Mia.

"Kick now!" Garbarino shouted.

All four of their legs struck the wall at the same time. It shifted back slowly, bricks grinding as mortar loosened.

They kicked again and this time the wall fell away.

Masters didn't shout as he dropped. He simply stared at them, his sad eyes and hate-filled face glaring at them all the way to the ground. He crushed a group of killers when he landed. A hailstorm of bricks struck next, slamming down more killers who hadn't already helped break Masters's fall.

Garbarino picked up the long board. "There are four more mills to cross. If we can make it the rest of the way without being seen, we might have a chance."

A roar, similar to Henry Masters's, but somehow more powerful, tore through the air.

They turned to find a second hunter emerge from the mill behind them.

"How did he get back up so fast?" Mia asked.

"That's not Masters," Garbarino said.

Mia saw that the giant man had no tattoo on his chest. His face was deformed like Masters's—missing cheeks, a perpetual grin, and frightening, but sad eyes. The only features on his white, shirtless torso were three scars—one long, curved streak on his side beneath the ribs, and two circular scars on the opposite side.

As the giant charged, Garbarino stood still, unable to move.

Mia tugged at him.

Garbarino took a step forward, staring at the charging monster.

"Garbarino!" Mia shouted.

"Oh God," Garbarino said as he recognized the scars, that when turned sideways, mirrored the smiley face the man always doodled during meetings. "It's Austin."

51

Austin landed short, just like Masters. But the transformed Austin still had all the skills learned over years of Secret Service action. With one arm wrapped over the top of the building, he began pulling himself up.

Mia stared at Austin long enough to confirm his identity, and then took Garbarino by the arm. "Let's go!"

They ran together, heading for the far end of the mill where they could use the board to continue on to the next building. But between Mia's battered body and Garbarino carrying the long, heavy board, they didn't manage much more than a brisk jog.

Austin on the other hand, unhindered by pain or fatigue, pulled himself onto the rooftop and pounded after them like an oversized Olympic sprinter.

The roof shook beneath Mia's feet. She looked back and saw Austin gaining. "Can you shoot him?"

Garbarino looked down to the holster strapped beneath his left arm. "Only one shot left."

Both knew that one shot would do little to slow Austin. But what other choice was there? Garbarino dropped the board, drew his weapon and turned. But Austin was already there, raising a hand up to swat Garbarino.

A loud crack rang out, but Garbarino hadn't fired his weapon. Austin growled as the roof caved in beneath his weight. He slipped down through the hole as though being swallowed by quicksand.

Garbarino holstered his gun, retrieved the board and continued to the far side of the mill with Mia by his side. They reached the edge without further incident, but neither believed Austin or Masters had given up the chase.

As they laid the board across the divide between them and the next mill, Mia was glad to see the ground below free of killers. "I can't believe it...Austin..."

Garbarino balanced the board between the buildings. "Makes sense."

Mia gasped at the thought. "What?"

"Austin saw himself as a protector of life. He could be violent, sure. Deadly. But to him, he was saving people. Protecting people. His mission, just like Masters's, was to save lives."

Her eyes turned down. "And now he takes them."

Confusion tore at her mind. The irony seemed too impossible to be chance or the way his genetics randomly responded to some physical change in the atmosphere, or food, or anything else. But the other possibility, that Austin—her protector, who thought of nothing other than saving lives and who brought hope into a hopeless world—could be damned? She didn't believe it. She couldn't believe it.

Garbarino crossed first.

Mia followed.

They wasted no time retrieving the board and running for the next rooftop.

"A fire escape leads down the side of the last mill building," Garbarino said. "If they haven't realized where we're headed yet, we should have a pretty good head start."

Wood shattered far behind them. The sound was followed by a roar. And then another. Both different.

Neither Mia nor Garbarino looked back. They knew Masters and Austin were there. They knew the pair would give chase. Their only hope was to outrun them and cross the divides between the buildings a little bit faster.

When they reached the far end of the next to last mill, Garbarino chanced a look back and saw Masters and Austin climbing up over the far side wall. He lay the board out and dropped it down, nearly losing it over the edge. He pulled it straight and stepped aside. "Go."

Mia crossed the board quickly. Garbarino followed. "Just run," he said.

"What about the board."

He jumped from the board and got to his feet. "Leave it, and hope one of them tries to use it."

Free of the board, they sprinted across the last mill building roof and reached the edge. A ten foot drop led to the top of an old metal fire escape that looked like it might fall away from the building at any moment.

"Give me your hands," Garbarino said.

They gripped each other's hands tight. Garbarino helped her over the side of the building, lowered her down as far as he could reach and then let go. Mia yelped, but landed on her feet after a short drop.

Garbarino looked back. Masters had taken the bait, stepping up onto the wall and then out onto the board. His body dipped down a little bit as the board bent under his significant weight. Austin, on the other hand, seemed to know better. He took several steps back while Masters took a step forward. The board snapped and Masters dropped down the four stories for a second time.

Austin charged and launched himself through the air. He landed short again, but had been expecting it this time and latched onto the side of the roof, quickly pulling himself up.

Garbarino rolled over the side of the building, hung down by his arms and let go. He landed with a clang and felt the fire escape shake beneath him. He looked down and was glad to see Mia already half way to the bottom. He gave chase, rounding the stairway quickly. Flakes of rust and paint scratched his hands as he gripped onto railings.

He could hear Austin's heavy feet above and each footfall shook the structure. He reached the final set of stairs right behind Mia. They hit the pavement running, but a nearby roar sent them to the ground.

Garbarino looked up. Austin had reached the edge of the building and stood above the fire escape. But he wasn't the source of the blast that had knocked them down. It was closer. He turned to the side.

Masters.

He stalked toward them, knowing they couldn't outrun him in the parking lot.

"We have to split up," Garbarino said quickly.

"What? No."

"He can't chase both of us, and Austin—"

A loud clang above turned their attention up to Austin. He'd jumped onto the fire escape. Metal screeched and scraped against brick. The top of the metal stairway tilted away from the building. A second screech followed as the top heavy staircase peeled away from the building.

Garbarino scrambled to his feet and yanked Mia up. "Run!"

Masters turned toward the noise above him. The fire escape toppled over, Austin's weight on top speeding its descent. It struck the ground with a boom, crushing Masters beneath a mess of hard iron. Austin fell away from the fire escape as it fell and landed on a car. He slammed through the roof and disappeared inside the vehicle.

Mia knew this was the last chance they'd get and she poured every ounce of energy she had left into her legs. The city streets next to the mills were empty of hunters and full of alleys and buildings to get lost in. If they could just reach one—

The crunch of metal turned her around. Austin pulled himself out of the car and locked his eyes on her. Despite the despair she saw in them, she also saw intention. Austin wouldn't let them leave.

The giant man gripped the ruined roof of the car and peeled a sheet of metal roof away.

Garbarino saw two bright orange signs ahead. Just beyond them were several road construction vehicles. The pavement on one side of the street had peeled away and several manholes had been marked with bright orange paint. One of the manholes was open, its cover leaning to one side. "There!"

Mia looked ahead and saw the manhole cover. For a moment, she felt hope return. Austin and Masters wouldn't be able to fit and she doubted they could force their way in. But when she looked back at Austin, she saw the sheet of metal spiraling through the air like some kind of giant killer Frisbee. It whistled through the air, arcing to one side and then angling toward her. A moment before the shard struck, she shouted Garbarino's name.

Garbarino turned when Mia shouted and saw the metal slice through the back of her leg.

She fell to the ground, unable to move, cringing in pain.

"Hold on," he said, and picked her up under the arms.

As Austin charged, Garbarino dragged Mia toward the open man-hole. When he reached it, Austin was nearly upon them. There was no time to climb down the ladder so he dragged her over the hole until her feet fell in and then dropped her. She disappeared into the sewer.

He followed her, leaping over the edge and catching himself on the ladder. With Austin only ten feet away, Garbarino reached up and pulled the manhole cover back into place. Before he could let go and climb down, the cover was struck from above. The force of the impact knocked Garbarino off the ladder. He hit the concrete eight feet below and struck his head.

The pair lay next to each other, both unconscious, while Mia's leg bled out onto the dry sewer floor. Austin pounded the manhole lid several times and let out a roar. But then he fell quiet as a sea of voices approached. The killers were coming, and unlike Austin and Masters, they would have no trouble entering the sewer.

52

Mia woke suddenly as a pulse of pain exploded from her leg and jolted up her spine. She gasped at the pain, sitting up. The quick motion made her throbbing head spin. I've got a concussion, she thought, feeling a lump on the back of her head. She probed her leg with her other hand and found a warm wet patch of blood. She drew her hand back, not really wanting to know the true extent of her injury. The pain and blood told her enough.

Voices pushed past the pain. The killers. But would they come into the sewer?

The manhole cover above began to twist, grinding bits of stone beneath it.

Of course they will.

Garbarino lay unconscious next to her. She winced as she slid over to him. "Joe. Joe, wake up!" She shook his arm. "Joe!"

For a moment she worried that he was dead, really dead, but then saw his pulse twitching beneath the skin of his neck.

Dust tickled her nose as it fell from above. She looked back up in time to see the manhole cover rise up. A crescent of light streamed into the dark tunnel.

The voices grew louder.

Austin's horrid face leaned over the hole. "Life," he growled through clenched teeth.

Henry Masters joined him, the pair looking like deformed conjoined twins cut apart at birth. "Peace," he said.

Mia began quickly slapping Garbarino's shoulder. "Dammit, Joe!"

She struggled to her feet. The pain in her leg nearly pulled her back under. Her vision turned black and her limbs tingled. She held on to the tunnel wall. Her head continued to spin, but her vision returned.

As the voices above grew louder and more urgent, Mia took Garbarino by the wrists and pulled him into the tunnel. Each step was agony as the partly severed muscles in her leg twisted and flexed. She felt an oozing warmth spread from her thigh to her calf. She would bleed to death if she didn't do something soon about the wound. But what could she do? Stopping would mean death, too.

But what held her attention more than the pain, was the continuing thought. I'm not ready. She felt like she needed just a few minutes of quiet to figure things out. She wasn't sure what she believed still and what she chose might very well determine her fate. Should she decide that the world had become a literal hell and the only escape was forgiveness from a God she never believed in before, she might actually long for death. But if this life was all that she had, and the people trying to kill her were really just mutated versions of their former selves, than she would fight to the end and do her best to stay alive.

But she had no time to stop and think. A loud whump and a crack filled the tunnel. She saw a killer lying on the tunnel floor beneath the open manhole. The man stood, but his leg bent at an odd angle and he fell to the side.

A second body fell to the concrete floor.

The killers were flinging themselves in with no regard for their bodies. The first man had broken his leg. The second, a woman dressed in a tattered power suit, lay unconscious.

But the bodies of the first two cushioned the fall of a third man. He stood immediately, and spun around, looking into the dark, oblivious to the fact that he was stark naked. Mia wasn't sure if the man could see her, but when he cocked his head to the side and then turned in her direction, she realized he could hear her.

Each step backwards was heavy. Her footfalls echoed. Garbarino's feet scraped along the floor. Until he woke up, stealth would be impossible. And after that, if there was an after that, she still had to do something about the blood pouring down her leg. She could feel it in her shoe now, squishing with each step.

The killer launched toward them as more dropped into the tunnel like lemmings over a cliff.

"Garbarino," Mia said, her voice pitched with fear. She shook his arms while walking backwards, unsure of where to go.

The killer gained quickly.

"Joe!"

Garbarino grunted. Mia raised her voice, shouting, "He's going to kill us, Joe!"

His arms tugged and then yanked away. Mia fell back and landed on her wound. The pain blinded her and she heard sounds of a fight. Garbarino shouted in pain.

She began to weep knowing that the killer would be on top of her any second. When a hand took hold of her she flinched away.

"It's me," Garbarino said.

She blinked as the pain faded and her vision returned. She looked beyond Garbarino and saw the killer lying on the tunnel floor, his neck twisted at an odd angle. But the man's neck moved slowly, twisting back into position. He'd be up and running in no time. Further beyond the immobilized killer, she saw more of them coming. "We're not going to make it."

"We will," he said. He helped her up and pulled her into the darkness.

He led them through a series of tunnels, turning left, then right and repeating at every intersection they came to. The only light came from small holes in the manhole covers and drainage grates leading to the streets above. They stopped a few times, hoping to exit through a manhole cover and hide in the city, but the thundering footsteps of Austin and Masters shook the streets above them, possibly following the voices of the killers that streamed through the tunnels behind them.

They rounded a corner and were struck hard from the side. They fell to the side along with a single killer. Mia rolled over and saw the woman jump onto Garbarino's back.

"I'm sorry," the woman said, and raised her hand to strike the back of Garbarino's neck.

Mia remembered what had happened to White when the killer struck his neck, and she knew that this woman could easily kill Garbarino with a single blow. From her position on the floor she snapped a kick up at the woman and struck her square in the face. Pain twanged up Mia's leg, but she ignored it and pressed the attack.

As the woman stumbled back, Mia stood and kicked again, this time with her good leg. She connected a solid blow on the woman's chest and sent her careening back, slamming into a second killer who'd just run around the corner. Mia had never used her karate to attack anyone, but dropping two killers on her own made them seem a little less unbeatable.

Garbarino pushed himself up with a grunt. "Thanks," he said, and then ran in the opposite direction of the two killers. Mia followed. The killers fought each other as they untangled and scrambled after them.

"We have to get out of here," Mia said. "We can't outrun them if they fill the entire system."

Garbarino knew she was right. Every turn could lead them headlong into a line of killers. But would the city streets be any better?

Light streamed out of a tunnel ahead of them.

"Looks like an opening ahead," Mia said.

"Run!" shouted a voice from behind them. The two killers were gaining.

"I don't want to!" The second voice was in front of them. A shadow moving through the tunnel on the other side of the light.

"Hurry!" Garbarino said, pushing toward the light.

Mia moved her legs as fast as she could, adrenaline blocking out the pain. But she knew it would be back, and far worse than before. She could feel the sinews of her ruined muscles snap with each step. If they survived, she'd have a limp for life.

As they approached the light, the three killers were only ten feet away on either side. Garbarino rounded the corner fast, yanking Mia with him. They squinted in the bright light, unable to see, but still moving.

The killers entered the light behind them and shrieked in agony. The noise sounded unlike anything Mia had heard before—pain-filled and horrified. What could make them react like that? Mia thought, and then the tunnel dropped away beneath their feet and she fell into the light.

53

Coffee. Mia smelled the most delicious coffee. It drifted past her nose and pulled her from sleep. But the warmth enveloping her fought to keep her asleep. She felt peaceful, like never before, and safe. More than that, she couldn't remember ever feeling unsafe.

She rolled over and felt a cool breeze brush across her face. It carried a trace of ocean air, cherry blossoms and earth. The scents invigorated her. She blinked her eyes open, squinting in the bright light of day.

She placed her hand down on the soft bed beneath her and smiled. The bed wasn't a bed. It was grass. Green and lush. The warmth came from a light above, like the sun, but too bright to see clearly. She lay beneath a cherry tree, thick with pink blossoms that drifted away with the breeze.

The sight made her laugh.

She didn't wonder how she got there.

She didn't question what happened to Garbarino.

These things and the horrible state of the world were no longer known to her.

She sat up and leaned back on her arms. The grass grew on a slope that led to a stand of tall reeds. Beyond the reeds was a sandy beach that led to the ocean where waves crashed, filling the air with the hypnotic sounds of roaring water followed by the sifting of sand.

Seagulls called.

And then a voice. Distant and high pitched. But familiar.

A shadow fell next to her and she found a wolf sitting in the grass beside her, its tongue hanging out as it panted. It glanced in her direction and then back out to the ocean. She felt no fear at the wolf's presence and saw no hunger in its eyes.

She held a hand out to the wolf and it scooted over to her. She petted the predator's head and squeezed it to her side. The stiff hairs tickled her.

She was naked.

Mia stood when the voice called out again. She headed down the hill toward the beach. The wolf followed her.

A worn path cut through the reeds. Mia walked through slowly, admiring the streaks of green as they reached up toward the sky and glowed in the bright light. She ran her hands through them as she walked, feeling the contours and listening to the gentle hiss of the reeds against her skin.

Then she stood on the beach, her feet sinking into the sand. Warmth spread from the sand and coursed through her body. The grains were smooth and caressed her feet as she walked.

The voice grew louder, coming from the water. A woman was there, concealed by waves as she danced in the water.

Mia called out, "Hello!"

A tall wave crashed, revealing the woman's naked back and flowing blond hair. She turned around with a broad smile that Mia recognized— Elizabeth, older and stunning.

She raised her hand to wave, but the brightness above exploded with white. The images around her disappeared. As Elizabeth's face was washed out, Mia's heart broke open and poured fear into her body. She shook, as the light became unbearably hot. The sand scorched her feet. The wolf growled and barked. The reeds behind her caught fire and blackened.

And then she was back.

She knew it by the smell. Death and destruction mixed with the dirty penny scent of her own blood. The pain returned next, pounding her body with each beat of her heart. Her vision cleared. The blue sky was now full of gray clouds, flashing with heat lightning.

Then Garbarino stood above her, his face twisted with worry. "You okay? You were just staring straight ahead."

But she couldn't answer. She had tasted freedom. From this world. From hate, fear, and pain. And she wasn't sure how, but she knew it was real. Dreams were never that powerful. Never that tangible. She could still hear the waves and smell the cherry blossoms. And the memory of the place hurt her more than the gash in her leg, the end of civilization or the death of Elizabeth.

She had never experienced such intense and all-consuming despair. She had tasted paradise only to have it yanked away.

But the feeling slowly ebbed as reality drowned out her memories of the place.

"Where are we?" she asked, but her voice sounded like someone else's. Rough and dry.

Garbarino looked from side to side. "We're in the crater. We fell a few feet and rolled a few more. The good news is that the killers won't come in here."

Mia had begun to detect the bad news before Garbarino said anything. Voices surrounded them, but no one spoke. She heard weeping and wailing, screams of agony and remorse. They were the very emotions she'd felt when she returned to the real world.

"The bad news is we're not alone," Garbarino said.

Mia turned to her side and saw a row of people. They would have looked normal enough if they weren't all naked and half buried in the ground. There were a mixture of races, and the ratio of men and women seemed equal. But what unified them was their despair. They all stared straight ahead toward the center of the crater, which was blocked from Mia's view by Garbarino—arms stretched out, desperately reaching for something. They screamed and cried for it. Tears streamed down their faces. They wanted something so bad, but it dangled just out of reach, taunting them with its closeness.

But they would never have it.

That's how the world worked now.

"What are they reaching for?" she asked.

"I don't know," Garbarino said. "I don't see anything."

He stepped aside and Mia looked down to the center of the crater. She saw a bright light and caught a scent of ocean water. Then it was gone. Loss and regret consumed her. She reached for the light, her voice crying out for it.

A shadow extinguished the light.

Garbarino stood in front of her again. "What the fuck was that?"

"You can't see it?" she asked, desperation filling each word. "Take me back. Please, take me back."

Garbarino looked over his shoulder and saw nothing but a football stadium-sized crater packed with people, all reaching down toward an empty swatch of blackened earth. If there was something there, he couldn't see it.

He pulled her up, careful to stand between her and the crater bottom. "We need to get out of here. They're not coming in, but they'll be on us as soon as we're out."

Mia looked back. The shattered sewer tunnel gaped open, a black hole into the earth. She could hear the shouting voices of killers within, but they stayed back from the light. Fifteen feet above that she saw the surface, a charred black rim of scorched pavement and the melted remnants of city buildings. There were voices up above, too, but they weren't getting any closer.

"They're afraid of the crater," she said.

"Actually, I think they're afraid of whatever they, and you, are seeing at the bottom."

Mia tried to look around Garbarino. She wanted to see the light again. To feel that taste of paradise one more time. More than anything, she wanted to run down to it, jump in and return to the beach with Elizabeth.

And Matt, she decided. She didn't see him there, but she had no doubt she would. "I want to go back," she said.

Garbarino looked her in the eyes. "You're not ready."

Having tasted the place, she didn't believe him. "Maybe you're not ready."

They stared at each other for a moment. Then a voice interrupted. It came from above, speaking quietly, but the word struck like an atom bomb. "Peace."

A second voice followed. "Life."

Mia turned around and saw Austin and Henry Masters standing at the edge of the crater. The pair seemed irritated by the light at the center of the crater, but were otherwise immune. The pair stared down at them, eternally smiling.

"Run," Garbarino said.

"Where?"

"Where do you think, Carol Anne? Run to the light!"

Nothing sounded better to Mia at that moment, so she turned and ran, looking into the light and reaching out for it as she ran. The empty patch of sloped earth beneath open sewer tunnel was congested with half buried people, but Mia pushed past them even as they reached out for her, jealously fueling their screams. Mia was headed toward the light. And as she neared it, she felt escape was at long last possible.

After pulling herself free from the swarm of reaching arms, Mia reached the bottom of the crater. The light hovered five feet above the ground, a glowing blue-white sphere. She stepped toward it and thousands upon thousands of voices roared in response. The sheer volume of the sound made her stumble. But she was almost there.

"Head to the other side," Garbarino said as he kicked loose of the crowd. "We can probably reach the top before—" He noticed Mia was no longer listening. She continued toward the center of the crater, arms outstretched. "Mia..."

The light was right in front of her. She reached for it, feeling its warmth, and closed her eyes. She stepped forward, into the light and felt its warm embrace.

For a moment.

Then it was gone.

She opened her eyes.

She stood inside the light. White haze surrounded her. A mirage. Nothing more.

Despair dropped her to her knees.

The combined howl of Austin and Masters put her on her stomach.

54

Mia felt her stomach lurch. She was starving, desperate to leave this world. The combined roars of Austin and Masters shook her insides. She convulsed, her body out of control. She lay below the sphere of light, but no longer desired it. Its allure had vanished with the realization that it wasn't really there.

Was it all a delusion? she wondered. The grassy hill. The wolf. The ocean. Elizabeth. It all felt so real. She wanted to go back more than anything she'd desired before.

The question was, how could she get there?

It became the background soundtrack in her mind on which she could never fully focus. I had years, she thought, why didn't I think about this before the world went to hell?

She tried to focus on the question of God, Hell, forgiveness and eternity, but the world around her drew her attention away.

"Get up!" Garbarino shouted at her. He grabbed her arm and pulled, but she just slid across the rough crater floor leaving a trail of blood behind her. Garbarino looked at her and his facial expression changed to that of a family member waiting by the bedside of a terminally ill family member. The look said, you're not long for this world.

He lowered her to the ground. "Don't take long."

He stepped away and she wanted to follow, but found herself rooted in place.

She couldn't move. She could only watch.

At the top of the crater, Austin and Masters jumped over the edge. They landed amid the crowd of people buried waist deep in the hardened ground. Those beneath the giants were crushed. The rest paid them no attention, their focus on the globe of light absolute.

Don't take long. Garbarino's words echoed in her thoughts. Her time had come at last. She would escape.

You're not ready, her inner voice said.

But a new voice, this one more confident, replied, I've been there. I saw Liz. I'm going back. I'm as ready as I'll ever be.

She had no doubt about it. She was a good person. She'd done bad things, but nothing like Collins. If God was real, he would see that. If God was merciful, he would understand. He had already shown her paradise. It was a gift. An incentive. She felt peace. And life.

Peace and life.

Masters and Austin charged down the hill. They tore bodies from the ground, ripping them in half and tossing them away. Others they simply stepped on, crushing them into the ground. A river of blood preceded them down the crater's bowl. When they roared, the people around them leaned away, a shockwave moving through the masses, like a crowd doing the wave at a baseball game.

Garbarino stood between her and the two approaching juggernauts. He held his gun in his hand. She knew it held only one round. It wouldn't even slow them. He turned back toward her.

"Are you ready?"

She started to say yes, but some part of her wasn't so sure. Was she forgetting something? The chaos around her kept her thoughts from solidifying.

Bodies flew.

Desperation filled the crater.

Monsters roared.

Her body quaked.

Ask, she thought.

Ask what?

"Are you ready?" Garbarino screamed it this time.

Austin and Masters were nearly through the crowd. She had ten seconds. Maybe less.

Ask what? Ask what!

"Please," she said. "Let me see Matt again."

"You're out of time!" Garbarino said.

"I'm ready!" she shouted.

Garbarino spun around and faced her. His face was full of fear, but his eyes burned with determination. She saw his hand come up, weapon steady.

One bullet left.

He'd been saving it, she realized.

For her.

Better to die by the bullet than torn apart by Austin and Masters. He was going to kill her—a final act of mercy.

She had just begun to mouth the words, "Thank you," when he pulled the trigger.

At the same moment the gun fired and kicked in his hand, Garbarino was struck from behind. The gun tilted down slightly as the bullet left the barrel. He looked up and saw Mia kneeling, her face twisted in pain. The bullet had struck her chest instead of her head. It was a kill shot for sure. Punctured lung. Close to the heart. She'd be dead within the minute.

But the anguish she felt at that moment was for Garbarino.

He looked down. A large hand had pierced his back and come out of his stomach. As it pulled back out, he could feel the thick arm scraping against his spine. Once back inside his body, he felt the fingers flex. A mixture of pressure and pain registered in his mind before he felt the hand pull back out. He felt his insides unravel in him, pulled out through his back. Numbness claimed his body. His thoughts drifted away. And he was gone.

Mia shook with sadness as Garbarino's body fell to the ground, dead.

But she couldn't cry. Not really. Her left lung was filling with blood. Each breath was shorter than the last. She'd drown in the stuff soon. If Masters and Austin let her live that long. But she was determined to last the minute, to make sure Garbarino had escaped. She pushed away from the monsters as they walked slowly toward her. They sensed the end coming and were in no rush.

She stopped moving when they reached her. They stood on either side, looking down at her.

Her mental count to sixty ended.

Garbarino was not coming back.

He'd escaped.

"Peace," Masters said.

Austin raised his fists. She thought she saw him give a faint head shake, as though disappointed. "Life," he said.

"Please," Mia said. "Let me see him again. Let Matt be there when I open my eyes. Please."

Four massive fists slammed into her body. In that split second of impact she felt her bones break, her organs burst and her life escape. Then everything went black.

55

Black became white.

Her body had returned, hale and healthy again. The broken bones, the wound in her leg, the fatigue and exhaustion were all gone. Warmth tickled her face. She smiled. Alive again.

As her thoughts returned, she could feel her body moving. Running. It felt wonderful.

There was dirt beneath her feet. Bare feet.

She smelled earth all around, and something else. Onions.

The white began to fade.

A breeze caressed her skin.

She saw colors. Dashes of orange.

Her eyesight returned in full. She blinked and elation filled her to the core. Matt lay beneath her, smiling, staring up into her eyes.

"Matt," she said, dripping with affection.

"No, no, no," he replied.

"Matt, it's me," she said. "It's Mia."

He screamed and she realized what she had taken for a smile was actually gritted teeth. His face was covered in grime and dried blood.

"No," she said, looking down. Matt's stomach was open. His guts were in her hands.

He screamed again and she realized her hands were yanking at his insides, eviscerating the fiancé she'd betrayed.

"I'm sorry," she screamed turning her head to the sky. "Make it stop! God, make it stop!"

But she didn't stop until Matt's body stopped moving and his own screams of pain faded. Then she was up and moving. She spotted several other killers and headed for them. She didn't want to be with them. She didn't want to hear their voices mixed with hers, but her body, and its actions, were not hers to control anymore.

"I wasn't ready," she screamed, her voice going hoarse. "I wasn't ready!"

A shuffling sound turned her around.

Matt was there, alive again, pulling his organs back together. He saw her attention and shouted, "No!"

But she was already running toward him, arms outstretched, fingers locked like claws. "I'm sorry!" she screamed. "I wasn't ready. I wasn't ready!"

ABOUT THE AUTHOR

Jeremy Robinson is the *New York Times* and #1 Audible bestselling author of over seventy novels and novellas, including *Infinite, The Others*, and *The Dark*, as well as the Jack Sigler thriller series, and *Project Nemesis*, the highest selling, original (non-licensed) kaiju novel of all time. He's known for mixing elements of science, history, and mythology, which has earned him the #1 spot in Science Fiction and Action/Adventure, and secured him as the top creature feature author. Many of his novels have been adapted into comic books, optioned for film and TV, and translated into fourteen languages. He lives in New Hampshire with his wife and three children.

Visit him at www.bewareofmonsters.com.

Made in the USA
Monee, IL
06 February 2023

27176210R00194